D0866379

Unless You Die Young

Also by GLADYS HASTY CARROLL

Novels

As the Earth Turns
A Few Foolish Ones
Neighbor to the Sky
While the Angels Sing
West of the Hill
Christmas without Johnny
One White Star
Sing Out the Glory
Come with Me Home
The Road Grows Strange
The Light Here Kindled
Man on the Mountain
Next of Kin

Nonfiction

Dunnybrook
Only Fifty Years Ago
To Remember Forever
Years Away from Home

Short Stories

Head of the Line

Anthology

Christmas through the Years

Unless You Die Young

A NOVEL BY
Gladys Hasty Carroll

W·W·NORTON & COMPANY·INC·NEW YORK

Copyright © 1977 by Gladys Hasty Carroll.
All rights reserved. Published simultaneously in Canada
by George J. McLeod Limited, Toronto.
Printed in the United States of America.

Library of Congress Cataloging in Publication Data
Carroll, Gladys Hasty, 1904–
Unless you die young.

I. Title.
PZ3.C2354Un [PS3505.A77533]   813'.5'2   76–57781
ISBN 0–393–08776–X

4 5 6 7 8 9 0

To
J. Randall Williams
in deep appreciation
of his long association with my work
as its editor, publisher, and loyal friend

Unless You Die Young

He that would pass the latter part of life with honor
and decency must, while he is young, consider that
he shall one day be old; and remember, when he is
old, that he has once been young.

—Samuel Johnson

It is a hard thing for the young in body to face the fact that
up the road a piece old age waits for everyone, and once it joins
us will not leave us and we never again be free of it on this
lovely earth. For what can the young in body know of age
beyond that which they see and hear and read of it?

>   . . . Last scene of all,
>   That ends this strange, eventful history,
>   Is second childishness and mere oblivion,
>   Sans teeth, sans eyes, sans taste, sans everything.

The concept, obviously, of a young man at the height of
his full physical vigor, who knew of age only what he observed,
and who, having recently escaped childhood, recalled only its
helpless vulnerability and innocence.

How could such a future be viewed other than with horror by one to whom his teeth, his eyes, his taste, his everything are the channels through which life flows? Yet there seems no way to avoid it, save by dying early, a course chosen by a few of the most fearful but fortunately not by many, since life is so precious in youth and one can never be certain that he has drained the last intoxicating drop of it.

A hard thing. A sad thing, too. Because it is a misapprehension, leading to unnecessary and fruitless suffering. Youth is a part of our mortal experience which is never lost and cannot be. The spirit resides in and is dependent upon the body only while what we most need to learn comes through the body. Then—unless it has been seriously damaged during that confinement—it emerges under its own power, tries its wings, and eventually soars.

I

This is the story of Alice. At the age of something more than threescore and ten, her story is complete though not finished. She is now on a plateau where she will remain because she is Alice and is beyond threescore and ten.

It is also a segment of the story of her son Philip and his wife Rhonda; of her daughter Emily and Emily's husband Jim; of Alice's grandchildren Gary, Weston, Vicki, Chris, Melissa, Sue, Desirée, and Margery, who range downward in age from twenty-five years to two; and of certain friends of Alice, her children, and her grandchildren.

But it is chiefly the story of Alice. Unless you want to know Alice, want to know what it really is—or can be—to have attained more than three score years and ten, and how it differs from being forty-three or thirty-eight or twenty-five or two or anywhere in between, this is the place to stop if you have indeed come this far.

It is late June and Alice stands in the doorway of a beach cottage. When Philip persuaded Rhonda to come to the island for the summer, he urged his mother to join them. Alice appreciated the thought, was pleased to think of being near Philip's family and once more on the island, but preferred to rent a small cottage for herself a mile down the beach from the house they had taken. She might have decided differently if Philip were spending the summer there—which very likely would have been a mistake—but he flies to his Chicago office every Monday morning, returning Friday evenings. He has found for Rhonda an excellent housekeeper who also keeps an eye on their three little girls. Rhonda is painting. Alice is accustomed to keeping her own house.

She stands there in her doorway looking out to sea, smiling a little, one hand shielding her eyes from the brilliance of the morning sun on the water.

She appears to have her own teeth, though some of them may be capped, and she has worn bifocals for years. She is not thinking of her teeth, her eyes, her everything; nor of Philip and his family.

Alice is a tall, rather slim woman, and her blue cotton skirt is briefer than she would have wished, but a skirt which fits her otherwise is always shorter nowadays than she would like and she is accustomed to it. The sleeves of her multi-striped shirt are rolled nearly to the elbows. She is wearing sandals and her bare legs are getting brown. A few varicose veins visible below her knees give her no pain, and tanning will eventually obscure them. Her once ruddy-brown hair has streaks of silvery white and blows in the salt breeze, for she has just taken out the night's pins. Her narrowed eyes are as blue as the sea. But she is not thinking of any of this. It does not matter.

There was a small book which Alice used to hold in her hands long before she had ever seen the ocean, before she knew that the black marks below the pictures were letters and made words. She looked at the pictures, mostly the first picture. Sometimes, after a while, she looked casually at those which followed, but they did not hold her attention and she soon turned back to the first one.

She is holding it in her hands now. The picture fills the small dog-eared page. It is of blue water, smooth white sand, and a little girl wearing a huge sunbonnet. She has a red sand pail with a red-handled shovel, but has put them down beside her and stands looking at the water. As Alice stares at the picture, she moves slowly under the sunbonnet, and no one is there but her. There never has been any strange little girl. Just Alice. The sunbonnet has been suspended, waiting for her. No sooner has she moved under it than this still, bright world of sand, water, and sunshine spreads out around her, extending endlessly in all directions. It is everywhere. It is all there is. It is Alice's. And she recognizes it for she has been here before.

The snow-capped waves roll in gently. The fine sand is like silk to her bare feet. The sun wraps all tenderly in a shining shawl. There is nothing but love, beauty, safety here. Nothing anywhere but love, beauty, safety, and Alice. She stands breathing it in.

Gradually she realizes that the waves are laughing very softly, singing very softly.

"Come, Alice . . . Come to meet us, Alice . . . Come play with us, Alice . . . Come, Alice . . . Alice . . . Alice . . . Alice . . ."

As she listens, she is suddenly puzzled. She is not, after all, the only one in this world. Someone else has come into it. Two other little girls. They are far away but coming toward her.

They are not in sunbonnets. They are running toward her along the white sand beside the blue water. They are hand in hand but the taller one is an arm's length ahead. Now they are near enough so that she can see their bouncing hair, one dark, one pale blond, and hear their laughter mingling with that of the waves. As she watches them, transfixed, the taller one darts into the water's edge, pulling the smaller behind her. They are still running toward Alice but before they reach her veer again and run farther into the water.

Now motion comes to Alice. She leaps out from under the sunbonnet, cries, "Wait for Garmie! Desirée! Margery! Wait for Garmie!" and runs into the water.

The children do not hear her. They hear only the singing of the waves, see only the fresh new world of early morning, feel only the silken sand and the icy caress of the sea. Alice knows this. She does not call again. She runs faster.

Just as she reaches them a wave playfully topples Margery and she disappears. The same wave staggers Desirée but she regains her feet and stands in the trough looking around in bewilderment for the sister of whose hand she has lost hold. A bigger wave is bearing down behind her. She sees Alice.

"We didn't go too far, Garmie," she says. "Margery fell down."

Alice, having scooped up Margery, reaches for Desirée's hand.

"Jump!" she cries. "Now! All—JUMP! . . . Oh, isn't this fun? Don't cry, Margery. This is fun. Here comes another wave. Now! All—JUMP! We're all jumping together. This is the way to do it, see? Keep hold of hands. Stand side to the waves, facing each other, and jump each one that comes in. Here's another! . . . Wasn't that fun? No, Desirée, we aren't too far out for you and me together, but a little too far out for Margery, who isn't so tall. You see, I'm holding her when we jump because we're too far out for her. Let's go in to where you and Margery can jump by yourselves."

Alice takes the other two little girls close to shore, places them facing each other, side to the waves, holding both hands, and then sits on the sand, hugging her knees for warmth, listening to their excited laughter, and shouting admiration of each jump. It is a lovely day on the island. A lovely, lovely day.

In a few minutes another little girl comes running down the beach. This is Sue. Sue is nine. She is panting and her hair is bouncing. Her hair is ruddy brown like Alice's and Philip's.

She screams, "Desirée! Margie! Get out of that water! This minute!"

They do not hear her, do not see her. They are watching the new wave coming in, to be ready to jump an instant before it reaches them. Sue starts into the water, not so much walking or running as stamping; and she is fully dressed in jeans, jersey, sneakers, and an angry scowl.

Alice gets to her feet, cups her hands, and calls, "Sue!"

Sue looks over her shoulder. Alice smiles and beckons to her. They move toward each other.

"What are you doing way down here?" demands Sue. "How did they get here alone? How did they find the way? Why didn't you call and tell us you had them?"

"They came to play with me," says Alice. "They found the way alone because they wanted to come. I didn't call because I didn't know they were here until I saw them in the water. Then I thought it best that I stay near them. I'm sorry if you were worried."

"I wasn't worried at first," says Sue. "I was asleep. Mrs. Batcheldor woke me when she couldn't find them, and sent me down the beach while she went up. Mummy is out somewhere painting or she'd be scared to death. I haven't had any break-fast yet. Why didn't you take them up to your cottage as soon as you saw them, and call us?"

"I was going to as soon as they had played a little while," says Alice. "I don't want them to be afraid of water. I want them to learn about it, but not to be afraid of it. We have to teach children what they should know. If we don't, we can't blame them for not knowing it. They know a great deal that older people once knew and too many have mostly forgotten. I'll go in and bring them out. You see, I'm already wet. I played with them at first. The water's glorious today. I think it will be quite warm when the sun gets higher."

When Alice, Desirée, and Margery come back to where Sue stands, Sue is no longer scowling. She looks only sober and hungry.

But she says, "What are you down here for?"

Desirée and Margery answer with happy smiles, "We came to play with Garmie."

"Why didn't you tell somebody you were coming?"

They stare at her in silence.

"Why didn't you *ask* somebody?" Sue presses them.

After some thought, "I don't know," says Desirée honestly.

"One wave was BIG," adds Margery helpfully. "Garmie and I jumped right out of it."

"They'll tell us next time when they want to come and play with Garmie," says Alice. "Because when grown-ups don't know where the children are, they worry. And when grown-ups worry they get headaches and red eyes and all such horrid things. It's something of a nuisance for children, but grown-ups can't help it. It's only because they love the children so much . . . Now, when I came down to the beach, I had just put a pan of muffins into the oven. If they aren't burned up, anybody who wants one or two may have them, buttered, to eat on the way home. Luckily, Sue, you left a sweater here both the last times you came, so Desirée can wear one and Margery the other. While I'm getting them, and the muffins, you call Mrs.

Batcheldor. She must have come back by now and thinks you are all three lost. Probably getting at least a headache and maybe even red eyes!"

As she fumbles on the shelf of the dark kitchen closet for the sweaters she thinks: "And Philip insisted on my having a telephone I didn't want and didn't feel the slightest need of! It's an ill wind that blows nobody good."

Later, when she is alone, still in wet clothing, she gets down on her knees a little stiffly, beside her bed, and thanks God for the book with the picture of the little girl by the sea, and for sending two other little girls to find her and play with her. Halfway to her feet she drops back again and adds:

"You know, Lord, as I ran through the water I asked you for help though I had no time or breath for words. Surely you know I was asking not only your help to reach the children in time but also to guide me in what I might say to them afterward. No one but you can know what it is right and best to say to children. Please, Lord, if I made mistakes, please correct them. For the children's sake . . ."

2

After lunch she walks up the beach to sit on a point of land running out into deep blue water and fringed with rocks piled helter-skelter as if a mad giant had undertaken to build a mighty wall and then forgotten his intent. It is good to sit there alone, idle, bare arms hugging one raised knee.

Alice was a nurse in a hospital where Harley was doing his internship. That is where they met. During Emily's last year in high school, when Philip was already graduated from college and doing graduate work in business administration, nursing care had been very difficult to get and cost more than many people could afford. Harley said the biggest problem he had was figuring out where to place his elderly patients when they were ready for discharge from the hospital but not yet able to care for themselves. Most of them lived alone, and their families felt they should go into convalescent centers, but they all longed for their own homes, and Harley said most convalescent centers were not really for convalescents but for terminal care. Alice visited them and saw that he was right. So she took one of his patients home from the hospital, stayed with her days, and arranged with her granddaughters to sleep nights on a living-room sofa in the apartment until that eighty-five-year-old lady could manage by herself again if someone brought in her groceries. By then Harley had another waiting for release from the hospital, and so it went. For over ten years, while Harley lived, Alice gave home nursing care to as many of his patients who needed it as she could. In the years since he died, she has continued on call for the doctor who took over his practice. It has been rewarding. It has been very good for Alice.

But she is not nursing this summer. She is on the island to be near Philip and his family, whom ordinarily she never sees except when she flies to Chicago to spend Christmas with them. She is not even thinking of nursing or, at the moment, of Philip and his family.

She is on a point of land running out into deep water, overlooking a wide border of tumbled black stones. She is alone and free.

So she becomes Alice seeing the shore and the sea for one of the first few times in her life, the very first time in late fall. Great-uncle Ezra and Great-aunt Molly have brought Alice and her grandmother out to the coast from the inland farm where they live with Alice's grandfather. It is a bright day with a chill in the air but still warm for November, and they are going to have a picnic. Granny and Aunt Molly have helped each other down to the first shelf of rock and found a corner with a windbreak into which the early afternoon sun shines. They are waving to Uncle Ezra, and he is unbuckling from the running board on one side of his high-hung, single-seated Overland runabout the wicker hamper which Aunt Molly packed before she left for church this morning in Port City. They are all very hungry because the Westons in the city and the Plaisteds on the farm usually have Sunday dinner as soon as they come home from church. Today only Grampa did. Uncle Ezra, Aunt Molly, Granny, and Alice have saved their appetites to enjoy the picnic after the hour ride down to the shore.

Alice has never ridden in Uncle Ezra's runabout as far as this before, and only a few times for shorter distances; and she has never ridden in any other automobile. She has seen only two others, the doctor's and the mailman's, until today. Two years ago the doctor was still going his country rounds behind a sorrel horse and with his black satchel tucked under the seat of his top buggy, while the mailman rode in a democrat wagon and his horse was roan. She remembers well the first time the sound of a motor preceded these couriers of health and communication over the Marsh bridge. It was about that time she first saw Uncle Ezra and Aunt Molly. Until they had the Overland, Port City was too far from the farm for them to get there and back in an afternoon, and an afternoon was all they had for outings. Uncle Ezra, superintendent of a mill in Port City, worked five and a half days every week, and Sunday mornings they went to church. Now they come two or three times each summer, because Aunt Molly is Granny's sister. In winter the Overland is put up on blocks in the Weston stable, to keep its weight off its tires.

Times are changing. Times are becoming exciting for Alice. There is more now for Alice to see and learn and feel than what happens next after Grampa tosses the cut potatoes into the furrows and she drops corn and peas and he covers all with his scraping hoe; how Granny kneads the dough to make bread, how Grampa draws streams of warm milk from the cow, and how the bread and milk taste when put together in a yellow bowl; how the brook sounds running over white and sparkly stones to fill the black Bottomless Hole; where the first strawberries, blueberries, cranberries ripen . . . how Old Bell's iron-shod feet thud on a sandy stretch of road, plod through mud and drip mud as she lifts them, clang on ledges while the iron rims of the wagon wheels grind slowly as she pulls up the hill. You see grass growing wherever soil still clings to the ledge, moss creeping in crevices, shadows swaying on the roadside as leaves and branches move in the wind. At the top of the hill, with a half mile of smooth, hard gravel ahead, Grampa reaches for the whip on the dashboard and flicks Old Bell's rump, so she arches her thin neck and begins to trot. Now you don't see each separate blade of grass, cannot trace each shadow to its source, but you still see them. And you are keenly aware of the sudden mingling of all the smells—horse, leather, grass, forest, spread manure, wet clay, hot granite, starched skirts, talcum powder—which companion a small farm girl going with her grandfather to market.

Riding in the Overland is altogether different. Fortunately, Alice's Granny is a tiny woman, so tiny that she can squeeze onto the seat between Uncle Ezra, who is not a large man, and Aunt Molly, whose figure is ample, and leave space for Alice to sit on the floor with her feet on the running board. Uncle Ezra says Alice is good ballast to offset the hamper buckled to the opposite running board and keeps the Overland hugging the road even when they go over thank-you-ma'ams. But Aunt Molly takes no chances, keeping a firm grip on Alice's shoulder all the way.

Sitting there, pressed against Aunt Molly's knee, you feel the slippery shine of Aunt Molly's long-skirted, dust-colored linen coat against the back of your neck, between your tight braids of hair. Sometimes a puff of wind wraps around your face the floating ends of the dust-colored scarf which holds Aunt Molly's hat on, and you are blindfolded for a minute, tangled in a huge spider web. Then the mists roll away, and the fields, woods, and scattered houses and barns come up out of nowhere and flash past you. You see nothing small, but all the big things you see look small. You wonder if people like living so far away from home. From your home, that is. Grampa's house is the hub of the universe.

Several times the Overland slows down, approaching a horse-drawn carriage, and overtakes it cautiously. Uncle Ezra is explaining that it does not do to blow the horn, as this startles a horse and might cause him to rear or run away and overturn the carriage. During these passings Alice has a clear view of couples or families dressed in their best, laps protected from the dust by fringed, embroidered linen coverlets, the ladies often plying palm-leaf fans. Some curly-headed little girls open and close smaller fans of pink or blue feathers. The glances of the carriage riders, inquiring, mildly anxious, meet Alice's. She feels she has nothing of interest to return for the curls and feathers, until it occurs to her to raise one arm and apply her forefinger hard to her cheek.

Now the carriage riders must be thinking, "That poor child! She cannot remove her finger from her cheek. It must be they are grown together. I suppose she was born that way. What a sad thing!"

This is gratifying, Alice smiles into shocked, sympathetic eyes. The Overland glides over the empty streets of villages where people rock on piazzas or play croquet on green lawns, and she continues to provide the sharp contrast of tragic disability to this peaceful scene.

Those looking up from their magazine or their game as the Overland goes by must be thinking, "That poor child! ... Does her arm ache? Does her cheek hurt? Would she have a terrible scar if finger and cheek were separated? See how bravely she smiles!"

Actually the arm is beginning to ache and the cheek to hurt, and when they turn into the coastal road, Alice ceases with relief to play the role.

Aunt Molly cries, "There's the ocean, Liss! There it is! See the blue, straight ahead and a little to the right?"

And Granny says, "Oh, I smelled it before I saw it, Molly. Didn't you? Nothing in this world so bracing as sea air."

Alice sees it, too, and smells it. Now larger cars—Maxwells and Hupmobiles, Uncle Ezra says—are blowing their raucous horns at the Overland and passing it in clouds of dust.

Aunt Molly says, "I had no idea so many other people would be here on a November afternoon. Did you, Ezra?"

He shakes his head. He has to watch the road and the other cars. Alice can look at whatever is to the right of the Overland, and what is to the right of it now is a narrow strip of smooth white sand and breaking waves. The strip of sand widens with every turn of the Overland's wheels, and now there are people walking on it and children playing, the children in hoods and mittens, the women holding shawls over their heads to fend off the wind. Alice tucks her bare hands inside her coat sleeves. Her lips sting with the cold.

Granny leans over to speak to Alice. Alice cannot hear her for the wind, the crashing of the breakers, and the roar of the engine. Aunt Molly repeats it.

"She says there's nothing now between you and England."

This is incredible, yet of course it is true. The coastal road is higher than the beach. Alice is looking across the beach, above the shawled and hooded heads, into the endless expanse of the Atlantic Ocean. She remembers how it is on a map. The jagged line of the Maine coast and then the empty blue all the way to the British Isles, which themselves are only small patches on the blue; like ships riding the waves.

Until now, on a rare summer day at the beach with her grandparents, having ridden across fields and through woods on a trolley car, Alice has never looked so far or thought so far, but been fully content with feeling the warm sand between her toes, dipping water in a small pail, and with a small shovel digging a hole to pour the water into and watch it disappear . . . *Nothing between Alice and England . . .*

The Overland comes to the end of the strip of sand and begins to climb by a narrow road over ledges and between thickets of wild-rose bushes. It goes on up hill and down dale, with the sound of the breakers growing steadily louder but often with no view of the water, until it emerges suddenly on a high point of rock which the waves smash thunderously against on three sides. Here there is no car but the Overland. At what seems perilously close to the precipice, the brake is set, the motor turned off.

"Oh—Ezra!" shrieks Aunt Molly.

But he does not hear her.

"That is what they call The Nubble," he says, smiling, proud to have brought his women here. But they can't understand him.

"What did you say, Ezra?" shouts Granny.

"I said—THIS IS THE NUBBLE!"

"Oh," says Granny, nodding. "The Nubble. I've heard tell of it. Never was here before. Quite a sight, ain't it?"

They are the only ones here. The only people in this world. They sit for a minute staring, and in Alice the realization is dawning that four is too many. She wants to be the only one. Once, somewhere, a long time ago, she was the only one.

She must be again. She must have a world all to herself.

Aunt Molly says, "Well, we've got to get out of this wind. Jump down, Alice, dear, and we'll see if we can find a fit place to have a picnic—"

But when Alice has jumped from her seat to the ground, the wind catches her up and she goes flying off across the vast tumble of stones giants or the gods of the sea have pushed up there, her toes barely touching as she springs over deep crevices, leaps from peak to peak, seeing nothing but gray granite and sea-blue and icy-white, feeling nothing but the wind and salt spray, and herself a part of both.

After a while she peers down from her world and sees three dark figures trapped in another. Two holding on to each other as they step from one smooth ledge the short distance to a lower level and inch their way toward a black boulder. One, the bigger one, moves her hand beckoningly to a third figure above them, and he begins to unstrap a basket fastened to the side of some kind of little chariot. She knows they are somebody's Granny, Aunt Molly, and Uncle Ezra; but not Alice's. Not *this* Alice's. She spreads her arms and flies again. They have to be there. They have to stay there. They can't get away. Because they are old. But not Alice. Alice is young; Alice is free —free as the wind; Alice can fly. And on she goes.

Some time later she swoops down from the bright clouds and rainbows, happily aware again of hunger, and skips across to where sandwiches, red Baldwin apples, stuffed eggs, and a coconut frosted cake are spread out on a red and white checked cloth which covers a stone table. Uncle Ezra is pouring hot brown tea from a thermos jug into metal cups. Alice has never seen a thermos jug before. She stands watching the steam curiously.

"Well, here you are, then," says Aunt Molly. "You didn't break a leg and you didn't get washed off into the briny deep."

"Of course not," says Alice, puzzled.

"No," says Granny. "Good thing I made her change out of her Sunday shoes and put on the sneakers Joel got for her to wear to school. Course I was thinking of the wet sand and keeping her feet dry. But them rubber bottoms must cling like leeches to the rocks. We ought to get us some, Molly, case we ever come here again. Well, now, eat up, everybody. My land, whatever did you mix with these egg yolks? It's *real* tasty."

And Alice is back with them, sheltered by the black boulder they found, chewing on a cheese sandwich, biting with hard young teeth into a Baldwin apple, sipping tea so hot and sweet it brings tears to her eyes.

3

Then suddenly she is alone again, no longer hungry, and with no urge to fly. She sits quietly, in complete contentment, idly surveying the world around her. The same old ocean and white sand she first saw in a picture book, and saw later on a summer day with her grandparents; rocks tumbled in the same way on the island shore as on the coast of Maine; white gulls swooping effortlessly as Alice has swooped. The late afternoon sun lies warm over all, and the rocks spread lengthening shadows on the sand. There is no wind, and the waves are gentle, breaking softly, sleepily, with a distant, bell-like sound. Time is no longer being kept. Once it was frightening when the kitchen clock stopped ticking. Now the cessation of time is more like the silence of the metronome when the practice hour has ended. . . .

Up the beach many figures of all sizes are still playing in and out of the water. So many that few are distinguishable from the rest, and they only as brief flashes of white or color. But one red streak at the water's edge does not vanish like a firefly. Instead it grows larger, coming nearer. Gradually Alice recognizes nine-year-old Sue.

Sue does not see Alice. She is walking very slowly, swinging both arms forward at one step and back at the next, and her ruddy-brown head is bent. She seems to be looking for something lost in the shallow water around her feet.

As she approaches the rocks, she still does not raise her eyes, does not spring over the deep crevices or leap from peak to peak, but takes one step after another without looking beyond it. Alice sits watching the child, wondering what preoccupies her, what has blinded her to this shining world.

They are close to each other before Sue sees Alice. Then Alice smiles and lifts her hand in greeting. Sue does not respond. She only keeps on coming until her knee touches Alice's. Then she sits down on the rock. It must feel harsh to her bare skin. The red swimsuit covers very little of her thin brown body.

"I didn't know you were here," says Sue.

"Were you looking for me, Susie?"

"No."

"What were you looking for?"

"Nothing."

"I've been watching you. All the way along the beach you were looking down into the water. As if you had lost something."

"I was just looking. Not for anything . . . Can I sleep at your house tonight? I left my pj's and toothbrush on your steps."

"Of course, if you want to. If your mother's willing."

"She won't care."

"Did you ask her?"

"She's not there. She hasn't been back all day. I told Mrs. Batcheldor."

"She'll probably be home by the time we get back to the cottage. We'll call and ask. Your father may be there by then too. It's Friday. He's coming tonight, isn't he?"

"I guess so . . . They won't care."

After a minute Alice says, "Oh, I think they'll both care."

"No, they won't. If we don't tell them—and Mrs. Batcheldor doesn't, and she'll probably forget—they won't even know I'm gone."

"Why do you think that, Susie?"

"Because all Mummy ever thinks about and talks about is her *pictures,* and she gets mad because Daddy doesn't listen to her. All he thinks about when he's home is the kids. He's always taking them off somewhere, or putting them to bed or something."

"Doesn't he take you, too?"

"How can he? He's only got two hands."

"Doesn't he put you to bed?"

"Course not. Nobody has to put me to bed. I go to bed myself. . . . It'll be worse than ever tonight. Mrs. Batcheldor'll be trying to tell every little thing about how the kids weren't there and how she hunted and how scared she was and where they went, and Daddy'll want to hear and ask questions and Mummy'll be trying to tell him what she's been painting or show it to him and he won't listen or look and she'll really go *bo-i-ing* . . . Garmie?"

"What?"

"Do you think I'm their own child? Or was I adopted?"

"What are you hoping I'll say, Susie?"

"I don't care. It doesn't really make any difference. I'd just like to know."

"Well, I know," says Alice. "I was there. You were their

very first baby. I sat for hours with your Daddy in a hospital waiting room. Until the doctor came and said, 'You have a little girl, Mr. Gilman. She's tiny but she's all right. Weighed in at just under five pounds.' "

"What did he say?"

"He said, 'Thank God' . . . Then he asked how your mother was, because just before that she had been very sick. The doctor said she was going to be all right, too."

"Was Daddy glad?"

"Very glad . . . The doctor told us we could go down the hall and see you through a window. We did, and your father was one big smile when he looked at you."

"What did I look like?"

"I thought you were the most beautiful baby I'd ever seen. So did your father."

"Then what did he do?"

"He went to see your mother for a minute. He was the only one the doctor would let see your mother that night. Because she had been so sick. I waited until he came back and then went home with him to your house. He showed me the bassinet they had waiting for you, and the bath table and scales, and a chest full of baby clothes. He kept saying how happy your mother was that you were a little girl."

"Was he, too?"

"Oh, yes."

"Why?"

"Perhaps partly because he already had two boys."

"Gary and Weston? . . . Garmie! You just said I was the first baby they had! How come there's Gary and Weston, older than me?"

"Well . . . because your mother is not their mother."

"Are they adopted?"

"No, your father is their father. They were born when he

was married to their mother. Out in California. Afterwards he married your mother, and you were *their* first baby."

Sue is silent, eyes on the surf. Alice doubts if she is conscious of seeing it.

"Do you think Daddy loves Mummy?"

"I'm sure he does."

"Then why doesn't he look at her pictures?"

"I don't know. Maybe he does, but not enough. Maybe he doesn't know what to say about them. Your father isn't an artist. Or maybe he is thinking of something else."

"That other one. Gary and Weston's mother. Did she die?"

"Oh, no. She is in California. Gary and Weston live with her when they're not in school or with you."

"Did Daddy love her?"

"I'm sure he did."

"But he stopped. Why does he stop loving people?"

"I don't think he has ever stopped loving anyone who loved him."

"Then she stopped loving him . . . Does she paint pictures?"

"No, she is an actress. In movies."

"Maybe he wouldn't go to see the movies."

"I don't know how that would have been if she had made any while they were married. But she was only trying out for parts then. She didn't succeed until later."

"Mummy hasn't sold any of her pictures. She says it's because nobody knows about them. She wants to—exhibit them as soon as we go home. Exhibit is hung in a big hall."

"I hope she will. I hope I can see them when I come for Christmas."

"When she tells Daddy that about an exhibit he doesn't say anything. That makes her mad . . . Every time he comes I hate her for trying to make him look at her pictures and talk about them. And then I begin to hate him because he won't, and for making her mad."

"I suppose we'd never get mad if we could help it, and we'd never hate—even for a minute—if we could help it. Because it hurts."

"Why can't we help it?"

"Why can't you help hating sometimes, Susie?"

"Well . . . there's nothing else I can do."

"Or if there is, you don't know what it is. That's the same reason people get mad, discouraged, frightened, and have other bad feelings. They don't know what else to do. But there always is something else. Something better."

"What?"

"That depends on the person and the time and the situation. Each one of us, each time, has to figure it out. It's like an arithmetic problem. Sometimes we can't find the right answer, but just trying is better than nothing. Isn't that what you're doing right now?"

Sue looks at Alice with interest for the first time.

"Me? What do you mean, Garmie?"

"You knew your father would be coming home tonight. You thought your mother would talk to him about her pictures again. You thought he wouldn't say much, wouldn't really look at them. You thought you would begin to hate them again, and you didn't want to do that because you really love them and deep down you are sorry for them. So you decided to go away by yourself and think what to do instead. But you remembered how it was when Desirée and Margery disappeared this morning, and you didn't want to frighten anybody, so you rolled up your toothbrush in your pj's and told Mrs. Batcheldor you were coming to spend the night with me. And then you walked slowly, all by yourself, all the way down the beach, thinking

. . . That was wise of you, Susie. You managed well. You are young to be so wise, but it's none too soon. I'm proud of you."

Sue smiles. But then she says:

"Only—now I don't know what to do next!"

"Shall I make a suggestion?"

"Yes."

"I suggest you give me a pull while I still have a chance of getting off this ledge, and we'll go up to my cottage and look for your bundle, hoping nobody's puppy dog has run off with it, and then see what we can put together for our supper. Do you like salad? I have some lettuce, and some oranges and bananas and a basket of strawberries."

"Could I have just strawberries? And a thick slice of bread and butter?"

"You certainly may. If you can get me on my feet."

Sue stands up and holds out both hands. Sue is strong. Alice secretly compliments herself on avoiding being pulled forward onto her face by Sue's strength and eagerness for the task. They cling to each other for an instant in the wind, both laughing and breathless. Then hand in hand they walk up the beach toward the cottage.

Sue gives a skip, and rubs her nose against Alice's elbow. Alice smiles down, Sue smiles up.

Sue says, "Garmie, how do *you* always know what to do?"

A bright little spring bubbles up in Alice's heart and sends a warm brook flowing round it, a fresh source of life and hope.

She says, "Oh, I don't, Susie. But, like you, I began trying to find out when I was about your age and I've kept on trying ever since. I've made a great many mistakes and when I knew it I tried to learn from them. In all these years, I hope I've learned *something*. But just one thing I'm sure of. Life is very complicated for everybody, and perfect for nobody, and we mustn't expect too much, but just try to see things as they are, clear-eyed, do the very best we can about them, and wait to see if the afternoon isn't better than the morning or tomorrow better than today. Because by and by it's going to be. It's *bound* to be."

Sue doesn't comment. Alice wonders what she is thinking.

As they approach the cottage steps, Sue runs ahead and calls back joyously, "It's right here, Garmie! Nobody's puppy dog ran off with it!"

"Oh, great!" cries Alice. "God bless every good little puppy dog in the world!"

Sue laughs.

"Puppy dog!" says Sue. "Nobody else says 'puppy dog.' It sounds funny . . . I want to leave the hulls on the strawberries, Garmie. I like them to hold on to while I dip the berries into sugar and bite them off."

She snaps her young, white teeth together in anticipation. Click!

4

Late in the evening, after supper, after a few guessing games, after sitting for a while on the steps listening to the surf while Alice's fingers separated and reseparated the locks of hair on the head in her lap, after Sue has got into her pajamas and brushed her teeth, after Philip has driven up in his rented dune buggy, come in blinking, looking tired and bemused as he does so often nowadays, exchanged a few vague remarks with his mother, taken Sue under one arm and rumbled off with her, Alice looks for something to read when she goes to bed.

She looks for the day's paper, remembers that she has not been to the store today to get one, turns to the single shelf of books beside the dark fireplace. It does not offer much of a choice, containing only a dozen battered paperbacks, a stack of dusty comics, and a few hard-bound cast-offs from several generations of summer renters. *The Eyes of the World,* by Harold Bell Wright; *The President's Daughter,* by Nan Britton; *The Valley of the Dolls,* by Jacqueline Susann; *Three Weeks,* by Elinor Glyn. . . .

Alice pulls out *Three Weeks* and opens it, smiling down at the stained page, remembering the copy Granny had once found under Alice's mattress, brought to the kitchen at arm's length, and would have burned in the firebox of the cookstove if Alice at the dishpan had not shrieked, imploringly, that it had been borrowed from a neighbor. This copy has a moldy smell. Alice puts it back on the shelf, and sees for the first time the oldest book there.

It is the binding which attracts her. Once tawny gold in color, it is now faded, spotted, smudged, but the design is familiar—a spray of three-petal leaves and five-petal blossoms like small black stars curving to enclose the title on three sides. There were bindings like this in Granny's bookcase in the front entry, on schoolbooks which had belonged to Alice's mother in the days when the scholars at district schools had been expected to buy their own books.

But this title was not there.

Ten Boys Who Lived on the Road from Long Ago to Now: A Classic for Home and School, by Jane Andrews.

Alice opens it to see when it was published.

"Copyright, 1885, by Lee and Shepard; S. J. Parkhill & Co., Printers, Boston' . . . To My Nephew, William Ware Allen' . . . Preface: In preparing this little book my purpose has been threefold. First, to show my boy readers that the boys of long ago are not to be looked upon as strangers, but were just as much boys as themselves. Second, in this age of self-complacency, to exhibit, for their contemplation and imitation, some of those manly virtues that stern necessity have bred in children. Third, to awaken an interest in the lives and deeds of our ancestors, that shall stimulate the young people to a study of those peoples from whom he is descended, and to whom we owe a debt of gratitude for the inheritance they have handed down . . . Jane Andrews, Newburyport, Sept. 29, 1885."

Does it matter in the late 1970's what Jane Andrews of Newburyport, Massachusetts, did or tried to do almost a century ago?

It does to Alice.

She takes this book to bed with her, though it, too, has a musty smell.

The title of the first chapter is "The Story of Kablu, the Aryan Boy Who Came Down to the Plains of the Indus."

The chapter begins with a quotation in italics.

Man is he who thinks.

Alice frowns in surprise and bunches up her pillow to raise her head.

Isn't this what she herself was saying to Sue a few hours ago? Jane says:

Are you ready to take a long journey, first across the Atlantic to Europe, then across Europe, through Italy, and Greece, and Turkey, past the Black Sea, and into Persia? Look at your map and see where you are going, for this is a true story, and you will like to know where Kablu really lived. We have passed the Persian boundary and are in Afghanistan, and now we must climb the steep slopes of the Hindus Koosh mountains, and in a sheltered nook we shall find a house. It is built of logs laid one upon another, and the chinks are filled with moss and clay. It leans against a great rock which forms, as you see, one whole side of the house. The roof slopes from the rock down to the top of the front door, which faces the sunrise.

Here lived Kablu, four thousand years, or more, ago . . .

Jane tells how early every morning Kablu and his father rub sticks together to make a flame on a broad, flat stove in front of their house. Kablu's mother and sisters pour the juice of the soma plant and then butter on the flame until it burns bright, shining with a clear yellow light, and his father prays to the sun-god.

Jane says: "This is Kablu's church, his Sunday, his everyday, his prayer, his Bible, his minister. He has no other . . ."

Jane tells how the family has a breakfast of cakes made from crushed grains baked in the ashes, eaten with curds and the flesh of the mountain goat. Then the mother combs out wool for spinning and weaving to make a new tunic for her husband, and her daughters help her while Kablu and his father take a wooden plow into the field to get ground ready for planting.

Jane says: "You might have woolen dresses without keeping sheep, and butter and cakes without getting them from your own cows and your own fields of grain, but it is not so with these Aryans; they must do for themselves all that is done."

Kablu asks his father, "What does *man* mean?"

His father answers, "Man means one who thinks. The cows and the sheep and the goats breathe and eat and sleep as we do, but when calamity overtakes them, they have no new way to meet it; man can bring good out of disaster, wisdom out of misfortune, because he can think."

Alice's eyes leave the fine print of the old book and fix on a bare white wall. This *is*, in its way, what she has said to Sue. How did she come by it? Sue said, "Garmie, how do you know?" Alice knows such things because they were taught her by her grandparents, rarely in words such as those used by Kablu's father, but every day by the way they lived. Much that children learn they forget while growing up and are unconscious of knowing in the middle years, but if you live long enough it all comes back. Sometimes you think you have just discovered it. But sometimes, as now, the source of it is revealed. If so, there is a flash of light which takes you back to where you were when awareness of this particular truth or principle came to you. You are where you were then, as you were then. This is perhaps the most surprising, the most delicious reward for having lived seventy years. You can go back and do it again, feel it again. Not everything you have done and felt. Only the ecstatic moments. You remember some of the times you were frightened, despairing, grieved, but those are only memories. By some miracle you are saved from, insured against reliving them, and return only to moments of such delight that no words can ever fully describe or account for them. They must be lived to be known, and once known they can and will be relived with all their original intensity from time to time when one reaches the age when no moments of ecstasy occur to cut off earlier ones from consciousness. Such reliving does not come on call.

If you wonder, "What was it like to look for the first time at a picture of an ocean beach?" there is no answer. If you ask, "How does it feel to run across a giant's rock pile on a November day, leaping over chasms?" you are not told. If you try to recall what your grandparents talked about while she was kneading bread and he was mending harness in the kitchen on a winter afternoon, or while you lay abed in the adjoining room, or what they said to you while you were missing a high-school year because you had been ill and were not thought strong enough to ride the five miles into town and back every day, you cannot remember much of it, if any of it. But when least expected, a glance at sea and sand, or a seat on a rocky ledge, or a shabby old book filled with truth will waft you back to it as on the wings of the morning. A little, perhaps, as hearing a few bars of "Melody of Love" may remind Emily of a teenage love, but more dramatically and more completely.

It is true that man can think, and by thinking can bring good out of disaster, wisdom out of misfortune. Can, does, always has, always will. It is true, it is true. And truth is the most beautiful thing in the world. Alice knows this and can bear witness to it with great conviction because she has lived a long time and seen it proven over and over and over again.

With God's guidance, of course. But God guides the human creature only through his own thought.

Alice snaps off the light and lies in the dark in which quiet waves break gently against stone and run softly over sand.

When Sue is seventy, will anything ever take her back to today? If it does, it will not be to the morning when she searched for little sisters who had disappeared, or to the afternoon when she saw and felt the black thunderclouds of hate rising to cover her sun. No, if to anything it will be to dipping red berries into white sugar and biting them off their hulls, to curling up on the steps with her head in somebody's lap, to being carried sleepily by her father to his dune buggy. She may or may not remember—in that way remembering differs from reliving—that someone once told her, "We mustn't expect too much, but just try to see things as they are, do what we can about them, and wait to see if the afternoon isn't better than the morning, or tomorrow better than today. Because by and by it's going to be. It's bound to be." But whether or not Sue remembers being told this, she will know it, because she has already begun to collect proof in her own experience, and her set of proofs will be fully convincing, incontrovertible, by the time she is seventy.

Alice sighs in deep contentment and murmurs a prayer of thanks.

As she drifts off to sleep, Granny is saying: "Alice finished a quilt top today. You'll have to get her some backing and cotton batting market day so she can put it together. I never thought she'd ever be such a hand with a needle, and have the patience to stick to it until she got a job done."

Grandpa finishes winding the clock. Alice knows he is now easing his shoulders out of his suspenders.

He answers, "Likely wouldn't if she hadn't been kep' out of school this winter. Head is always in a book if she's got one to stick it into."

And this is strange, because the patchwork quilt, stuffed and backed, is already over Alice, keeping off the cold in which February winds wrap the small farmhouse, while she lies warm and secure, falling asleep. Maybe she will start some new patchwork tomorrow, in a new pattern. Now that she has made one quilt it should be easy to make another, and not take her so long. Maybe by summer she can make her own dresses to wear back to school . . .

5

Last night Alice had a telephone call from her daughter Emily. From the house in the Boston suburbs in which Emily had done the last of her growing up and to which she had returned with her family to live after her father's death. It is a larger and better house than Emily and Jim could afford to buy, a big brick house with wide lawns and fine old trees in front, space enough in back for producing not only flowers but vegetables. Sometimes they have difficulty maintaining and heating it, with all their other expenses. It was also more than Alice needed or could afford to maintain for her own use, but she owned it, it was the home Harley had provided for his family, and none of them wanted it to be sold. So for ten years now

Alice has occupied a three-room apartment in the wing which once served as Harley's offices, while Emily has had the main house with the long living room, the formal dining room, the spacious kitchen, and four bedrooms. On the whole this arrangement has worked well.

Emily called to say Melissa was steadfastly refusing to go to camp another season and also insisting that she did not want to go with her parents, Chris, and small Doan, born in Vietnam, for their annual visit to Jim's brother in Colorado.

"So we don't know what we're going to do with her, Mom!" exclaimed Emily, in mock despair which in no way concealed the naturally lilting notes Alice has always loved to hear. "She certainly can't stay alone all day, and Vicki has this lifeguard job she loves and really needs to pay for the clothes she'll have to get for college this fall. We don't even want Vicki to stay here while we're away. We'd planned to close up the house. Neighbors and police will keep an eye on it. Vicki can stay nights with friends. But what on earth to do with Contrary Melissa?"

"Well, I don't know, Emily. Would she want to come here with me?"

"Oh, *of course* she would. *You know* she would. When did she ever not want to be with you? But we've told her you're on vacation, you're having a summer off, you went there to spend time with Phil and his family, you can't always be at her beck and call . . ."

Alice has never known how Emily feels about this second daughter's special attachment to her grandmother, which began as soon as the Eustaces moved into the Dr. Harley Gilman house when Melissa was two years old, and has continued ever since. Alice is sure of very little about Emily beyond the obvious externals. Does it seem to Emily that Melissa would be closer to her mother if she were less close to her grandmother, and therefore that Alice is a usurper? Does Emily long for a more intimate relationship with Melissa? Does she wish Alice would agree that it would be difficult to have Melissa here at the cottage for two weeks, with the result that Melissa would have to accept her parents' plan for her and go with the family to Colorado? If so, Alice would like to do it. All Emily's life it has been a joy to Alice to please Emily. But how would Melissa interpret this decision, after having made it plain what she wants to do? She couldn't be expected to figure out the reason for it. Would she resent being obliged to do what she did not want to do and so withdraw further from Emily and Jim while at the same time feeling rejected by Alice? For Melissa this would be quite possible. Alice, at the telephone, caught a fleeting picture of a dark, slight, hurt, angry twelve-year-old silent in a corner of the back seat of a Volkswagen van, riding, riding, riding west through the midsummer heat . . . And what if all the time Emily had really hoped she and Jim, Chris, and the baby could make this trip by themselves, and thus sacrificing Melissa would be worse than useless?

Emily and Jim have the most successful marriage Alice has ever observed. It began well and has grown in perfection every one of its twenty years. They are both goal-oriented and their goals, when not shared, are complementary. As they work toward one they already have another one beyond, usually several in sight. And they are in love, more so all the time. Jim and Emily are idyllically happy in the rare times when they can be alone together and free. Chris is a younger Jim, and Doan clings to Chris, needing little of anyone else. Chris and Doan do not prevent Emily and Jim from feeling alone; and do not mind being overlooked, as Jim would not mind—might welcome—being ignored by everyone but Emily. Emily is perfectly adjusted to her menfolk and to babies. It is womankind that she confuses and perhaps is confused by, though she may not be conscious of it. Melissa is probably conscious of it, Vicki may be, in her different way. And Alice is.

It is probably always best to speak the truth when you are asked a question, if you know what the answer is. Certainly it is absurd to hesitate long about doing so on the chance that the asker may want you to say something else when you have no way of knowing what he wants, or whether he knows.

Alice said last night, "I'm always glad to have Melissa when she wants to come and you want her to. How would she get here, if you decide to send her?"

"Oh, Jim could put her on a plane," said Emily. "If you're sure she won't tie you down. You could meet her, couldn't you? Rhonda has her car there, doesn't she? Of course, I don't know what we'll do about this. I thought I'd find out from you what the chances were before I bothered Jim with it. Now I'll talk to him tonight. If he's willing, I'll probably ship Melissa out no later than Wednesday. I'll let you know. We want to start early Friday morning. Jim talked with Everett last night, and they hope we'll get there early next week because they're eager to try out a lot of new camping equipment Beck gave Ev for his birthday. We're going to have at least a week in the high Rockies. Jim's so thrilled. How he loves those mountains! Me too. By comparison they make ours look like pygmies. And Ev's boys will take Chris on some overnights out of camp. He'll like that, and it will give Ev and Beck and Jim and me some evenings all to ourselves. Jim and Ev grew up on cards, and they've kept at it until Beck and I are pretty good, too. I can hardly wait for Jim to get out there, it always does him so much good. He's been working terrifically hard on the Waite case, and going to meetings just about every night on the plans for solid waste disposal, or whatever is going to be done to close the open dump. They don't seem to have got far on that, there's such strong opposition to every idea that's proposed. But he did win the Waite case. I suppose you read about it in today's paper. The jury brought in the verdict yesterday. I couldn't go because it was my day at the hospital, but I picked him up at the office afterward. He was limp with relief, and when I found out he hadn't eaten a thing since breakfast, I called up home to tell the kids we'd be late, and we went over to the Crown for dinner to celebrate. I had one of their marvelous curry dishes, but I insisted Jim get a good steak. After that he was quite revived and slept fine last night. Until he called Ev I wasn't sure he would be up to going anywhere by the time he was through with this case. But it seems to be all working out . . ."

So now it is Monday and Alice is walking slowly along the beach, tossing a small, smooth stone loosely imprisoned in her hand. She is thinking of Emily and of Melissa, of Rhonda and Phil, knowing she will not ask Rhonda for the use of her camper, which is all Rhonda has to take her to the remote parts of the island where she prefers to paint. Rhonda must need the isolation she seeks every day. No, Alice will get the island taxi to take her to the airport, and she will be there well ahead of when Melissa's plane is due, standing tall at the gate where twelve-year-old Melissa may see her as the plane comes in and will surely see her as she comes down the ramp; though if it is foggy the plane will be late, or the flight out of Boston may be canceled at the last moment. Sometimes when this island is fogged in, incoming planes land at a neighboring island. What would Melissa do in that case? It is a chancy flight for a child alone. Is Emily thinking of this too? Does it worry her? Alice thinks Emily would say confidently, "Oh, Melissa can cope." Perhaps she can. Perhaps she always can. Alice hopes so.

When Alice was twelve, she had only seen a plane and

that only once, high above her grandfather's field. She had seen it coming over the marshes, shrieked, "Granny! Grampa! Quick! There's an airship going over!" and raced toward the hill, where she stood leaping like a jumping jack and waving both arms like a semaphore in her excitement. The plane was flying quite low. The noise of the single engine was deafening. She could see the pilot (he was wearing a white shirt with the sleeves rolled up), and he saw her and waved. She was sure she saw him smile. For years she believed he would come again someday, land in her grandfather's field, turn off that noisy engine, get out of the cockpit, stride toward her smiling, and say, "Did you think I had forgotten you? I came as soon as I had a plane of my own. Will you fly with me?"

Not long after that Alice had her first ride on a train, going to visit her grandfather's sister, Aunt Em, in Lawrence, Massachusetts. Like Melissa, Alice traveled alone. Her grandparents had driven her behind Old Bell to the little station they called The Depot on the riverbank. They bought her a ticket at a window in the wall. The stationmaster came out to raise a metal flag which would tell the engineer he had a passenger waiting here. The passenger was Alice. She stood between her grandparents on the platform. It was very quiet. They could hear the telegraph clicking in the ticket office, see the river flowing between banks covered with alder bushes. There was a blue butterfly soaring, dipping, lighting, and soaring again. Grampa took out the big gold watch he carried in a vest pocket and looked at it lying in the open palm of his hand, as Alice now held the small, smooth stone.

"She's due," said Grampa.

As if the engineer had heard him, a black engine, puffing black smoke, came round the bend, along the riverbank, so far away it made almost no sound. But now its whistle blew for the crossing, the same *too-oot, too-oo-oot, toot, toot* Alice had heard in the distance so many nights as she lay in her cot in the step bedroom.

Granny tightened her grip on Alice's hand and drew her back, close to the dun-colored clapboards of the station house. The engine seemed now to be sliding along the track, drawing three red cars behind it. It was not moving fast but it was so huge! The nearer it came the louder its noise, and from its great iron wheels blew a strange wind which did not push against you but sucked you in like a whirlpool. Alice was sure that Granny's old straw suitcase, leather straps and all, left out there alone in the middle of the platform, would be dragged under those giant wheels and chewed up. She would have run out to get it, but Granny held her hard by the station wall.

Then the train stopped. In the sudden stillness a man in a blue suit with gold buttons and a blue cap with gold braid appeared on the steps of one of the red cars, looking at the watch in the palm of his hand as Grampa was looking at his.

"You're a minute late," said Grampa, handing up the straw suitcase.

"Not bad," said the man on the steps.

Granny let go of Alice's hand and pushed her forward.

"This my passenger? Traveling by herself?"

"As far as Lawrence," said Grampa.

"All right, little lady. On we go." Over his shoulder, he promised Grampa, "We'll make it up between here and there. We'll be on time in Lawrence. Somebody meeting her there, I think's likely?"

"Yes. Her Aunt Em and Uncle Eben. She's got her ticket."

Alice held out the ticket. She could hardly have lost it. It stuck to her hot fingers.

"Well, now, you just hang on to that, little lady. We'll find you a seat now. We'll give you a good ride. Lots for you to see between here and Lawrence." He spoke again to her grandparents. "Don't worry. I'll look after her." And then, "All-ll aboard!"

The train was starting on as Alice sat down on the scratchy red plush seat with the straw suitcase beside her. She waved through the sooted window glass to her grandparents, alone on the platform, and saw tears running down Granny's brown cheeks.

Alice had a fine ride. The man in the blue suit, who told her he was the conductor, came by often to talk to her. He even let her punch her own ticket. She loved hearing him call out the names of the stations where the train stopped.

"Jew-ett!" *Jew*ett!" . . . "Eli-ot! *Eli*yot!" . . . "Ports-mouth! *Ports*mouth!" . . .

But the best part of the trip was when he called, "Law-rence! *Law*rence!" and Alice, looking out of her window, saw Aunt Em nodding vigorously, smiling and waving a lace-edged handkerchief from the protection of the brick wall of the Lawrence station, while Uncle Eben in a white linen suit and white panama hat with a polka-dot band, smoking a long cigar, strolled confidently toward the still moving train . . .

Alice will be at the gate, in full view, when Melissa's plane lands.

6

She turns at the far end of the beach and, walking slowly back toward the cottage, hears a rattling roar in its vicinity. This roaring when at its height suddenly ceases. She is near enough now to the cottage to see two figures come around it from the back, swing up the steps, and disappear inside. She has never yet locked her door on the island, though Phil and Rhonda have told her that this summer they do whenever there is no one in the house, and always as soon as dark comes down.

By the time she is in front of the cottage, the two figures are noisily emerging. Two young men bare to the waist, in khaki fatigue pants and desert boots.

One waves his arm.

The other shouts, "That you, Garm? Don't know who we are, do you?"

She shades her eyes with a hand, studying them.

"Well, for goodness' sake! I know you're Gary and Weston—but I don't know which is which. And where on earth did you pop up from?"

"I'm the elder," says one, dropping an arm across the bare shoulders of the other. "I'm the firstborn, heir to the throne, and all that. This is the no-'count younger son, known to his peers, he tells me, as Crayfish."

"He's Weston," says Alice. "And you're Gary. Well, what a surprise! Did anybody know you were coming? Your father didn't tell me. Shall we sit on the steps or go inside?"

"Anywhere you say, Garm."

"I vote for inside," are Weston's first words. "May be food in there. We haven't eaten since morning. Thought there'd be grub on the boat, but there wasn't."

"No beggars allowed in my kingdom," Gary says, grinning. "And nobody under twenty-five has a vote. You're not twenty-five yet, are you, Crayfish?"

"Near enough," says Weston. "Give me any more harassment I don't need and I'll start a revolution."

"This island is *my* kingdom," says Alice, "and Article One in the constitution says nobody here goes hungry. Inside with you, both of you . . . Now, while I rustle up something to eat, tell me—where did you drop from, how long are you going to stay, and how did you know where to look for me? It's so long since I heard from you, or anything about you, I thought maybe you were in foreign parts. Some place like Nepal, or Turkey, or Siam, or Uganda."

They draw tall glasses of water at the kitchen sink, stretch out on the floor with their bare backs against the wall, lie there drinking and talk.

They say they had not seen each other for a year, until they decided to have a reunion by making up a small caravan to cross the country, from sea to shining sea. At that time Gary was just back from India, where he had been studying transcendentalism until he wore himself out with so much thinking and decided what his system needed was a shot of action.

"About then," says Gary, "old Crayfish here was in the same mood after two years of lounging around grad school, doing a so-called dissertation on a minor Roman poet. So we put the screws on the Queen Mother to set us up with a couple of motorbikes, took a quick dip in the bland Pacific, and headed east."

"Will you stay for the rest of the summer?" asks Alice.

"Staying is what we're getting away from." Gary, now at the kitchen table, grins as he holds a dripping lobster sandwich in both hands. "Especially poor old Crayfish. He can't rest until he gets out of the country. Never has been anywhere, you know, since the Queen sent him on a guided tour of Europe when he got through prep. If he ever finishes eating and starts talking, he'll tell you what he thinks of guided tours. No, we're taking the next boat back to the Cape and rolling north into Canada. Some morning up there he may wake up and find me gone. This kid has to be on his own before long or he'll never grow up."

"May your muffler drop off before *you*'ve been on your

own a hundred miles," mumbles Weston. He tells Alice, "Gare doesn't know one end of a bike from another. Helpless as the Queen with a motor."

"The place to go," says Gary, "is Amco. We've heard that on every TV set we've turned on across the country. Amco must own all the American networks by now."

"You haven't seen your father," says Alice. "He just left this morning, but he'll be back Friday night. Surely you can wait—"

"We should be across the border before Friday night. We're the Pepsi generation. Something else we learned from TV."

"Then you'll come back this way?"

"We may never come back, Garm. Who knows? Right now the wilderness is what grabs us. We may throw up a little shack in the tall timber and start ourselves a commune."

"If a shack is thrown up," says Weston to Alice, "you know who'll throw it."

Alice sits watching them eat, her arms folded on the edge of the table.

"It's not right," she says firmly, "that you shouldn't see your father while you're this near. He hasn't seen either of you since Weston graduated from college. And then you were in Kenya with the Peace Corps, Gary. He will be very disappointed."

"You really think so?" Gary asks, raising heavy dark eyebrows.

"I know so," says Alice.

"The Queen said something like that. She gave us his address here and we found out at the post office where their place is. But I figured she just wanted her baby to check in somewhere. Crayfish was dutiful, though. So we came over and went up there. Nice spot they've got on the bluff. But nobody was home except the kids and a woman we assume is their jailer."

"Cute kids," says Weston, reaching for an éclair and pouring another glass of milk. "They told us where you were. Wanted to ride over with us. We would have taken them, but She wouldn't let them come."

"Be reasonable," says Alice. "How was Mrs. Batcheldor to know you were who you said you were? If you told her who you were. She is responsible for those children when their parents are away. Rhonda was probably out painting. She'll be home by late afternoon and would put you up—or I could—the rest of the week. So you would be here when your father comes. It's not a bad place at all to spend a few days. In fact, your father loves this island more than any other spot he has ever been. We owned a cottage here, you know, when he and your Aunt Emily were children, and spent every summer in it. But we had to sell it to buy a good house for them to grow up in. When your parents used to visit us there, your father always made a point of bringing you boys over on the boat to spend a day here. But I suppose you can't remember it. You were very small."

"Bet the Queen didn't come," Gary says, grinning.

"Once, I think."

"That would be enough. Too primitive for the Queen."

"Don't worry, Garm," says Weston, putting down his empty glass, pushing back his chair, and looking straight at Alice with wide, warm dark eyes. "If you say Dad would be sorry not to see us, that's enough for me. We'll see him. At least I will. Not now but later. If not here, then in Chicago on our way west. You can count on it."

"I will," says Alice. "And so will he. I hope it will be here, when he can show you the island. And maybe more of the family will be over then. I'd like for Emily and her family to know you. None of her children has ever seen you, and that's a situation which should be changed."

"Garm believes in families," Weston says to Gary. "Something to keep in mind if you ever start thinking again."

"Meantime," says Gary, "we'd better be off or we'll miss the boat. Anyhow, you've seen us, Garm. You can tell Dad we're chips off the block, two magnificent human specimens, burning up the macadam on our way to throw up great sheets of Canadian gravel, in unabating search of Truth, Reality, the Ultimate, and the eventual achieving of the Great Gilman Dream."

"Don't let Gare put you off, Garm," says Weston, pulling Alice against him on the back steps of the cottage, and kissing the top of her head. "Funny thing is, he half means it. Maybe more than half."

They swing onto their motorcycles, as Alice watches, and roar out of the grassy driveway into Dock Street. As the sound dies away, the world seems strangely still.

Clearing the kitchen table and washing the dishes at the old iron sink, she wonders what is to become of Gary and Weston, who have never lived with a father since they were six and four years old; whose mother since then has belonged to her career as an actress, to her public, and to her admirers around the world; whose only homes have been a succession of schools; and who have learned, from books and other people and the workings of their own minds, nobody knows what.

She remembers a boy in the district school whose eyes were narrow and blue like Gary's. The children called him Tommy, and he was in Alice's class; just those two in the class for a year or so; then Tommy went ahead of Alice. He seemed to read a page at a glance and remember everything on it but never to be really thinking about it. You could not tell what Tommy was thinking. The teacher called him Thomas. Once he said suddenly, loudly, so loud that everyone in the room turned and stared at him, "I wish you wouldn't call me Thomas." The teacher said coldly, "Your name is Thomas. The schoolroom is no place for nicknames." At recess the children asked him, "What do you care if she calls you Thomas?" Tommy said, "I hate it. It's what my aunt calls me. And my father." Tommy had no mother. The summer he was twelve years old, his aunt told his father to drown the five baby kittens he was keeping in a basket under his bed. Tommy threw himself over the basket, but his father dragged him off and carried the kittens in a grain bag to the river. Tommy set fire to the mother cat, ran to the shed across the road, and shot himself with his father's hunting rifle. Alice cried when she heard about it; cried all day and couldn't stop. Grampa told Granny, "You hadn't ought to said so much before her. Young ones have to get used, more gradual like, to Satan's works . . . Never you mind, lovey. Tommy's all right now. God's taking good care of him. I wouldn't be surprised but he's got a dozen kittens, and never a one of 'em ever going to get bigger, or get into fights, or die." Alice thought, sobbing, "It was the kittens he had he wanted to keep. Tommy isn't used to—to heavenly kittens."

But Gary has survived being twelve years old, and sixteen, and twenty. Perhaps it is better not to know a father than to know one you hate, better to have a mother who is busy being a famous actress than to have none, better to have a brother than to be an only child as Tommy was. Somewhere along the way Gary has developed his own wry sense of humor, so that he can laugh good-naturedly at others and also at himself; laugh even at his own desperate search, and that of others, for what is so far unknown and may long remain so. This may be what is saving Gary for the time when he will understand what he is here for. He is actually, Alice thinks, very much like his father. Phil, too, though he grew up surrounded by a loving family, always seemed to be searching for what he could not find, and still is. Gary's humorous twist, which he has acquired on his own, might have been a great help to Phil.

Weston, Alice thinks, resembles his mother in looks and perhaps in disposition, though she never felt acquainted with Delores, and she cannot remember ever seeing her show more than a superficial affection. Delores called everyone darling, did a good deal of kissing, and could make her purple eyes shine like sun on the sea, at will; but one felt that she never really noticed or responded to anyone but Delores, that whatever she did was for the purpose of promoting Delores, of leaving behind when she spun away an imprint she assumed would be indelible. This is obviously not true of Weston. He loves his brother. He would like to know his father. He went out to Alice, spontaneously; that was in his eyes, his voice, his touch.

She hopes Weston will marry and make the family he has not yet had. She wonders how he feels about girls, how girls feel about him, what kind of girl would want to marry him and be a good wife to him. There is so much Alice does not know about Weston. Does he? Does anyone?

She remembers another boy. His name was Tim Corcoran.

7

Tim had the use of his mother's driving horse to take his sisters and himself the six miles to high school from the farm where they lived, and Grampa paid him fifty cents a week for Alice to ride with them. From the first Granny had dark reservations about this arrangement. She said nothing specifically against it, since there seemed no other way for Alice to get into town to school, but her reservations were in her eyebrows and voice every morning as Alice left and every afternoon when she came back.

It was not so much, though partly, that Corcoran was a new name in the old neighborhood; nor so much, though partly, that Inez Rundlett (and the Rundletts had been among the first settlers) had married and brought home a city boy who had a stiff shock of fiery red hair and an impudent grin, and who had been born and brought up a Catholic, to which faith Inez was soon converted. So the Corcorans, as the first and so far only family to go into town to mass early every Sunday morning, were already back home and in their old clothes when their neighbors walked or drove past in hats, gloves, starched shirts and skirts, silk neckties and ribbon sashes on their way to worship together at the clean, bare, plain little Baptist church which their grandfathers had built and bought family pews in and which therefore belonged entirely to them and God with no intermediaries needed or wanted. It was more, Granny implied, that one just never knew about the Corcorans, had no idea what they might do next, and therefore in any association with them it was essential to maintain a safe distance and be constantly on guard.

The Rundlett farm was far enough east of the Plaisted farm for the Corcorans to have prepared for high school in another district than Alice's. Until she began riding with them, she had never been near enough to speak, had rarely seen them.

But how quickly and easily she had come to feel she knew them very well!

Mary Corcoran was a senior that first year Alice rode with them. Mary sat in the front seat of the democrat wagon beside Tim, who was a junior and drove Mavourneen, the horse. Theresa Corcoran, like Alice, was a freshman. They sat in the back seat, in the mornings finished together as they rode the problems and passages of translation which had baffled them the evening before, and at school were inseparable. After Mary graduated and went off to secretarial school, she was replaced in the wagon by Pansy (she had another name but the Corcorans and Alice called her Pansy). Theresa and Alice preferring the back seat because they wanted to be together. When Tim had graduated and Alice returned to school after her year's absence, Theresa had taken over the reins and Alice sat with her in front, leaving the back seat to Pansy and to Michael, who was a freshman now.

It was like that with the Corcorans. Whatever one of them left behind, a younger one picked up.

It was true that no one could tell what a Corcoran would do next. Alice found this enchanting.

The first two years they might all be singing at the top of their voices as they came within earshot of where Alice stood waiting, bare-armed and bareheaded in early fall and late spring, raincoated and rubbered in the between seasons, huddled in the brown plush coat and blue hood and fringed scarf in winter, but always with lunch box in one hand and lumpy green felt book bag in the other.

She could not be sure they were all singing until she could see their mouths. The voice she missed if it was not raised was Tim's sweet tenor. Mary and Pansy both sang alto, Theresa and Michael soprano. Corcorans sang if they were happy. They sang because they were happy. If one Corcoran was not singing when other Corcorans were singing, he or she was staring straight ahead with stormy eyes, chin on chest, gripping reins or whatever lay in his lap so tightly that the cords of the fingers showed white at the knuckles. Most often it was Tim who was not singing, and on those mornings Alice worried about him, but the other Corcorans didn't. They just sang louder than ever, and livelier tunes, and laughed a lot, sometimes poking fun at him.

"Come ON, Tim! Snap out of it! Quitcha crybabyin', will ya? Wake up, Timmy, and hear the birdies . . . My gosh, Tim Corcoran, you look more like a horse than Mavourneen!"

Of course Tim did not look like a horse. Who ever saw a red-headed horse with freckles and dimples? Tim could never banish his dimples, however hard he tried, but they were more like scars when his eyes were stormy.

Alice found it impossible to sing, laugh, chatter, or even work out a translation or an algebra problem as long as Tim was unsmiling; and she hated the others for making fun of him— until it performed a miracle, as she came to see it usually did.

She climbed silently into her place, at such times, sitting pressed into the corner as far as she could get from merry Theresa, and waited.

"Hey, Tim, looka here, you're scaring Alice. She prob'ly thinks you're about to have a conniption fit. I mean it she's getting tears in her eyes and her mouth is getting all quivery. She may not dare to ride with anybody that looks so mean. She may try to jump out and get all tangled up in the wheel. How would you feel then, Tim Corcoran? You want Alice to kill herself?"

Alice held on, staring straight ahead as Tim was staring, and waited.

Nearly always, after the other Corcorans had in this way drawn her into the teasing, in a little while Tim roused himself, usually only to say, "Oh, lay off me, will ya?" and give Mavourneen's rump a slap with the ends of the reins to urge her on; but once he had spoken at all, the spell was broken, and soon he would be talking, laughing, or singing with the others. Sometimes the first word he spoke was over his shoulder to Alice.

"How about your homework, kid? Finish it last night?"
Then her day could begin.

"One algebra problem I couldn't get."

"Which one? Read it out."

Tim was very good at algebra, and liked geometry even better. He was taking solid geometry now.

Once or twice when he did not speak all the long, slow ride into town, she spoke to him before she followed Theresa into the school building. She had to, very low.

"Tim? Are you—are you all right?"

Then he grinned down at her, scars turned back to dimples, and sunshine peeked through the clouds in his green eyes.

"Sure, kid. I'm okay. I bog down sometimes, but I always bounce back."

In following days, while she waited mile after mile, she had this to remember and to count on.

The year after Tim graduated Alice never saw him. The next year—Alice's and Theresa's senior year, for Alice had made up her work to graduate with her class—he was working in a grocery store in the nearest city, came home Saturday nights and went back Monday mornings, riding into town with the other Corcorans—and Alice—and taking the trolley car from there. He was a little taller now than when he went to school and considerably broader shouldered. His strong, ruddy hands were very clean, with close-clipped nails, and had fine gold hairs growing on the backs. Now he had stories to tell, all funny, about the customers in the store, the people to whom he delivered groceries from a basket on the bicycle the store gave him the use of, the grumpy lady who ran the boarding-house where he lived, the moving pictures and carnival shows he went to at night.

On those Monday mornings, when the Corcorans stopped for Alice, Tim handed the reins to Theresa, came around to put Alice's book bag and lunch box under the seat, gave her his hand up, and climbed in beside her.

At first he explained this by saying, "Likely Alice hasn't finished her math. How do you ever get a passing grade when I'm not around, kid?"

Theresa went off into a gale of laughter at that, asking, "Who you think you're fooling, Tim Corcoran?" and Pansy and Michael joined her.

But Alice too was older now.

She said lightly, "By the skin of my teeth. I can tell you that, Tim."

After the first time he made no excuses, and after that first time Alice always had difficult problems awaiting solution. Alice loved Monday mornings. It was like having every week begin with Christmas Day.

Granny said, "I don't see why that great boy can't find some way to get to work besides riding with you young ones. It's too much of a load for the horse."

Alice answered demurely, "He's talking about getting a motorcycle."

Tim had said expansively, "Tell you kids what I want. I want a motorcycle. A Harley-Davidson. Have one, too, first thing you know. Maybe with a sidecar. If I do, you can take turns riding with me Sunday afternoons."

"If you do," said Theresa, "I know who'll get ten rides to one for any of the rest of us."

Alice thought, "She means me. And Tim means me. But how could I? Granny would never, never let me."

One morning early in the spring she saw Tim scribbling on a piece of her yellow scratch paper, after a proposition had been proved and marked Q.E.D. with a flourish. Before tucking the book into her green bag, he thrust the paper inside it.

She read his scribble in the girls' coatroom while the first bell was ringing. It said: "There's something for you in a hole in the fourth post from the northeast corner of your pasture fence. If you want to know what it is, better get there ahead of the birds and the mice. Now tear this paper into bits and throw them away. See you next Monday."

The rest of that school day was an iridescent blur.

She flew from the wagon into the kitchen, hugged Granny, crying, "It's spring, Granny! It's spring! As soon as I've changed my clothes I'm going down in the pasture and see if I can find us some pussy willows. I've kept thinking about pussy willows all day!"

Granny settled her glasses, smoothed down her apron, and said, "I don't think's likely they're out much. Your grandfather tapped the maples today; I told him the days ain't warm enough yet for sap to run good, but he's got a hankerin' for a taste of syrup."

Alice was already at the top of the steps, dropping her pleated plaid skirt in a swirl around her feet, pulling off over her head the new crushed strawberry sweater Granny had knitted for her between Christmas and Easter, and unbuttoning her pongee blouse.

Ten minutes later, in a winter dress too short for her though the hem had been faced, a winter mackinaw with sleeves which did not reach her wristbones, outgrown rubber boots which pinched her feet, she was at the northeast corner of the pasture. From here the fence ran in two directions and Tim had not told her which one to take. It did not matter. If she chose wrong, she could choose again. She stood still for a minute, looking at the trees and the sky, listening to the silence, feeling on the threshold of something beautiful and postponing discovery in favor of the delicious taste of anticipation.

Then she chose wrong. The pasture fence posts were old

railroad ties (Grampa called them sleepers) into which side openings had been bored to admit the ends of poles; but the fourth one south from the northeast corner was still solid, clutching its poles stoutly.

She was glad she had chosen wrong. Now everything was still ahead of her. She walked slowly back to the corner, stood there for another minute, looked up at the sky and whispered, "Thank you, God, for letting me be all alone, for not having even a leaf out or a bird singing," and then moved toward the west where the sun was going down, spreading a rosy-gold banner along the horizon behind the bare branches of birches and poplars and the almost black pyramids of firs and pines.

The fourth post to the west had a deep hollow in its top. The weathered wood had rotted away; ice had formed in the hole and worn it a little larger, a little deeper each year; probably birds had nested there. The posts were not all of the same height. This was one of the tallest ones. Alice had to climb onto a pole to look down into the hollow, after reaching up to find it with her fingers.

It had felt and now it looked packed nearly full of dry marsh grass.

Standing on the round pole, keeping her balance with one hand, she dug gently into the grass and felt something hard. A corner of a box . . . Four corners of a small box . . . She drew it out slowly, as incredulous as if she had not been told it would be there. She had not been told it would be a box. She had supposed it would be a letter. She looked at the box in the palm of her hand, half disappointed, half excited in a new way. Her first conscious thought was that she wished she had not torn Tim's note into bits as directed.

But surely she would never forget a word of that note; always be able to see again his penciled scrawl on yellow scratch paper.

There's something for you in the fourth post from the northeast corner of your pasture fence . . .

Comforted, she let herself down from her perch, squatted to make a lap—the ground was too wet to sit on; water oozed up around the soles of her boots—undid the knot in the twine, which held a cover on the box, and took off the cover.

Inside there was a folded sheet of blue-lined composition paper which might have been torn from Teresa's loose-leaf notebook. It had punch holes along one side.

When she took out the paper, something fell into her lap. Had she known it would? Was that why she had so carefully made a lap?

She did not look to see what it was. There were words on the paper, and it was words she wanted most of all. These words had a beginning and an end.

"Dear Alice" . . . He had never addressed her as Alice before. Always, if he called her anything when he spoke to her, he called her "kid," exactly as he did all his sisters and brothers except Mary. ". . . Your true friend Tim Corcoran."

"Alice . . . Corcoran." Alice Corcoran. *Alice Corcoran.*

And now becomes then. Then is now. Alice is not remembering. Alice is there, scooched, squatted, sitting on her wet heels, staring at the words on the slip of blue-lined paper, words written for her eyes alone.

Dear Alice

I will leave something else in the same place next Sunday if you will come for it. This Friday I will get off early from work and be in the village in time to ride home with you and the kids after school.

If you will come to get what I leave next Sunday will you wear this pin Friday so I will know?

If you will come I wish you would come on Sunday around the middle of the afternoon when I would be there. If you will, then wear the pin on either the right or the left side.

If you can't come Sunday but you will come after that wear the pin in the middle. Under your chin.

If you will come Sunday I will be there from noontime right up until dark.

Your true friend Tim Corcoran

She reads slowly, disbelievingly, rereads, and reads again. These are Tim's own words, written in his own hand. She sees his hands, one moving a chewed pencil, the other pinning down the paper, sees the strength in the fingers, the deep-set nails, the hairs on the backs; sees the set of the head, his intent eyes, his underlip thrust out to blow a stray lock off his thick sandy eyebrow, the motion in his throat as he swallows. All this she has seen many times before. But he is not writing now of cubic feet or acreage or isosceles triangles. There is no Q.E.D. on this paper. This is not the end of anything, but the beginning of everything. The beginning for Tim, and the beginning for Alice.

The beginning of what? No one knows. When something begins, no one ever knows where it will take you, or where it will end. And it hardly seems to matter at the time, beginnings are so small, or so instantly exciting, or so magically sweet. The beginning, if you notice it at all, is in itself as far as you can bear to go, as much as you can bring yourself to face.

Alice does not know how long she stays in that crouching position. It seems, when she sees the water has reached her ankles, that she has always been there, has grown there like the surrounding tussocks of marsh grass. She looks around in bewilderment and starts to rise as if from a dream. She has totally forgotten the pin, hears it drop with a small splash, and stoops again, feeling for it frantically in the cold, muddy water. The pin she is to wear. Or not wear. In this place or that place, depending.

She retrieves it, and now looks at it for the first time.

A bar pin. A slender, wet gold bar with tiny blue enamel forget-me-nots blooming all over it.

Forget-me-nots.

How could she forget? She will never forget . . . But this is more than an ornament. This is a sign and a symbol. What will she do with it? If Granny finds out she has it, she will not be allowed to keep it. Not only that, but then Granny would find out where she got it, and Alice would not be allowed to go into the pasture alone for a long time, if ever. So how could she return the pin to Tim? Maybe Granny would return it to Tim herself, and say that Alice would no longer be riding with the Corcorans. Then maybe there would be no way Alice could go to school . . . finish the year . . . graduate . . . So today would not be the beginning of everything, after all, but the end of everything.

No, the only safe way is to put the pin and the letter back in the fence post, pretend she never found them, pretend she lost Tim's first note before she could read it or that, having read it, she decided at once that it would be improper for her to go into the pasture to look for whatever he might have left for her, just as Granny would have prayed she would do.

But she cannot do this.

Tim will know as soon as he sees her on Friday that she did go to the pasture. Though his pin is nowhere to be seen, he will know, because there has been a beginning. There has been a change in Alice. She is not the same person she was yesterday. She is someone new, with sudden springs bubbling up inside her, now hot, now icy. She is so newly alive she tingles. Tim will know this. Tim will look straight at her as he climbs into the wagon, and she will be unable to look back at him. Her eyes will fall. He will see only her eyelashes brushing her cheeks. And he will know why.

Besides, she cannot leave Tim's letter and pin for him to find under the musty grass in the fence post, telling him she has not seen them or touched them when she has and he will know she has. That would be cruel. And it would be a lie. He does not deserve it, and if he did she could not do it to him. Perhaps if she wrote out an explanation to leave with them. . . . But she has no paper except what he has written on; she has no pencil; and what explanation could be given except Granny's? Alice is not Granny.

She realizes she is very tired. She wants to cry. But she must not cry. Granny would say, "What in the dear Lord's world have you been crying your eyes out for?"

She knows she will cry if she does not run.

So she runs toward home, in and out among the trees, leaping over some of the boggy holes, plunging blindly into others. Seeing the cleared field before her, she pauses uncertainly, on impulse unbuttons the blouse of her dress, tucks the letter inside her camisole, fastens the pin securely under her arm where she can feel it by pressing her arm against her side, and runs on again across the uneven ground Grampa plowed last fall.

She remembers to take off her boots in the back entry, but when she reaches the kitchen stands still on stockinged feet and looks around as if she had never been in the room before. A lamp on the table has been lighted.

Granny, stirring at the stove, says, "Well, where's the pussy willows?"

Almost without knowing she is going to, Alice says, "What? . . . Oh, just like you said, they've hardly started to come out."

What a tangled web we weave, when first we practice to deceive.

This is in one of the old books which used to belong to Alice's mother. The book has a worn green cover and is on the bottom shelf. It has "Emma Mary Plaisted, 1899" written on the flyleaf in delicate script with airy curls on the capital letters and at the end of the "y." Alice did not know until Granny told her when she was old enough to go to school that her own name was not Plaisted but McIntire.

Granny tells Grampa at supper that it certainly was too early to tap the maple trees, for Alice just spent more than an hour hunting all over the pasture for pussy willows and could not find one branch to pick.

Grampa says nothing, dipping again into the bowl of fish hash, and taking a big spoonful of Granny's piccalilli.

But on his way to the milking the next night he lays a bunch of pussy willows, glinting white at the tops of their shiny dark casings, on the kitchen table and says to Alice, "Don't know where in thunder you looked."

Alice stares at them, only half seeing. She feels Granny's exasperated glance as from a great distance. It is Tuesday now. Tomorrow will be Wednesday and then the day after tomorrow will be Friday. How can she wear the pin, if she decides to? What will she say when Theresa cries, "Hey, you've got a new pin! Where'd you get it?" Tim does not know Theresa will do that, but Alice does. That will happen in the morning, of course. If Alice waited to put on the pin just before leaving school, it would be even worse. Theresa would cry, "Where on earth did that pin come from? You didn't have it this morning."

Usually Alice dries the supper dishes while Granny washes them, but tonight she insists on doing them alone while Granny gets at the mending. Then she pulls a chair close to Granny's and begins to patch a mitten.

"Hadn't you ought to be studying?" asks Granny.

"I've only got a little to do tonight," says Alice. "I'll do it later. I'm not a bit sleepy."

Granny is pleased. Grampa is hard on mittens.

Now he is reading his newspaper on the other side of the lamp. Alice keeps an eye on the pages as he turns them. If she is going to speak, she must do so before he reaches the last one, because then he will say it is time to go to bed. It has never been any use to ask Grampa to buy you anything because he just says, "What does your grandmother think?" But it often helps to have him hear you ask her.

The only way you can do it is to *do it.*

Alice draws in a breath and forces words out on it.

"There's something I wish *so* I could have."

Granny bites off a thread.

"What's that?"

"A middy blouse."

"What's a middy blouse?"

"Kind of like shirts sailors wear. Just about every girl in school has got one but me. Some are white and some are blue. They have sailor collars, with braid, and they don't go inside your skirt to be always pulling out like other blouses; you wear a middy over the top of your skirt, and some of them lace up on the sides."

Granny sews silently for a minute or two. Grampa has turned to the last page.

"Think some girl would lend us a pattern?" asks Granny.

"They don't make them. They buy them all made. I've seen them in the window of the dry-goods store."

"Humph," says Granny. Then, "Seen any prices on them?"

"They cost a lot," says Alice wistfully.

"Shouldn't wonder. All made up . . . How much?"

"A dollar—and a half . . . And everybody wears a big black silk scarf with them. Tied in a square knot . . . They're handsome, Granny."

"Yes . . . Well . . . Maybe sometime . . . We'll see."

Grampa is folding his paper and getting up. Alice draws in one more breath.

"Oh, Granny . . . If only I could have it to wear to school the rest of this year! Like the other girls! Could it be my graduation present? After graduation, if I start nurse's training, I won't have any place to wear a middy except in my room at night."

Granny sews on, peering into the oncoming future, visualizing Alice alone at night in some strange little room, exhausted from a long day's work with the sick, lying on a cot bed in a sailor blouse and a black silk scarf she did not have in time to wear where it could be seen. Just as Alice intended she should.

"I told you, Alice," Granny says. "We'll see."

The next morning she says, as Alice picks up her lunch box, "You can go into the store after school and find out just what one of them middy blouses costs—there may be different prices."

"And the scarf, too, Granny?" asks Alice with shining eyes.

Because it is in the middle of the square knot in the scarf that bar pins are worn.

"You can find out," Granny says. " 'Twon't hurt to know."

Friday morning Alice is ready, waiting at the end of the lane in spring sunshine as Mavourneen pulls up her load of Corcorans on creaking wheels. Alice's jacket is unbuttoned.

"Look, Treece!" cries Alice. "Grampa got me a middy yesterday when he went to market! I'd begun to think I'd never get one until I was too old. You've been wearing them for over a year, and Pansy got hers for Christmas."

"None of ours is blue, though," says Theresa, slapping Mavourneen with the reins to start her on, "and we don't have a scarf between us. Seems like the sky fell right over your head, Chicken Little. Lucky you!"

But she sounds as cheerful as always, as if it is not very important to Corcoran girls whether they have middies or not, or what color they are, with or without scarves. What Corcorans have they like. What they don't have they don't especially want. Except Tim. Tim and Alice dream.

"I know," says Alice demurely. "I was surprised he got me a blue one, and a scarf too."

Perhaps she had been a little surprised, but not very. She had made it as plain as she could just what she wanted.

"And the bar pin in the scarf," says Theresa. "Did he get you that, too? It's awful pretty."

"No," says Alice, easily, like a memorized line in a play. "I found that. I don't know who it belonged to. But nobody was wearing it. Looks like it might have belonged to my mother when she was a girl."

"Lucky you," says Teresa again.

And Pansy says, "Maybe I'll get a scarf for my birthday. My birthday's next month."

So another crisis is surmounted, another step taken. Somehow the school day passes. The afternoon is almost hot, and Alice's jacket lies across her knees as Tim crosses the square from the trolley to the wagon. She reads the conflicting reactions on his revealing face as he sees his pin, and where she wears it. She tries to reassure him, when he climbs in beside her, with the brightest smile she can muster, though tears are close to her eyes and she wonders if he can see them. She can hardly bear to have Tim in the least disappointed after waiting out a long work week. Can it have been as long a week for him as for her?

As soon as she can, she engages him in a half-done geometry problem on which her writing is so fine that Theresa surely could not read it even if she tried, and which has worked carefully into it, "Find fishhook tin in mailbox Sun."

When Tim comes to this, he does not raise his eyes from the paper, but spots of color appear on his cheeks and neck. His hand, holding the pencil, trembles for an instant. At the end of the lane when he helps her down from the wagon, he squeezes her arm, and when he gives her her book bag and lunch box their hands touch.

The next day, when Saturday morning's work is done, Alice tells Granny, "Now I'd like to take an hour and see where Grampa found those pussy willows. It's so nice out! I could almost smell lilacs and apple blossoms when I hung the dish towels on the porch."

"Well, that was your imagination running away with you, right enough," says Granny. "But likely you can find pussy willows now if you're a mind to. Sap's running good the last day or two, and we'll start boiling down this afternoon."

"Oh, that's always fun," says Alice, enthusiastically. "And it makes the whole house smell so good!"

She gives Granny a quick hug, which Granny seems as always scarcely able to endure without protest, though Alice knows she likes it, pulls on the old boots and the mackinaw, and is free to run bareheaded down across the field and into the shelter of the pasture pines. She does not need the mackinaw for warmth, only for its pockets, one of which contains a small tin box which once held fishhooks and now holds the note she wrote to Tim in bed last night long after her grandparents were asleep.

"Tim, dear . . ."

She had been obliged to rewrite the salutation several times because sometimes it seemed she must not go beyond "Dear Tim," and at other times she felt driven to make it "Tim, dear," since at those times she so longed to say, "Tim, darling," or even "My darling Tim."

Tim, dear,

Thank you for coming today even though you knew I didn't dare to. I wish I could have, for I'd love a chance to talk all by ourselves without the kids listening and interrupting, and I wish I could tell you how much I love my beautiful pin. I just hope you know that. But I'm in a bad spot. Living with grandparents isn't like living with parents, I guess. My grandparents love me a lot and do a lot for me, but they're so old they think I'm just a child and hardly let me out of their sight except to go to school. If I asked them if I could meet you here I know they wouldn't let me and if I wanted to ask you to our house they wouldn't let me either. I guess you wouldn't want to come, either. It wouldn't be any better than riding with the kids, probably worse. I can just feel them worrying about me all the time. I don't know why they worry, but they do, and it's awful. Sometimes I feel as if I can hardly breathe.

Oh, Tim, what can we do? I like to be with you. You know I do. I have since the first day we rode to school. Now all these years have gone by, and we've never, never, never had one chance to talk alone. If we did, I'd have so much to say that I can't say to anybody in the world. And I guess you would, too. We can't always keep it bottled up inside of us, can we?

Think, Tim. Think hard what we can do. And then find a way to tell me. Because you're so much older and smarter than I am, maybe you can figure it out like you do math. I can't.

I'm lonesome, Tim. Are you?

I'll wrap this around a match so you can burn it before you go home.

See you Monday morning.

The letter has no signature. He will know who wrote it.

Alice runs in and out among the scrub pines, comes like a homing pigeon to the corner post of the fence, turns her eyes to the west—and there, leaning against their mailbox, Tim is smiling at her.

"Tim!" she whispers, her fingers clenching the fishhook tin in her pocket.

"Who—else?" he asks; but has to clear his throat between words.

It could be nobody else, of course. To find anybody else here would be horrible.

He comes toward her. He stops quite close to her. Now Alice cannot see his face for he is taller than she and she cannot raise her eyes.

She hears him say huskily but with a singular gentleness, "You're all out of breath, Allie."

She has never been called Allie before. Now it is Tim's name for her. Nobody else must ever call her Allie as long as she lives.

She whispers, "I ran all the way. I have to find pussy willows and get home as soon as I can."

"I know where there are pussy willows, right near. Come, I'll cut you an armful. Then you'll know you have them. While we talk."

He doesn't waste time with questions. He doesn't need to. He knows why she has to find pussy willows and has to have them first. He reaches for her hand and plunges into the scrub, drawing her behind him. A little way in beyond a clearing, on the bank of the pasture brook, there are masses of pussy willows. Tim lets go of Alice, pulls a jackknife from his pocket, grasps several branches in one hand, cuts them off with the other, and pushes them against her, laughing now and suddenly at ease. She stands there while he cuts and pushes until her arms are full. Then he straightens triumphantly, snaps the knife shut, and throws back his head, far enough away so that they are looking at each other. His eyes are the clearest green she has ever seen them.

"What if Granny notices they're cut?" Alice asks, low. "She knows I don't have a jackknife. Girls don't. When you break off pussy willows they have strings on the ends."

"Tell her a boy at school lent you a knife to play stick knife," says Tim. "And you forgot to give it back."

He takes his knife from his pocket and comes close to drop it into hers. It clinks against the fishhook tin.

"I'll bring it to you Monday," whispers Alice.

"No need to whisper," says Tim. "Nobody's here but us."

No, nobody there but them, in a clearing in a wilderness. Nobody anywhere really, but them. Another Adam and Eve, in their own Garden of Eden.

"How did you get here?" asks Alice softly. "I mean, how did it happen? How?"

"To wait for you, Allie. You said yesterday I'd find a note Sunday. So I came over here as soon as I got home. The note wasn't here yet. I waited until so late I was sure you wouldn't come last night. And I've been here since right after breakfast this morning. Look, I even brought a rubber blanket for you to sit on. How's that for a Sir Walter Raleigh?"

He strides across the clearing, disappears, and she hears his footsteps crackling through the thicket. What if he never comes back? He comes back, fish pole against his shoulder, and on his arm one of the two worn black coverlets the Corcorans have on the seats of their wagon to be unfolded and spread over their knees when it rains.

For an instant Tim and Alice have all they need, all they will ever need. Each other, a blanket against the weather, and a pole for catching fish in the brook.

Tim props the pole against a tree, takes her armful of pussy willows and lays them on the ground, shakes out the blanket, sits on it, and lazily reaches up to pull her down beside him.

"All right," he says, "where's my fishhook tin?"

"You don't need it now."

"Yes, I do. Where's my fishhook tin?"

"It isn't your fishhook tin. It's my grandfather's."

"Then darn the old fishhook tin. What's in it is mine. Give me what's in it."

"It's just a letter."

"Give me my letter."

"Maybe—when I—go—"

"No. Now. You've had a letter from me. I've never had a letter from you. Give it to me."

"You weren't here when I read your letter. I'm not supposed to be here when you read mine."

"But you're going to be." He repeats that, with a note of exultance in his voice. "You're going to be. Right here beside me. Where we can talk about it as I go along. *Give me my letter, Allie.*"

She tries to shake her head. He laughs, reaches into her pocket and pulls out the tin, cries, "I thought that was what clinked!"—and laughing lips brush her cheek swiftly.

Brushed her cheek . . . Laughing . . . How many times, alone, she has tried to imagine this. Just this. Now it has come to her, and she is enveloped by the touch as by the silvery mist when sun begins to penetrate heavy fog.

As the silver brightens to gold she sees that Tim is reading.

" 'Tim, dear,

" 'Thank you for coming today even though you knew I didn't dare to . . .' "

He senses that she is watching now, and throws her a blinding Corcoran smile, puts a hand on her knee, and says, "I'm here today because by today you would dare to come."

He goes on reading.

" 'I'd love a chance to talk all by ourselves . . . ' "

He turns his head toward her, and she looks down at her hands twisted together in her lap.

"Now we've got it. Let's not blow it . . . *Say something, Allie."*

"I'm talking in the letter," murmurs Alice. "Saying things I'd never say out loud. Never."

After a minute of silent indecision, he reads on. About her grandparents, how she is not allowed to meet him here or ask him to her house.

" 'Sometimes I feel as if I can hardly breathe . . . ' "

He drops the letter on the blanket beside him, takes his hand from her knee to put his arm around her shoulders and pull her hard against him, covers her hands, and begins gently untwisting them.

Into her hair he says tenderly, "Poor kid . . . Poor Allie . . ." Later he says, exultation creeping back into his voice, "You're breathing all right now, Allie. Must be. I can feel your heart beat. Can you feel mine?"

She nods, but says nothing. Should she be feeling the pounding of Tim's heart? Is it right for her to feel it? She has written and he has read, "They wouldn't let me . . . I don't know why they worry, but they do . . . They love me a lot and do a lot for me, but . . .

Later, having freed her fingers, he picks up the letter. To see it, while keeping her pressed against him, he has to hold it where she sees it, too.

Oh, Tim, what can we do? I like to be with you. You know I do. I have ever since the first day . . . and we've never, never,

never had one chance to talk alone. If we did, I'd have so much to say that I can't say to anybody else in the world . . .

He drops the paper again, and draws her forehead against his neck, plays with the buttons of her old mackinaw.

"Say it, Allie . . . Say it . . . Tell me . . ."

She can say nothing. If she made a sound, the world would burst into tears. In this world there is only a silken thread between incredulous delight and black despair.

"Say a little of it, sweetheart. You wrote there, 'We can't always keep it bottled up inside of us' . . . Come on. You can tell old Tim anything . . ."

She tries. No word will come out. She wants to indicate this by shaking her head, but he is holding her so close movement is impossible. Yet he must have felt it.

After a minute he says, "Maybe you can't talk yet, Allie. But I can. So I will . . . Living with parents isn't that different from living with grandparents. My folks wouldn't want me to bring you to our house either. They'd be afraid I was falling in love with you, planning on marrying you someday. They probably think it will kill them if I marry a girl who isn't Catholic."

Then Alice hears the astonished croak of her own voice. "They—*do*?"

Tim laughs, giving her a quick squeeze.

"Sure, kid. But I don't let that bother me. They'll find out in time that it won't . . . Time, Allie. That's all we need. Where you make your mistake is you seem to think the way things are now is the way they'll always be. They're not. You say 'never' a lot. There's no never in my book. You're 'most through school. Before long I'll be earning enough to support us. When we're on our own, we won't be tied to our folks and can do what we want to. Between now and then we just have to make up our own minds what that is. We won't let anybody else do it for us, will we? Just us, Allie. You and me . . ."

He buries his face in her hair. He kisses her temple gently. He puts a strong hand under her chin and lifts her face up to his, smiles down at her, kisses the tip of her nose several times . . .

His mouth finds hers. She cannot draw back. She does not want to draw back. Her mouth clings to his. And now there is nothing else in the world. Nothing, nobody but Tim . . .

"Alice!"

The sound from another world is a loud rumble and cuts through.

"Alice, I've come to take you home."

It is Tim who draws back, starts to get to his feet. Alice, blinking in bewilderment, sits there looking past him and sees her grandfather just inside the clearing. He is not looking at Tim. He is looking at Alice.

"Your grandmother is worried," he says. "You've been gone so long. Come along with me now."

His voice. She has always loved his low voice. It has ceased to be loud. It is slow, quiet, in the usual way. But the lines around his eyes, the clefts in his thin cheeks, are deeper than she has ever seen them before; and his eyes are narrow with anxiety and sadness.

"Oh, Grampa—"

She is up and running toward him. He holds out a brown, veined hand and she takes it, pressing her cheek against his arm, wanting only to comfort him.

But he is turning his eyes on Tim now.

He says, "Tell your folks not to stop for Alice again. It'll be so I can take her to school the rest of the time until she's through."

That is all he has to say to Tim.

He says to Alice, "Them your pussy willows?"

She whispers, "Yes."

"Well, gather 'em up, then. If you want 'em."

She stoops for the pussy willows and, as she rises, gives Tim one last, despairing look. *Do you see now, Tim, how it is? It is never, like I thought, and it will always and forever be never. This is goodbye. Goodbye . . . darling Tim.*

Her grandfather has turned his back, is already at the end of the clearing, and she follows him, shaking with sobs.

Tim is left behind, alone among the scrub pines, alone with his fish pole, his rubber blanket from the Corcoran wagon seat, and her letter.

. . . Think, Tim. Think hard what we can do. And then find a way to tell me. Because you're so much older and smarter than I am, maybe you can figure it out like you do math. I can't.

I'm lonesome, Tim. Are you?

But you can't figure it out, Tim. Because nobody can. This isn't math. It's people. Either we're going to be lonesome the rest of our lives, or our folks are. I don't know why it's so, but it's so. Maybe—maybe we can stand it better than they can. I don't know, but we have to try . . . Tim—oh, Tim . . . Tim . . . Tim . . .

Alice must have finished the dishes. She is now turning on the light in the bulb which hangs from the ridgepole of the narrow, unfinished loft which is the only bedroom in the beach cottage. She snaps the switch which plunges the rude staircase into darkness and looks back to assure herself that she has left no light on the floor below. It is increasingly eerie how much one who has lived a long time does automatically, with no recollection later of whether or not it has been done. Comes of one's being transferred so often without warning to another place and time altogether, even to a quite different body and mind and heart.

She thinks, "But I wouldn't have it any other way. Surely

wouldn't exchange this miracle, this most interesting part of me, to be able to concentrate constantly on what I am doing with switches, keys, steps I am taking, what the clock says, what the calendar says this very day, this very hour and minute. Today is just countless grains of sand . . ."

Ready for bed, she pulls off the light, raises the shades of the two windows—she wants the sky and the water to surround her while she sleeps, and to be wakened by the sunrise streaming in—but does not want to go to bed yet. She is still too wide awake, too close to the experience of being Tim's Allie in the clearing in her grandfather's pasture. So she steps out on the balcony, sits in her nightgown on a bench there, hidden by the dark, her bare feet almost touched by the rolling waves she can hear and smell but cannot see.

. . . Her feet had been heavy as lead following Grampa out of the pasture and up through last year's stubble. They reached the barn first. The house was on the other side of it from the pasture. It was not until they were close to the barn that the searing thought penetrated the roiling black clouds which filled Alice—*what will he tell Granny? What will she say to me?* . . . But Grampa never looked back at Alice. The big door in the end of the barn was half open, and he walked through it without a word or a glance. Alice stumbled on alone up to Granny's back porch and kitchen door.

That is one of the worst parts of being young; perhaps the worst. Whether or not something of awful importance has just happened, it may be about to; and you cannot know what it is, or how far-reaching its consequences will be. You are forever on the brink but unable to see over the edge to know whether the slope is gentle and sunlit or precipitous and deadly.

Granny said without looking up from the bread she was kneading, "Find the pussy willows?"

Alice whispered, "Yes."

"Well, better get 'em into water. 'F you want 'em to last any time."

They never mentioned Tim to her again. If Grampa ever told Granny where and how he had found Alice—and she supposed he did, at least part of it—Alice did not hear him, and Granny never spoke of it to Alice. They all went through the motions of everything being as it had always been. But it wasn't.

For the two months left of Alice's last year of high school her grandfather had the horse harnessed into the buggy every school-day morning when it was time for her to leave—a little later than usual, for Bell pulling only two people could make better time than Mavourneen pulling five or six; and every afternoon when she came down School Hill he was waiting at the foot to drive her home. And not only that. Alice, who had to suffer, had to do it behind closed doors, alone—as Tim was alone—and not admit it, not let it show more than she could possibly help. She no longer studied at one side of the kitchen table after supper, but carried her books and papers and a lamp to the sewing table in her room. For the first week or two she could not study when she got there, could only suffer, and the marks on her papers reflected her preoccupation with pain.

Would those weeks have been harder or easier if her grandparents had united to confront her, that day they took her away from Tim, with what she knew they regarded as a breach of faith, as the actions of a weak, silly, unreliable girl, as a poor return indeed for having devoted going-on-to-twenty years of their hard lives to caring for her and bringing her up as best they could? Or if she had found Granny in her rocker moaning, sobbing, and Granny had exclaimed, "Oh, Alice! What have you done? Why did you do it? How could you treat us so? You have broken our hearts! I wish I were dead." Would Alice then have been able to tell her truly just what she had done, why she had done it, just what Tim had done and why he had done it, how she loved Tim and why? Not likely, since Alice was too young to know the answers herself; it was all too new and strange. But if she could have, could Granny have understood it, accepted it? If she could have, could Grampa have? Then could they have comforted each other, even if they still could not agree with Alice on what was best for Alice? Would this at least have prevented Alice from going away to suffer alone, and so kept them together as they had been a few weeks ago?

Nobody would ever know, because this was not the way of Alice's grandparents. They did what they felt they had to do in the only way they knew to do it. Whatever had happened had happened; that could not be changed now; but they had put a stop to it. The future would have to be dealt with when it came.

After the first dreadful week or two of riding to school and back with her grandfather and trying to avoid Theresa's eyes, Alice became aware that not only Theresa's but the eyes of other girls—and boys—were not so much curious as understanding, not critical or amused but warmly friendly, newly admiring, frankly intrigued.

As Alice hurried up School Hill one May morning, Ev Scott caught up with her.

"Hi, Alice."

"Hi."

"The old boy won't let you out of his sight lately, will he?"

"You mean my grandfather? I don't think you should call him 'the old boy.'"

Ev laughed.

"Aw, I didn't mean anything out of the way. I'll call him your grandfather if you want me to. He's trying to see to it you don't go out with fellers, isn't he?"

"Who told you that?"

"Theresa."

"Theresa—talks too much."

"Don't blame Theresa. You always came to school with her. Now you don't. You don't even speak to her. Everybody's been pestering her to find out why. She had to say something."

"Why didn't you ask me?"

"Now, that's a foolish question. Way you've been lately, nobody dared ask you anything. Look at the hot water I've got into asking you a question now."

They had reached the school building. Ev held open the heavy arched door at the top of the granite steps. She looked up at him for the first time. Ev Scott was the son of a village minister. He had blond hair that curled, and bright brown eyes. He was on the football team, she knew, though she had never seen him play. She had seen him last winter skiing down the hill and taking the jump over the wall as she and Theresa and the younger Corcorans turned in at the gate at the foot of the walk. And he was the president of this year's graduating class.

His big white teeth flashed in an easy grin.

"Not that hot, was it?" Alice said with lifted eyebrows. "If you really want to know, what Theresa says is true. But don't blame my grandfather, either. He just doesn't realize I'm old enough."

Climbing the inside stairway, joining the girls crowding the coatroom, she thought, incredulously, "But I *am*. I really am. Or Ev Scott would never have talked to me that way. I couldn't have answered him that way. We never even spoke to each other before."

Light was coming through at last. Almost blinding. The faces of the other girls stood out against it.

She said, "Hi, Ruth! . . . Hi, Glenda . . . Oh, hi, Treece—"

Over fifty years later, sitting by herself in the salty dark, listening to the waves strike harmlessly against the rocky point of Harley's island, Alice knows all the rest of this story, or all anyone will ever know.

The day Ev Scott first spoke to Alice, she ate her lunch with Theresa as she always had until two weeks ago. She had prayed for death every night during the first week. What if her prayer had been granted?

Now the two girls sat together beside a budding lilac bush, their knees touching, unwrapping sandwiches.

"You're all okay again, huh?" said Theresa, hungrily taking her first bite.

Alice nodded, breaking off a corner.

"What did Tim tell you?"

"Just that your grandfather would take you to school now. We needn't stop. He wouldn't say any more. He didn't have to. I could figure it out."

Well, Theresa was a year older than Alice.

"Kids ask questions?"

"Sure. I told 'em to forget it and M.Y.O.B."

"Good for you."

They finished their sandwiches. It was warm and peaceful by the lilac bush.

"Tim okay, too, you think?" asked Alice, looking without caring to see what remained in her lunch box.

"Sure," said Theresa. "I guess so. He doesn't come home any more."

"Doesn't come home?"

"Not since the first weekend after . . . He's gone into the Navy."

"The Navy?"

"He wrote Pa a letter. Said he'd been thinking about it quite a while, so he went for the exam and they took him. He said he'd see us first leave he gets."

Alice thought he might write to her, but he never did. Or if he did, she did not get his letter. She could not believe Granny would keep a letter which came in the mail addressed to Alice.

As time went on, she thought, "Of course he's not going to write. There is nothing to say."

She had talked to her teachers about nurse's training and applied for admission to programs in hospitals whose addresses they gave her. At a class meeting she had been chosen to write the Class History to be delivered on Class Day during Commencement week. Everyone was talking about the dance which would follow the Alumni Banquet. Those seniors who could dance were teaching the few who couldn't. Those few included both Alice and Theresa.

"Come *on.* Dance with me," urged Ev. "Or this may be the last time I'll ask you."

They were around the old square piano in the corner of the main room. Doris's stubby, hard little hands were pounding the yellowed keys. Several couples already spun in the spaces between the piano and the screwed-down desks and chairs, between the piano and the platform from which Mr. Morrison conducted the opening exercises every morning with his staff of teachers seated along the wall behind him. Even Theresa was on . . . Alice gave herself up to Ev. He gathered her in . . . Now Alice was on, too. Flying and spinning . . . Spinning and flying . . .

When the music stopped, she swayed uncertainly, but Ev steadied her.

He said, "Pretty good for a first try. At least, you didn't fight me, the way some girls do. You'll be better at it tomorrow."

She would be better at everything tomorrow.

Word came from three different hospitals that she would be accepted there for training. Her grandparents looked proud.

One of the hospitals was in Portland, Maine, one in Manchester, New Hampshire, one in Boston.

Grampa said, "Best you stay in your home state. Portland's fur enough off to go."

Alice said, "I'll ask my teachers."

The teachers said the Boston hospital had the best course, promised the brightest future.

Granny said, "Well, now, she's right the teachers ought to know better than we do about such things. Once she gets on the train, what difference will it make if she rides a half an hour or so longer?"

Boston!

Her classmates told her at rehearsals they really liked her Class History. They said it was not dry as dust, like most. On Class Day she could see her grandparents, and Aunt Molly and Uncle Ezra, all dressed up, sitting next to the center aisle looking pleased and proud at her in the ruffled blue organdy Granny had made by hand and the silk stockings and bronze slippers which were her graduation gift from the Westons. She heard her own voice growing louder, clearer, more assured . . . That night, after the banquet, not only Ev asked her to dance but nearly all the other senior boys who danced at all. Whenever she was not dancing, Paul Chisholm came and sat with her. Paul had lost a leg in a train accident when he was ten and gone about on crutches ever since. People said a new leg would cost a lot and Paul's family couldn't afford one for him. She felt close to Paul that night. The seniors all felt closer to one another than they ever had before, but she felt especially close to Paul, somehow. He asked her what she was going to do now she was through school, and when she had told him, she asked what he planned to do. He said he thought he would work in his cousin's shoe-repair shop until he had learned the business and saved enough to have a shop of his own. She wondered what it would be like to mend a pair of shoes and then another pair of shoes and another all day, all week, year after year, when you could wear only one shoe. If he mended enough shoes, would he get the money to buy a new leg? Or would it be too late then? Was it already too late?

Sitting with Paul, thinking of Paul, she thought of Tim, by now probably swinging high on rope ladders, leaping into and out of hammocks, springing confidently across wet, sloping decks, and setting off on shore leave nights his ship was in port.

Lucky Tim!

She was glad and proud that she was going to learn to do what would help people like Paul who had been hurt as he had been hurt or in other ways.

8

Years later, having been home to care for Grampa in his last illness and then taken Granny to the Gilman house near Boston to spend the winter, she and the children, at Granny's insistence, had driven her back to the farm in the spring and stayed a school vacation week to help her get the house clean and comfortable.

One day as they stood at the sink, carefully washing and drying the sprigged company china the children were bringing a piece at a time from the parlor cupboard, Alice said: "You know this is going to be too much for you alone, Granny. I'd like—"

"Nonsense. 'Tain't neither. Nobody but myself to do for. House will go now till fall anyways. Maybe then you can come up and give me a hand 'f you want to."

"Still . . . Harley and I have talked about it. We'd like to arrange with somebody in the neighborhood to come in for a day a week at least. Somebody you'd feel free to call on the telephone if you should need to."

"Don't intend to need to."

"Of course you don't, but one never knows. None of us do. Can you think of anybody in the neighborhood I might get?"

"No. Only ones I know are old as I am, or else sick-abed, like Hattie Welch."

"Any young Corcorans still at home or living nearby? What about Theresa who went to school with me?"

"She the oldest girl?"

"Next to oldest."

"She got married and went off years ago. A Navy man, folks said. The oldest one died, I think I heard."

"The oldest girl, you mean?"

"Yes."

"Her name was Mary . . . There was a younger one, too, who went to school when I did. They called her Pansy."

"She may be the one that took over the farm, along with her husband, a few years back when her folks moved to Dover. I don't know which one it was. There was quite a flock of them. But one of them married a Canadian and he's a farmer. Folks say he's bringing the Rundlett place back pretty well. Name's Legere, or something like that. Corcorans had let Rundlett's run down. Especially after he got sick a year or so before they moved out."

"Would you be willing to have Pansy—or whichever one it is—come over one day next week if I ask her and she wants to?"

"Well, there, no harm in giving it a try, if it would ease your mind. But don't say anything about making it regular, till I see how it goes."

"Of course not, Granny."

The next day Alice drove up to the Rundlett-Corcoran-Legere place, toward evening. The buildings were newly painted. The yard was neat. Lilacs were budding beside the porch. A man's voice called the cattle up the pasture lane for milking.

"Co, co, boss; co—"

A chubby pink-cheeked woman with floury hands came to the screen door when Alice knocked.

"Hello. Are you Pansy?"

The woman laughed. "I've been called that, but not much lately. How did you know?"

"We went to school together. I was Alice McIntire. Alice Gilman now."

"Oh, my gosh! Treece's old sidekick! Tim's girl friend once, too, wasn't you? Well, come along in. I'll have to let you open the door. I'm all covered with flour . . . Take a chair. Have you come back to live at Plaisteds'? No sign of life there all winter—"

Alice explained her errand, saying she would have to leave her grandmother in a day or two and the cleaning and settling would not have been entirely done. Was it possible Pansy could come over one day the first of next week for at least a few hours to see what Granny needed help with? Pansy said of course she could, well as not, be glad to, like to look after the old lady as much as Alice wanted her to. Alice said, well, Granny didn't consider herself an old lady, didn't think she needed looking after, would have to be handled with kid gloves.

Pansy said comfortably, "I've always got along good with old folks. I like 'em, that's why. I didn't want Ma and Pa to leave here after I got married, but someway they couldn't get along with Pete. He works hard, but he's one that don't seem to, and Pa had always been so drove he couldn't understand that. Ma couldn't stand his being so upset all the time, sick as he was, so she thought they'd be better off living with Tim. Didn't do Pa much good, though. He died a few months after they moved. Ma said Tim's kids bothered him awful."

Tim's kids . . .

Pansy laughed. "Hadn't ought to, had they, after the tribe he used to have around him here? But everything's different, I guess, when you're old and sick. You got kids, Alice?"

"Two."

"I'll tell Treece that when I write to her. She's got seven. One's a new baby. Funny thing, Pete and I've never had any. I never thought but all of us would have a lot of kids. Sometimes I wish we had, but other times I think it may be just as well. Pete's never said anything about it, one way or the other. Anyway, gives me plenty of time to help out your grandmother when she wants me."

They agreed on an hourly wage and that Pansy would call Alice collect after the first day to tell her how long she worked and how it had gone, and Alice would send her a check. Pansy wrote down Alice's number. So that was settled.

"Your mother is still living with Tim and his family?"

"Oh, sure. That is, Tim built on two rooms just for her, a bedroom and a kitchen so she can be to herself as she wants to. But far as I can tell, the kids are in her part more'n they're in their own. He and Celia've got five, three in school but two of them still real small, youngest one's named for me. Ma and Celia take turns looking after them while the other one helps Tim in the store. Works out good. Ma's crazy about the kids, and she'd rather tend store than go to the movies. Tim praises her up. Says if she ever quits he'll lose a lot of steady customers."

"Tim has a store then?"

"Oh, you didn't know? He saved enough while he was in

the Navy to buy into that one he worked in before. Now he owns it, lock, stock, and barrel. Corcoran's Fresh Fruit and Vegetables; Fancy Groceries. Right on the main street in Dover. Lower square."

Alice said it was wonderful to have up-to-date news on so many of her old school friends, she couldn't say how much she appreciated Pansy's willingness to look in on Granny, she would be going home with a much easier mind, and now she must run because it was almost suppertime.

The next day she told her grandmother she wanted to get in a good supply of groceries before she left, thought she would go to Dover to shop, and was taking the children, so why didn't Granny come along for the ride?

"I s'pose I might's well," said Granny. "Nice day, and I ain't likely to have a chance to go that fur again for a while."

. . . In gold letters on black; Corcoran's Fresh Fruits and Vegetables; Fancy Groceries.

Alice pulled into the parking space in front, facing Tim's sign.

Seeing Alice looking up, her grandmother looked up, too.

"Fancy groceries." She sniffed. "Now, I don't need anything fancy."

Alice laughed.

"I doubt if all of them are fancy, Granny."

"Corcoran?"

"It belongs to one of Pansy's brothers. She told me yesterday. Her mother works here. I thought it would be fun to—see how they're doing."

"Well, 'twill," said Granny, opening her door with unexpected alacrity. "If they're letting it run down way they did Rundlett's, don't buy any mysteries."

Tim's store was large, well lit, crowded with merchandise, busy, and shining clean. It was self-service, and Alice and

Granny moved along the aisles pushing a bright metal cart on which Emily rode on the jump seat and Philip walked beside them, soberly taking from the shelves what his mother pointed out and stacking it around Emily's feet.

Here and there other children not much older than Philip —a boy of perhaps fifteen who looked eerily like Tim at that age; another of ten or twelve, small for his age, short and slight with sandy hair, quick-motioned and intent on his work; and a girl of probably thirteen or so, with a round, pink, dimpled face which reminded Alice of Pansy—were wheeling up carts full of cartons, opening them, and placing cans on shelves.

In a wall near the clanging cash registers there was a window with the word MANAGER above it. Tim's office must be there, Alice supposed; but she could not see through the window because a woman stood outside it, one hand on a small child's stroller and the other holding the end of a strap encircling the waist of a boy around four who was climbing everything he could reach. . . . The woman was short and slight with sandy hair, like her second son, with his quick motions, the same strength disproportionate to size, and she was talking rapidly, laughing, telling some story with as much ease as if she had no baby to watch, no little monkey to keep from climbing too high. . . . This was Tim's Celia . . . Tim's and Celia's family.

And the chubby little woman with bright, birdlike eyes at the cash register nearest the office must be Mrs. Corcoran.

"Are you Mrs. Corcoran?" asked Alice, when she and Philip had unloaded their cart.

"That's right. I'm Tim's old lady," answered the cashier with a quick, twinkling glance, square fingers, their knuckles distorted by arthritis, rapidly punching buttons.

As she pushed the sales slip across the counter and Alice handed her a bill, Alice said, "We used to be your neighbors when you lived on the farm. You remember the Plaisteds? This is my grandmother, Melissa Plaisted. I was Alice McIntire. I rode to school with your children."

"Well, I'll be blest!" cried Tim's mother, smile broadening. "Quite a surprise to see folks over here from up-country! Tim! TIMMY! Celia, hark a minute and tell Tim to come over and bag these groceries for me!"

Celia turned her head. Her skin was a girl's skin. She looked too young to be the mother of five, the oldest perhaps fifteen years old. She must have married when she was no older than Alice when . . .

"Oh, Donald should have noticed you're getting a line there, Ma. Don! DONNIE!"

"Leave Donnie alone," Tim's mother shouted back. "Don't want Donnie. I said TIM!"

The office door swung open and Tim came to the checkout counter, picked up a paper bag. He looked older than Celia. He had put on weight, and his thick red hair was graying at the temples. He looked as old as Harley and he wasn't. But his eyes were unchanged, still had that haunting depth, that capacity for fury, for intense melancholy, for aching tenderness—and for sudden emergence of inner light. Whatever Celia had been telling him had pleased and amused him. He was still thinking of it.

"Wake up, Tim," cried his mother. "These ladies lived near us on the farm. Know who they are?"

Tim straightened and looked at Granny with a smile, trying to recognize her.

But of course he did not know Granny. Probably he had never seen her before.

His eyes moved on to Alice, seeking a clue. She could not bear their scrutiny of her thirty-five-year-old face.

She said quickly, offering her hand, "Hello, Tim. I was Alice McIntire. How are you?"

The inner light flamed now. He dropped the package of margarine he was holding, and the hand which grasped hers was cool and damp from it.

"No!" he exclaimed. "Are you Alice? Where on earth did you come from? Long time no see! Boy, what a surprise! Ma, this is Alice Mc—"

"Sure, I know," his mother said. "Wondered if you would. And that's Melissy Plaisted, her grandmother. Now, if you'll just move them and their groceries over by the window, I'll get this line along while you all have a visit."

By the window Tim's words fell over one another.

"These your kids, Alice? . . . Emily? Emily, you're a doll. You're a living doll . . . Philip? Hi, there, Phil! Where you living now, Alice? . . . Oh, Big Town, huh? Like it? I don't know as I would. Size of Dover just suits us. Look, I want you to meet my wife and kids. Celia, come over here! KIDS, come here! Alice, this is my wife, Celia, and our two youngest. Mike is the rascal. Pansy's our baby. Alice used to ride to school with us, Celia, in our horse-and-wagon days. Remember buffalo robes, Alice? And the beach rocks we used to heat to put under our feet on winter mornings? Emily, look what I do with Pansy!"

He lifted his baby out of her stroller and tossed her in the air. She shrieked with laughter.

"Bet you wouldn't let me do that to you, would you, Emily?"

Emily, staring as if hypnotized, bent forward on her jump seat and held out her arms.

"You would? Well, by golly, here we go then."

Tim thrust Pansy into Alice's arms, caught up Emily, and tossed her, leaning back to laugh up at her until her small, incredulous smile grew into rollicking sound. And there they all were in a warm knot, Celia pulling on Mike's strap to keep him from climbing his father's leg, Alice cuddling Pansy, who felt small and very light compared with sturdy Emily, and Tim's three older children coming doubtfully into the circle to be introduced by their mother.

"This is our oldest, Donald. And Mary, the only girl we had till Pansy. Charlie, he's ten; named for his grandfather. These ladies lived near Daddy, kids, when he went to school. This one rode to school with him. Before they had buses. They didn't even have a car. Daddy drove a horse with a wagon hitched to him."

"Your Daddy's horse had a long name," Alice told Donald and Mary and Charlie Corcoran, rubbing her chin gently across Pansy's soft, reddish hair.

"You don't still remember it?" demanded Tim, looking around from Emily poised on his hands in midair.

"I'll never, never forget it," Alice told him and his children. "It was Mavourneen."

"That's right, kids," said Tim, laughing. "Mavourneen it was!"

"Heavens!" exclaimed his mother, from the cash register. "I hadn't thought of that horse for years. That was my horse, but I hardly ever got to pull a rein on her long as we had kids in high school."

Granny chimed in, "I don't doubt that. Country folks in them days done without a lot of things to get young ones educated."

"You said a mouthful there," agreed Tim's mother. "But it all paid off, didn't it, Melissy? They've all turned out pretty good."

She returned to her customers. Donnie began bagging groceries. Alice said they must go, as she had to get ready to go home the next morning. She kissed Pansy and passed her to Celia. Emily refused to let Tim put her down. He said he would ride her to the car. Alice took Granny's elbow. Philip carried the groceries.

With Granny settled in the front seat and Emily strapped in to ride beside Philip, Tim came around to where Alice and Philip were trying to close the trunk and did it for them.

He told Philip, "Glad to have met you, kid," and rumpled his hair.

Philip, abashed, scuttled away and got into the car.

Tim looked after him, chuckling, and then turned to Alice.

Once more—the second and last time in her life—they were alone together.

He took her hand, there by Harley's car in a city parking space, and asked: "Life good to you, Allie?" *Allie!* "Everybody been good to you?"

"Yes, Tim. . . . Oh, yes, it is. And they have been, and are. Everybody."

"That's all I need to know. I've thought of you sometimes. I've wondered."

"As I have about you. I can see you're happy, too. Now we won't need to wonder any more."

His eyes twinkled. "Once we'd never have thought to hear Ma and your grandmother agreeing on something, would we?"

So that had struck him, too. She shook her head, smiling.

"Natural enough that it would be on how much they sacrificed for us. Because they did."

Tim nodded. "And now we've got where we understand what that means."

Alice moved around the car to the driver's seat. Tim followed and closed the door behind her.

He said to all of them, through the open window, "Come again when you can. Corcoran's is open seven days a week."

"We will, Tim," Alice said, and Granny added unexpectedly, "You've got a real nice store. Nice and neat, and a good stock, and prices reasonable. You must be doing a real good business."

"No complaints," said Tim with a grin. He reached in to touch Emily's cheek. "Bye, doll."

Emily was still waving at his retreating figure as he crossed the sidewalk and went through the door of Corcoran's Fresh Fruits and Vegetables; Fancy Groceries.

Alice started the engine and put the gear in reverse.

No complaints . . .

In the dark of a beach cottage balcony, thirty-five years later, Alice in her nightgown, with the sound of ocean waves below her, leans suddenly against the wall and trembles, receiving and returning young Tim Corcoran's kiss.

Afterward, spent and happy, half lying against clapboards as if against his shoulder, she whispers, "Thank you, dear Tim, for showing me the way . . ."

9

Promptly on the evening of the sixteenth day after Melissa reached the island, her mother calls to say that the Eustaces are home again, she and Jim and Chris and the baby have had a marvelous time in Colorado, Vicki has replaced a man as head lifeguard and her pay has been increased so that she is now saving fifty dollars a week toward college expenses, is Alice worn out from Melissa's visit, and may Emily speak to Melissa.

Melissa comes to the telephone and says, "Hi," warily. Then, as she listens, her expression brightens, and when she speaks her voice has Emily's own lilt.

"Oh, there's no hurry, Mommy. We've been having lots of fun. I take care of Uncle Phil's children every morning, and afternoons Garmie and I go swimming. I can swim more than twice as far as I could when I came . . . Oh, I think so. I'm almost sure—but I'll ask her . . . Garmie, is it all right with you if I stay until next weekend? Not this very weekend coming but the next one?" Alice is already nodding, but Melissa hurries on. "Because Daddy can't get away this weekend, and Vicki'll be on duty, and Mommy's got the house to air and clean; and they'd all like to take the Sunday boat over to the island and stay until evening and bring Vicki's new boy friend. . . . Yes. She says yes. . . . Okay, Mommy. See you a week from Sunday. Look for us on the dock. Garmie says she loves to meet boats or planes any of us are coming over on . . ."

From the first, Melissa has reacted to the island as to an enchanted garden in which she was born, from which she was early spirited away, and to which she has now been suddenly and miraculously returned. To her everything and everyone there is beautiful, living and moving in perfect harmony; and it has been effortless—indeed restful, exhilarating, delightful— for her to become instantly and to remain an integral part of what she sees and feels around her and to respond in kind.

She has waked each morning enveloped by a faintly golden haze and emerged swiftly from it into a bright blue world. Preparing breakfast with Alice and eating it wherever they chose to eat it—never two mornings in the same place— and then helping to put kitchen and cottage in order, Melissa has been completely at peace, deeply involved in her domestic role, admiring of every object she touched. She has said, "Oh, Garmie, I'm so happy!" so often that one morning she asked, "Do you get tired of hearing me tell you how happy I am?"

But if by nine o'clock she could not see her cousins coming down the beach, she was off to meet them, sometimes to run all the way to her uncle's cottage and bring them back, Margery clinging to one hand and Desirée to the other, Sue either trailing behind, gathering shells, or running ahead to find Alice.

In all ways, Melissa and Sue have kept a respectful and appreciative distance from each other. What Melissa wanted those mornings was to be an ideal mother, while Sue was more than willing to transfer big-sisterly responsibilities already carried too long. That Desirée and Margery preferred the company of an ideal mother to the sometimes desperate authoritarianism of a reluctant older sister surprised no one, and, far from grieving Sue, filled her with a relief Melissa does not in the least understand or try to, but accepts as natural on this wondrous isle where whatever anyone wants is exactly what everyone else wants him to have.

Every forenoon, rain or shine, Melissa has spent apart with Philip's little ones and then given them their lunch, leaving Sue free to swim with Alice, go to the store with Alice, walk the beach and sit on the ledge with Alice, and finally to picnic with Alice. After lunch Melissa takes her charges home, followed by Sue, and tucks them in for their naps. She must have come as a ministering angel to Mrs. Batcheldor, a heavenly easement to her calloused feet.

"Now I think of it," says Alice to herself, "that is the part Melissa has been playing to the hilt throughout her visit. I wonder if she was aware that the sun broke through clouds and flooded the whole island with warm light as her plane taxied to a stop. Does she feel that she dropped down from heaven and brought a piece of it with her, a piece just large enough to cover the island? Anyhow, she must know, consciously or unconsciously, that this is the role she needed and wanted to lose herself in."

Melissa has served as ideal mother to Desirée and Margery—and incidentally as angel to Sue and Mrs. Batcheldor—until their naptime seven days a week, varying her program for them only on Sunday mornings, when she has put on a crisp, brief cotton dress, walked up the beach to her Uncle Philip's, arrayed his little ones to match herself, and led them to Sunday school in the island's tiny old stone church. When she takes them home on Sundays, she is always invited to stay for dinner and usually spends the afternoon on the sun porch Rhonda uses as a summer studio, its floor bordered along the inner walls with canvases turned back to the light. Here Melissa has become a breathlessly eager student of art. Having first stood on the sun-porch threshold as if uncertain whether it was hallowed ground, she eventually ventured to ask her Aunt Rhonda in a hushed voice if she might turn just one canvas to see what was painted on it. Rhonda in some surprise shrugged, rose from a chaise longue, and turned one of them, even lifted it to an easel.

"Oh-h-h," whispered Melissa. "Oh, did you do that? . . . It's beautiful . . . It's so beautiful! . . . How—how could you paint twisted scrub pines so they look peaceful—and make me want to crawl under and between them along the ledges, and as if I could, even had—as if I had gone through and am looking back from them—only I don't show because they hide me?"

Rhonda stared at the canvas.

"It was the first one I did after I got here," she said. "I didn't think the trees looked peaceful. I thought they looked tortured. They're desperately trying to hang on, and maybe they can't much longer. Don't you see?"

"No, no!" cried Melissa. "Didn't you think that because you didn't know them yet? Now you know them, you must see how proud they are because they did hang on in those crevices when it *was* hard! Now they're all dug in deep and safe, and they know it, and they're strong and proud—and *kind*. They're protecting me, Aunt Rhonda, as they must be protecting you. You feel that now you know them, don't you?"

Rhonda's gaze had shifted from the canvas to Melissa's ecstatic face. Rhonda was moved and impressed, but unconvinced. She shook her head.

"That isn't what I saw," she said stubbornly. "If I didn't paint what I saw, it can't be good . . . For some reason, I tried the same scene last week. Let's see how that looks to you."

She searched among the pile of canvases, extracted one, and put it on a second easel beside the first.

Sue, crouched sorting her shells on the boardwalk to the beach, had heard the conversation through the open window, and now came into the sun room, fingers and hair tips dripping sand.

Philip, who had appeared to be sleeping after dinner in a big wicker chair by the living-room picture window, opened his eyes slowly and reached for his pipe. But he did not turn in his chair to look into the sun room. He was only listening.

"Oh, yes!" exclaimed Melissa, nodding vigorously, her eyes radiant. "By last week, you had got to know them better. They're even stronger now because they've reached still deeper down. And their branches are not so close to the ledge. *Look* at the difference! The branches tilt up at the ends and let light in! Sunbeams are running across the ledge at the foot of the trees. They're dancing, really. Oh, Aunt Rhonda, this is exciting, like—like a serial story—"

"It's a false light," insisted Rhonda. "You've heard of the will-o'-the-wisp? Like that. It tempts you, but if you follow it you plunge into the sea. You said of the first canvas that you had crawled under the trees and were looking back from beyond; but you couldn't be, Melissa, because the trees grow to the very edge of the cliff and the drop-off there is a sheer hundred feet or so, with surf crashing at the bottom of it."

"No, no, no!" shouted Melissa. "I didn't go that far. The outermost trees stopped me. They took care of me. They're my friends. I pushed against one of them and felt how strong it was. Then I turned and leaned against it and looked back. I'm doing it now and watching the sunbeams from the other side. And they're not false, Aunt Rhonda! They're true as true. Honestly. Sue! Susie, what do *you* see in these two pictures?"

She held out her hand to Sue, took Sue's sandy fingers in her own Sunday-school clean ones, and they stood side by side, joined for the moment, for the first time.

Sue did not speak quickly. She stood and pondered, while Melissa and Rhonda—and Philip—waited.

Finally Sue turned her huge, dark, haunting eyes on Rhonda and said earnestly, "I think like Melissa does, Mummy. If it was like you say, wouldn't I feel sad—and frightened? But I don't. The one you did first makes me feel good, and this other one makes me feel happy . . . I didn't know you could paint pictures that would do that!"

"See?" cried Melissa triumphantly, hugging Sue. "Uncle Philip! Uncle Phil, come and vote! It's two to one now—"

He pulled himself slowly out of his chair and came in on bare feet, carrying his pipe, a quizzical, indulgent expression on his face. Philip was incapable of denying a child anything he understood it wanted.

"Is this picture sad and scary, or just dark and strong?" demanded Melissa. "And then is the light in this one false, a trick, or is it real sunbeams dancing? Which, Uncle Phil? Which?"

He dutifully studied one painting and then the other, then returned to the first. Melissa and Sue were in front of him, back to the canvases, their small hands locked together, their eyes fixed on his face. He was aware, too, of Rhonda watching him from the other side of the narrow room. He felt helpless. He shook his head.

"Sorry, kids," he said. "I'm no judge. Sounds to me as if whether a picture is scary or just dark depends on who's looking at it. And I don't know how you can tell whether a dancing light is true or false. But I take it any picture which sets off so much discussion and so many fireworks must be pretty good, whether the artist thinks so or not. And one thing I do know —that's Weyanoke Point. Anybody who can paint Weyanoke Point so I can tell it from any other of at least a dozen points on this island is no mean painter."

"Is it Weyanoke Point, Mummy?" asked Sue.

Rhonda was looking through the open window at the sea. It was a minute before she turned her head. When she spoke, her voice had not completely steadied.

"Yes," she said. "It is Weyanoke Point."

She was not looking at Sue but at Philip.

Sue and Melissa reached her at the same instant. They were separated now, one on each side of her, each clutching one of her hands. "Where is Weyanoke Point, Mummy?" . . . "Will you take us there, Aunt Rhonda?" . . . "Will you show it to us, Mummy? I mean now. Right now!"

"Why, I suppose," Rhonda began vaguely, looking at Philip. "It's about a fifteen-minute walk. There's no road."

"Oh, a walk, Sue! To Weyanoke Point! Won't you love it?"

"Can we take the pictures with us, Mummy? So we can compare?"

"You'll find they're not alike," said Rhonda, glancing down at the girls as if they were small strangers. "The point and the pictures. You may be disappointed."

"Neither are the pictures alike," crowed Melissa. "If they were alike, they'd just be copies. Real artists don't paint copies,

Aunt Rhonda. Oh, this *is* exciting, isn't it, Sue?"

In their excitement, the girls hugged each other fiercely.

Philip said, "We'll all go to Weyanoke Point. I'll carry the canvases. Been meaning to get over all summer. Used to be a favorite hiding place of mine. Because nobody else seemed to go there."

"You took me out the first time I ever saw it," said Rhonda softly. "The first time you brought me to the island. The summer before Sue was born."

Alice heard about this from Philip later that afternoon when he drove over to tell her Rhonda would bring Melissa home after supper, in midevening, after she had taken him to the plane. He said Melissa and Sue had persuaded Rhonda, after returning from Weyanoke Point, to let them watch her begin a painting.

"They are watching so close I don't know how much freedom of movement she'll have," he said, chuckling. "She's trying to do a sea gull for them just as it spreads its wings to take off from one of the black boulders out front. There are always a dozen of them there, coming and going, but her model keeps shifting. I'd think that would be a problem. And they want sunset colors in the sky because the bird is gray on the black rock."

He told Alice only what had been said and done in the sun room which served Rhonda as a summer studio. He did not tell her the tones in which each of them had spoken, or the direction in which each looked, or how anyone felt, or of the sand which dripped from Sue's hair and fingers when she came in from sorting shells. But it was not necessary. Alice knew.

She said, "That's good, Philip. Very good. Good for both children, and for Rhonda and you, too. When a wife and mother applies herself as steadily as Rhonda does to her painting there has to be a reason, a driving reason. Rhonda's reason may be that deep inside she knows she is a painter. If so, she needs the support of her family if she is to stay close to them while doing what she has to do that she must do alone . . . She may be right, you know, Philip."

Philip, big brown fingers through the handle of his coffee mug, eyes on the sky beyond the small window of Alice's island cottage, said, "Yes . . . Yes, in spite of myself, you might say, I'm beginning to suspect she is . . . I guess I've been looking the other way because—the record shows I'm no good at keeping a career gal as a wife."

Alice waited a minute. She did not want to sound insistent or importunate or overly concerned. Philip must and would come to his own conclusion and act on his own judgment.

"But how many other elements in the two relationships are the same, Phil?" she asked gently. "How much is Rhonda like Delores? Especially how much is Rhonda now as Delores was before her acting talent was recognized?"

He thought about that.

"Apparently not much," he answered honestly. "But how can I know? There's bound to be a difference in temperaments between people who want to act and people who want to paint. Delores was hardly ever home because she was out chasing rainbows—attention, contracts, opportunities—and when she caught one she vanished on it. Rhonda is hardly ever home because she is out painting. If she has an exhibit and people like her work and buy it, how do I know she won't vanish into a studio?"

"I suppose that depends," said Alice slowly, "on how much she wants to live with you while she paints. Which in turn must depend to a considerable extent on you—your feeling for her and her painting . . . I don't know Rhonda very well, not even as well as I knew Delores. Rhonda is much more difficult to know because she withdraws and conceals while

Delores was never at ease unless revealing everything she was and had and wanted to be and have. Delores had a very strong, I'd say exaggerated, ego. Do you think it ever mattered to her what you thought of her ability? I don't, because you weren't a producer or anyone with influence in the world she wanted to be a part of, preferably to dominate. Probably Delores should never have married. The fact that she hasn't married again bears that out. She has no need of a husband . . . But I believe Rhonda does, and that she would find a place in the art world a poor substitute for a secure place in your heart . . . Though she may feel it would be better than nothing, and I hope it will be if it is ever all she has. I think it would be a great mistake, Phil, to harbor any notion that the reason Rhonda married you and has stayed with you is that she can't support herself. I'm sure she loved you and still loves you. That is a great deal on which to build security for both of you—if you want to."

Now Alice was afraid she had said too much. But Philip's thoughtful expression had not changed as he listened.

He lifted his mug in both hands. When he put it down, he looked straight at his mother for the first time, and smiled a little.

"What if what I wanted all along was a wife who both loved me and couldn't and didn't want to support herself?"

"Then you made not only one but two serious mistakes," said Alice promptly. "You are an able man, Phil. The only such woman you could possibly have both respected and loved would have had to be an invalid, and you knew perfectly well that both Delores and Rhonda were in vigorous health . . . No, if that was what you think now you wanted, surely it is because your experience with Delores has shaken your confidence. You're obviously fearful the same thing will happen again, and I can understand that. But it won't if you want it not to enough to take steps to prevent it. Rhonda is not Delores and, as you say, a painter is not an actress. For one thing, an actress has to go where the world can watch her work. A painter can have her studio at home, if that is where she works best and is happiest . . ." Impulsively, Alice put her hand on her son's wrist. "Oh, Phil, dear, if I sound as if I'm absolutely sure about all this, of course I'm not. But it is what I believe. And I do so want you—and Rhonda, too—to know the full joy of a good marriage, and for Sue and Margery and Desirée to grow up whole, not—not fragmented like Gary and Weston. Though I do think the boys are coming through much better than we once expected. I did enjoy them the hour or two they spent here a few weeks ago, and hope they'll come back when you're home so you can enjoy them too. But home life in the early years may be even more important to girls than to boys . . . You will do all you can this time, won't you, for all our sakes? You made a good start today, all going together to Weyanoke Point. I loved hearing about that. I'm sure it meant more to Rhonda —and the children, too—than you can possibly know. Now just build on that, and you may get some wonderful surprises."

Philip's smile reached his eyes. He looked at his watch and rose.

"In that case," he said, "I'd better get home and start building. Have to catch a plane in exactly five hours. Take care, Mom. See you next weekend."

A little later Melissa came tearing down the twilit beach like a young colt, sprang up the steps, and burst in upon Alice with, "Oh, *Garmie!* You wouldn't *believe*—Garmie, did you know Aunt Rhonda is an artist? *Really* an artist? Have you seen her pictures? I never had until today, and they're marvelous! I mean, *really* marvelous! I think she's going to show them in Chicago. You know, rent a gallery for a week, maybe more, and exhibit them for the art critics and art patrons and art buyers to see. She and Uncle Phil were talking about it when I left. It's all so exciting! Uncle Phil's going to make some inquiries this week. I can hardly wait until he comes again next weekend. Oh, if she does have a show, I'll die if I can't go out there to see it! Really, Garmie, she's done some terrific things. To think I never saw any of them before! Well, let me tell you what happened—"

Then Alice heard the whole story from Melissa's point of view and lived it with her far more completely than she had been able to with Philip, for while she had never been a man who felt threatened by his wife's talent and ambition, she had been a girl little older than Melissa in experience and emotional maturity, though considerably older in years, encountering for the first time a creative gift. She remembered Carmen Ferrari and wondered fleetingly how long it had been since she had thought of her.

"She must," she thought, "have come to my mind when I first met Delores. If so, did my feeling about Carmen affect my judgment of Delores? Did I unconsciously reveal this to Philip and affect his judgment?"

Well, no matter now. Delores had gone her way, and Philip's wife was Rhonda, in whom today Emily's daughter had discovered qualities which transported her as Carmen's had swept young Alice briefly into a new, magic, and breathlessly exciting world.

"Go on, dear," Alice said to Melissa. "How did you feel when you saw Weyanoke Point? How did everyone else seem to feel? What did you all say to one another?"

Melissa ended her account with, "And guess what? Aunt Rhonda asked Sue and me if we thought we could take her pictures safely home. It was time for Margery and Desirée to be waking up, and she and Uncle Phil wanted to stay there a while longer. Of course we were so proud to! At least, I was, and I think Sue must have been. You know how quiet Sue is, mostly. I told her on the way she must be so proud she could hardly bear it. Imagine your own mother being an *artist!* I'm practically out of my mind she's my aunt! She just said, 'I think Daddy really likes that picture, don't you?' I said, 'How could anybody help it that saw it?' And she said, 'Well, he certainly looked at it. He looked at it a lot.' I had a feeling that meant more to Sue than anything else. But just wait till the critics look at it and all her other things! She's done at least a dozen here this summer and says she must have a hundred or more at home. Oh, Garmie, if she does have the show, could you and I go out to see it? I'm almost sure Mommy wouldn't, and they probably wouldn't let me go alone. Maybe they would, but I'd rather go with you. I'm sure you'd like it. I simply couldn't bear to miss it. I want to stay the whole week. Could we go, Garmie? Could you just say 'maybe'?"

"If Rhonda has a show in Chicago," said Alice instantly, "I certainly shall go. You, too, if your parents are willing, and I expect they will be. Maybe your mother will come with us—"

"Oh, Garmie!" cried Melissa. "Garmie, Garmie, Garmie, I don't think I've ever wanted anything so much in my whole life!"

"I know," Alice said with a nod. "Believe me, dear. I do know."

"How?" whispered Melissa incredulously.

10

Then Alice took Melissa with her into a Boston hospital in the fall of 1921.

Two young girls together, in petal-pink and white striped uniforms with long sleeves, starched white cuffs, and full, swishing, starched skirts, they scurry along a corridor on their way off duty. All the patients have been served supper. Now it is time for theirs and, as always, they are ravenously hungry.

But one of them pulls the other to a halt in front of the door to Room 1601. The door is closed.

"That's where she is, isn't it?"

"Who?"

"You know. Carmen Ferrari."

"Sh-h-h. We're not supposed to know where she is."

"We do, though. She isn't awfully sick, is she?"

"I guess she was when they brought her in, but they took out the oxygen tank today and didn't take in another one."

"She must be much better then."

"Probably."

"I've prayed they'd let me take in her tray. Or bring her a pitcher of water. Or anything."

"Silly. Her own nurses do everything. She has specials around the clock."

"I know *that*. But I do so long to see her."

"Why that bad?"

"Well, I never saw a real actress, a real celebrity. Did you?"

"No."

"She must be great. She's had all the big female parts in the Shakespeare festival, they say. She was doing Lady Macbeth when she collapsed. Right on the stage. Remember reading *Macbeth* in school? Did you ever think you'd be this near to *Lady Macbeth?*"

"So near and yet so far."

"If I could only hear her voice. Just once. She must have a beautiful voice."

"She may still be hoarse."

"I don't care . . . I'm going to tap on the door."

"You wouldn't! She may be asleep."

"I'll tap very lightly. Besides, she's supposed to be eating supper."

"She probably can have it any time she wants it. I've heard that actors and actresses always dine after the performance. Around midnight."

"Well, at least we know she isn't performing."

The girls giggle nervously.

"I'm going to tap. If she says, 'Come in,' we'll hear her voice, and then we'll go in."

"Then what?"

"I don't know. But we'll have heard her speak. And seen her."

"If she doesn't say, 'Come in'?"

"She will if she's alone, I think. Unless she's asleep. If her nurse is there, she'll open the door."

"And tell us to get out of here. As fast as our feet can carry us."

"But maybe we'll have caught a glimpse of her! Of *Carmen Ferrari!*"

Almost without her own volition Alice taps softly on a heavy oak panel. She can hardly hear the tap herself. But both girls begin to tremble, aghast at her daring.

Through the transom come the husky, melodious words.

"Did someone knock? See who it is, will you, darling?"

The door opens. In it, practically filling it, stands a young man in white whom the girls recognize as an intern they have occasionally seen about but who has never spoken to them and whose name they do not know. They would run away now if they could, but it is too late.

"Yes?" he says icily.

"Would—would Miss Ferrari like her water pitcher refilled?"

"*Two* pinkies to fill one water pitcher?" he asks, with a quizzical, penetrating gaze they cannot meet. "I'm sure Miss Bridges has provided her with fresh water."

"Two what?" asks the husky, melodious voice behind him.

"Two probationers," replies the intern, turning his head. "Sometimes called pinkies, otherwise stripeys. Because of their uniforms. Means they're just out of high school, starting their training with some hope—very likely vain—of being allowed to stay on to finish it."

"Oh? Let me see them, darling. You don't know how all your starched white depresses me. I might as well have spent the last week in a morgue. Come in, pinkies; do come in."

"She says for you to come in," growls the intern wryly. "And that's exactly what you were counting on, isn't it? Don't think you won't pay for this bit of mischief if word of it gets to your supervisor, as it very likely will."

He stands aside, and closes the door after them.

There she lies, bolstered high by stark white pillows, her sloping shoulders draped in a scarlet silk shawl heavy with Eastern embroideries, long, dark, slender fingers tipped in lustrous scarlet raising a small gilded cup the girls assume is pure gold toward lips that are a splash of vivid red against the olive skin of her thin face. A diminutive Portia, a youthful Lady Macbeth with languorous, midnight-black eyes, in a bower of heavily perfumed roses, lilies, carnations, sweet peas, and other blossoms the girls have never seen before and do not know the names of . . . *Carmen Ferrari* . . .

Suddenly she puts down the little gold cup and leans toward them, laughing delightedly, enchantingly.

"Why, Pietro!" she exclaims. "They're children! Fresh,

sweet, innocent children! You don't mean they're—darlings, do you really want to spend your lives shut up in a horrid place like this? I don't even understand why Pietro—but then Pietro is a man and a man need never be caged as women can be. I can't see why girls like you would even think for a minute of entering—what do you call it?—the nursing profession, if only because of the awful smell as soon as one comes through the outside door. Sick as I was, simply devastated, when they brought me in here, it revolted me. Carbolic, or something. It's even in the bed linen. I *will* have my own put on my bed tomorrow. I will not sleep another night between hospital sheets. Pietro, you hear me? If my own linen is not brought in and put on this bed tomorrow morning, I'll leave. If I can't walk out and you don't have me carried out, I'll jump out the window."

"It's sixteen stories down, darling," he drawls, draining a shallow, stemmed glass of what the girls suppose is Italian wine.

"Don't tell me!" she cries, her laughter long gone and replaced by a mounting fury. "I don't want to know. I don't care. My Katy shall bring my linens first thing in the morning, and if they're not put on this bed, I go *out,* any way I can get out! Remember that! I cannot bear this another day. I shall go mad!" A small, hard gleam of madness flashes in Lady Macbeth's eyes.

But as she turns them again to the girls, the gleam softens to a dreamy tenderness and honest wonder. She reaches one hand toward Alice and lets it drop on the hated sheet, gentle, tawny, crimson-tipped.

"But *you* are *staying* here! How long have you stayed here, darling?"

"Ten weeks, so far," Alice answers almost in a whisper. "Ten weeks and a half."

"Why? Tell me *why,* darling."

"We like to make sick people feel better."

"But as soon as they're better they leave, and the beds fill up with other sick people! Always more and more sick people, week after week, year after year. And they don't all get better. Some of them must *die!*"

Alice nods gravely.

Carmen Ferrari nods emphatically, dramatically, and spreads both arms, letting the scarlet shawl slip back to bare them and her lovely, tawny shoulders. She twinkles the bright-tipped fingers of her right hand.

"One of you come around to this side . . . That's it. Now, darlings, each of you take my hand, and listen closely. I am much older than you, and I know much more of the world than you do—or than you ever will if you shut yourselves up in any one place or any one profession. You are both so pretty and may have many talents of which you are unaware. How can you know unless you explore yourselves and the opportunities out-side a—a place like this? I must have been a born explorer, for I cannot remember when I was not exploring; reaching hun-grily, fighting savagely, struggling painfully, but always explor-ing, always excited, and often making a discovery more wonder-ful even than any I had dreamt of. Of course the theater was my world; I knew that from the age of three. You are already late, but not too late if you begin now to uncover who you *are*, what you can do, what is effervescing inside you, and then to think of ways of life that appeal to you and to make associations with those now living that way, to broaden your knowledge of what is possible for you before you make any final choice. Will you do that, darlings? Will you promise me to do that?"

The girls nod, gripped by her hands. Alice feels an electri-cal charge stinging her wrist.

"And will you always remember it was I who pointed the way?"

"Oh, yes," whispers Alice. "Yes, Miss Ferrari." How could anyone ever forget an experience like this?

Portia–Lady Macbeth has become a tired angel of mercy. Her fingers loosen. She slowly draws in her scarlet shawl as if it were heavy, and the lids lower over the dark eyes.

She says drowsily, "Oh, I shall sleep better for this tonight. Thank you for coming, darlings . . . Will you take away this ugly tray?"

The girls pick it up and have nearly reached the door when she says suddenly, almost sharply, "Wait!" Her eyes open wide. "Pietro, you said something cruel to them. About their paying for this if their supervisor hears of their coming here. I don't want them to have trouble from it, understand? It was a joy to me to see them. If any question arises, you say that I said so. If they want to be nurses, nothing must prevent them. Goodness knows this place needs people who want to be nurses. But they are more important than those they try to make feel better, to themselves, and I want them to be whatever they truly want to be; but I want them to be *sure* they know what that is. You hear me, Pietro?"

He shrugs and says, "I hear you, angel," raising black eyebrows in the direction of the girls, with a movement of his hand in dismissal.

But she has told them to wait. So they wait.

She turns toward them, lies on her side, raises herself to lean on her elbow. Each of her motions is like music, each attitude she assumes like a painting.

She smiles bewitchingly, tantalizingly, as if privy to a secret she cannot or will not tell.

"You've never seen me in the theater, have you, darlings?"

They shake their pink-capped heads.

"No, of course not. What did I tell you? You know so little. You're like empty boxes. Such pretty, fragile boxes waiting to be filled. I both pity and envy you, darlings. If only I could get back on stage before the festival ends, I'd have three good seats saved and make Pietro bring you! But I'm sure that is impossible, as next week is our last. I open the following week in *A Midsummer Night's Dream* in New York . . . Well, well, I'll keep thinking. I won't forget you, darlings."

She drops back against the pillows and her eyes slowly close, but the enchanting smile lingers.

The girls slip through the door, close it softly, and are back in the cold, bright light of the empty corridor. There they stop, the tray between them littered with gilt-edged, blue-sprigged china and the little gold cup half full of coffee on its little gold saucer.

"These must be her own dishes," murmurs Alice. "If they are, it can't be they are supposed to go to the kitchen. It must be her nurses wash them up . . . *I* don't know *what* to do with them . . . I think we'd best leave them here, right beside her door."

She lowers the tray to the corridor floor gently, reverently, and the two tiptoe away together. They may be too late now for supper in the nurses' quarters, but they are no longer hungry.

II

Lying on her back in the hammock on the beach cottage porch, knees drawn up, staring into the dark, Melissa says, "She wasn't a bit like Aunt Rhonda, was she, Garmie? Except—"

"Except in the feeling she gave us. The feeling of having come very close to something much bigger than ourselves, something bigger even than herself, something so extraordinary we had no way of knowing what it was, only that it was, and we had seen what it produced."

"What *was* it, Garmie?"

"The creative spirit, dear, I can only think. That's what I call it. We all have some of it. At least, I've seen sparks of it in every human being I ever met. But when you feel its flames, as from an underground fire, as I did from Carmen Ferrari, as you do from Rhonda, you have met someone who is suffused with it, and that's a very rare and precious experience."

"Yes," says Melissa. And after a little silence, "But I don't really feel it from Aunt Rhonda. Just from her pictures."

"Isn't that where it should be for a painter? I suppose it could be and sometimes is in a painter's personality, too, but surely it doesn't have to be. A painter doesn't have to reveal it that way. I've always thought Rhonda very reserved, a very private person."

Melissa is thoughtful again.

"I guess so. You mean—like she has this inside her, and when she sees a place, like she saw Weyanoke Point, she doesn't just look at it the way the rest of us would. She draws it inside where the fire is, and the fire does something to it—"

"Purifies it?"

"Yes, and—and makes it crystal clear, and tells her the meaning of it, and when it's ready pours it onto the canvas *through her brushes!*"

"Oh, I think so, Melissa. I think that's exactly how it is."

Melissa sits up in the dark.

"So that's why, even though Uncle Phil had been to Weyanoke Point so many times and could tell what the picture was of when he saw it, he seemed to like the place better when we were out there today than he had expected to, as if he could now see more in it than he ever had. And I kept thinking it was just like the picture but still I didn't believe it would look the way it did to me if I hadn't seen the picture first."

"Yes, darling!" They are both excited now. "Rhonda's fire had illuminated it, revealed it for what it *is,* all of it, so those of us who haven't the gift to see it so could know for ourselves what is there and even recognize it as you did. As a poem so often says what we have always known or felt but could not express and didn't even know we knew. Probably Rhonda does that for many places besides the island scenes she is painting now because this is where she is. If we go to her show, we may see what she does when she is in Oak Park close to Chicago. A corner of the Universalist church designed by Frank Lloyd Wright, maybe. Or laundry on a line strung between two windows of a tenement house. Or unused and rusting railroad tracks entering a tunnel. Or away out at the edge of an Illinois cornfield a rotting cart that used to be horse-drawn, with tipsy wheels and smudges of blue paint—"

To herself Alice adds, "Though probably none of them will hold Phil's attention like Weyanoke Point. He loves this island."

Melissa does not hear.

She says urgently, "Garmie, we *have* to go. I couldn't bear it—"

"But you can see how different it is with actors. The Carmen Ferraris have to take *people* into their fires and then *become* those people so completely, in every detail, that their audiences will believe they are actually looking at and listening to those people. The product of the painter, as you say, rushes out through his brushes. That of a great actor flows through every pore of his body, his inflections, his eyes, his every movement and expression . . . And Carmen Ferrari was acclaimed as one of the brightest stars of the theater in her time."

Melissa has come back from visions of Rhonda's show.

She says in a small, troubled voice, "I don't see how when a person keeps on being other people all the time they have any chance to be themselves. Do they?"

Now it is Alice's turn to be thoughtful.

After a minute she says, "I've wondered about that, too. Especially for a long time after I took Miss Ferrari's tray out of her room. I don't suppose anyone knows about that except actors themselves and people who know them very, very well outside the theater. It *seems* as if, in a way, they are always onstage. She certainly was, lying in a hospital bed, with no audience but two scared pinkies and a brother who was paying her no attention. But perhaps when they are alone or with people they love and who have loved them for a long time—"

"Oh, was that doctor her brother?"

"Yes. Yes, Pietro was her brother. Her half brother. His last name was Amalfi, not Ferrari."

"Anyway . . . anyway, it must be the most wonderful thing in the world to have that much of what you call the— the—"

"Creative spirit? I'm sure it can be. It is certainly one of life's greatest blessings for us who profit by what it produces. To those who have it there may come great rewards and some moments of intense ecstasy, but these are hard won and always uncertain. A great fire within, constantly burning, constantly consuming, must put a human being under terrific pressure. Of the few born with it too many are destroyed by it, some before they ever reach the point where they can understand, accept, and control it, and so produce nothing at all. Others give so much to the rest of us that too early they have given all they have, and the fire goes out, leaving a void that never again can be filled. I've always thought that to be the keeper of such a fire is one of the greatest responsibilities, one of the greatest challenges, on earth."

"It hasn't destroyed Aunt Rhonda," Melissa says proudly.

"No, darling. No. Thank God."

Alice's lips move in a fervent prayer, but Melissa cannot see them.

She jumps out of the hammock. It thumps against the side of the cottage. She comes to Alice, leans against her, breathes a sigh of contentment, and says, "Oh, Garmie, this has been a beautiful day!"

12

"Yes," Alice thinks, after Melissa is asleep beside her under the eaves of the cottage roof. "Yes, Pietro was Carmen Ferrari's half brother."

Miss Ferrari must have left the hospital soon after that night. Perhaps she was not allowed to use her own bed linen. Anyhow, Alice and Millie (who, Alice still remembers, had never uttered a word in the presence of the actress) were the very next day, whether by coincidence or as a warning they never knew, sent upstairs for three months of duty in the children's ward, and never saw her again.

But Alice noticed now when a voice came over the loud-speaker, "Dr. Amalfi! Calling Dr. Amalfi!" and watched to see if he passed along the corridor on her floor.

One day she met him there face to face, and looked up curiously, but he did not recognize her. Otherwise she certainly would not have done what she did next, for she had disliked intensely the little she had seen of him and had no wish to see more. But the lack of recognition annoyed her unreasonably.

Did he notice anyone or anything but himself?

So she said, "Good morning, Pietro."

This brought his languid gaze down, and he paused.

"Pietro?" he asked coldly.

Now she saw nothing for it but to continue the mischief.

"It's the name she calls you. She didn't say what your last name is. Is it the same as hers?"

"Who?"

"Carmen Ferrari."

Now he was getting an inkling. He studied her face and figure, and she was surprised to find she enjoyed it. She could feel the impish sparkle in her eyes, the flush rising toward them, the I've-won-the-first-round in her slight smile.

"You're one of those impertinent pinkies who barged into her room one night before she went home."

"We didn't barge. We knocked and were invited in."

"So now you work in the children's ward."

"*So?* Is that why? I like taking care of children."

"Do you?"

"Yes. How is she?"

"Who?"

"Miss Ferrari, of course."

"She is very well."

"I'm glad to hear it. Please remember me to her—Pietro."

"I am Dr. Amalfi."

"Are you?"

Suddenly he grinned. It made an astonishing change in his face.

"And you're Miss Impertinent."

"I am Alice McIntire."

"I should report you to your supervisor, Alice McIntire."

"What, *again?* Excuse me, Dr. Amalfi. A light just went on."

Alice has never forgotten a word of that conversation, for she reviewed it in her mind frequently by day and by night, like memorizing a poem. It was a high point in her life at the time because it revealed to her a side of herself she had never seen before. She could stand up to a superior, if need be! She could even puncture an inflated ego by gently, merrily poking fun at it! She had not only dared to try but discovered she knew how, and so had succeeded! She had taken a long step away from the vulnerability of childhood.

"I'm grown up at last," she told herself triumphantly.

But was not, of course, as mature as she thought. There was much more to be learned, just as Carmen Ferrari had told her.

Later meetings with Pietro Amalfi have dimmed in the years between. She slowly recalls, as she lies in the dark and hears the wind rising outside, the surf crashing against the rocks, that the next time he spoke to her it was abrupt. Without even a greeting he asked gruffly what time she would go off duty. When she told him, he said, "Look for me in the lounge then," and hurried on as if he might be under surveillance.

She felt challenged. Now she must prove that she could follow Granny's old rule, *Begin as you can hold out.*

She went to the lounge. No one was there but Pietro. He was lying back in a big chair and motioned her to one beside his. She perched on the edge of it. He looked sulky, and sulkily told her: "I spoke with Carmen on the phone last night . . . Told her I saw you last week, and gave her your message."

"Thank you, Dr. Amalfi."

"She wants to know if you have seen any theater yet. Have you?"

"No."

"Then she wants me to take you to a play."

Alice thought about it and him. He was growing sulkier and sulkier. He didn't *want* to take her to a play!

"Well, if that's what your sister says," she told him, "I suppose that's what we have to do."

"I don't do everything she says."

"I believe that. So are you going to do this or aren't you?"

"What kind of play would you want to see?"

"I have no idea. I've never seen one except in our high-school auditorium."

He sighed.

"You'd probably prefer a silly musical."

"I might."

"I detest them."

"Too bad. Well, I have to run or I'll miss supper. Again."

Alice jumped up and was halfway across the lounge before he could pull himself to his feet and speak her name.

"I'll see if I can get some seats for *No, No, Nanette,* and let you know."

She laughed aloud.

"Thanks a heap—Dr. Amalfi. I guess."

Strange how the words, even the tones, come back now to her ear, distinct through the noise of wind and waves . . .

Pietro, she found, was a man of great variety in moods. In the months that followed he took her many times to the theater, to the opera, to symphony concerts, to big restaurants glittering with chandeliers where they were waited on elegantly by black men in red uniforms, to little holes-in-the-wall where an aproned woman brought them dishes which he said were specialties in European countries and which she could not pronounce the names of until he repeated them several times; and he took her in his car to Lexington and Concord to see the battlegrounds, to Revere Beach to ride a roller coaster, a merry-go-round, and more ridiculous machinery which made her scream in terrified delight, to Gloucester to watch the fishing boats come in. All one Sunday afternoon they walked in Boston's North End, where happy people of his race crowded together on doorsteps and called to one another from high windows. But he knew none of them, and none of them knew him. Nobody waved from step or upper story, calling, "Hey, there, Pietro, who's your girl?"

Anyway, she was not his girl. He knew it, and she knew it.

By intermission at *No, No, Nanette* his sulkiness had been replaced by indulgent amusement as he obviously found her unconcealed delight in what was taking place on the stage more worth watching than anything he could see there. From then on for several weeks his attitude swung back and forth between that of a sophisticated, fondly teasing older brother and that of a paternal world traveler lately back from fruitless wanderings alone in far places and now trying to get reacquainted with a daughter he had never really known, by introducing her to all she had been ignorant of while growing up in the convent school where he had placed her.

During that period he seemed driven by his own curiosity to expose her to as many different environments as possible. Though he sometimes asked her where she would like to go, and she always suggested a place they had already been or a play they had already seen, she knew as she did so what he would say.

"You liked that, didn't you? Sometime maybe we'll go again. But there is so much to do you haven't done. Why not a new place tonight?"

"I don't know anything about the places I haven't been."

"But I do. I was thinking of taking you to the Oyster House."

"All right."

She loved the Oyster House. It had crude, heavy dark tables and benches, sawdust was inches deep on the floor, the waiters looked like old sailors and wore unbleached canvas aprons held up by straps around their necks and tied behind in bowknots of wide tape curled from many washings.

It did not matter to Alice where he took her, or what his mood was. Being there was what mattered to her. She was deep in a love affair with everywhere, almost oblivious of Pietro except as a guide. Such gratitude as she felt—and she was often swept and shaken by surges of it—was to God for making the earth and everything on it and to Carmen Ferrari for insisting that she go out and see it.

Then quite suddenly he became critical, often viciously so, as she came toward him through the front hall of the nurses' home, as he looked at her slantwise from a seat next to hers in subway or auditorium, as he faced her across a table or in a theater lobby where she waited for him to finish a cigarette in a chased gold holder.

"Is that the only coat you have?"

"Yes."

"Do you know the back of your head looks like a country boy's?"

"It's shingled."

"Who shingled it?"

"Millie."

"Who's Millie?"

"My roommate."

"I thought as much. Why don't you let it grow awhile and go to a hairdresser?"

"No time. No money. Besides, I like the way Millie cuts it."

"Don't you ever use any makeup?"

"Just powder on my nose."

"Your eyebrows are too light and thin, and your eyelashes are too short. I'll get you some mascara if you'll use it."

"I wouldn't. I'd be afraid it would smear and I'd look like somebody in a minstrel show. I'm always excited when I go out, and being excited makes me hot."

"I never knew a girl like you. Sometimes I'm not sure you are a girl."

"I am."

"You are a girl?"

"Yes, and always sure of it. When I think of it. There is so much else to think of."

"Can you dance?"

"No." Not with him, anyhow.

"I thought not. From your walk. You walk like a colt . . . I'd take you somewhere and teach you to dance if you had a decent dress and would get your hair done and at least put on some lipstick."

"There are plenty of girls with decent dresses, fancy hair-dos, and lipstick you can take dancing, and I haven't a doubt in the world you do."

"That isn't teaching you anything. Do you want to get to be an old woman without a man ever telling you you're beautiful? Or graceful?"

"I don't know. It's nothing I worry about . . . Come to think of it, colts have always seemed graceful to me."

His critical moods did not distress Alice. His opinion of her was of little or no importance. Sometimes she only half heard him, being lost in where they were going, where they were, or where they had just been. Often she did not even answer, if he had not asked a direct question. She was out to see, to feel, to drink in, to listen to a thousand other sounds than Pietro's rumble.

From this he turned to tucking things into her coat pocket when she left him at the door of the nurses' home.

The first time it was a bottle of perfume, which he covered by saying, "So you won't smell like the hospital at *A Doll's House* next week." She had never had perfume before and this was French, the container cut glass and brilliant, and she was pleased. Though she almost forgot to put a drop under each ear before going to *A Doll's House,* she did remember just in time, and he noticed and spoke of it; but she was by then identified with Nora and never remembered afterward what it was he said.

The perfume was followed by a long, narrow, sheer blue silk scarf she was happy to wear evenings in place of a hat which was more difficult to forget, a tiny pair of earrings (she lost one the first time she wore them, not having screwed it in tightly enough), other bits of jewelry which did not look expensive, and a tiny, mottled green fountain pen which she carried in her bag for years. Sometimes a flower box with her name on it was on the long golden oak table in the front hall of the nurses' home when she came off duty. None of them contained a card, but she knew who sent them. The flowers she liked best were a bunch of violets she put in a white ironstone bowl she had brought from home because it had been her choice for crackers and milk as long ago as she could remember.

She was always careful to thank Pietro for each gift the next time she saw him, and then forgot about it, settling into what the evening offered.

"How selfish I was!" thinks Alice now. "Giving nothing and taking whatever he offered as if it were my right, as if it were owed to me! Is that typical of a girl of nineteen? If so, it's no excuse."

Perhaps she did give something to Pietro. She hopes so. But, if she did, it was unintentional, unconscious, and in no

way to her credit for she made no effort, being absorbed whenever she was with him in her own impressions and reactions,
deaf and blind to him in the suspense of watching a curtain go
up, breathlessly appreciating entertainers, eavesdropping on
the conversation of those at a neighboring table . . .

During the weeks when he seemed to want to be with her
only for the opportunity it afforded him to attack her, she
suspected that each evening she saw him might be the last.
This suspicion led her to increasing concentration on what she
wanted to gather up and squeeze out of the evening before it
was over. And what she wanted to gather up certainly was not
and did not even include Pietro.

When the little gifts began coming and his mood grew
gentle and quiet, she thought it was his way of preparing to say
goodbye. He did call her less frequently. After months of taking
her out every week, he let the dates separate by two weeks or
more; and, though she enjoyed the free weekends which allowed her to go to moving pictures with Millie and the other
girls on her shift, the places where Pietro took her were so
much more real and at the same time so much more magical
that she welcomed each invitation from him, whenever it
came, even more eagerly than before.

He often spoke now of where he had been in the weeks
between and whom he had taken there, sometimes describing
the gown the girl had worn, her wrap "black velvet with an
ermine collar," her silver slippers "with toes sharp as needles,"
how beautifully she danced, how late he took her home. ("She
doesn't have to get in early; she can sleep till noon.") But Alice
scarcely heard, might not have heard at all but for the way he
seemed to come to life when he talked of it, like an actor in
the role he had always longed to play. It did not matter to Alice
where he went, or with whom, if she was not there.

Then, suddenly as always, his mood changed again.

It was spring and he wanted to walk instead of taking taxis, to window-shop along the way. He drew her attention to gray silk crepe dresses with wide white lace collars, to flowered satin negligées, to wide-brimmed straw hats with wreaths of tea roses around the crown; and pointed out strings of pearls, wristwatches in a circle of diamonds, putting an arm around her as he did so.

"I'll get that for you if you'd like it, Alice."

"Oh, no! Of course not, Pietro. I couldn't accept it. Anyway, I don't need things like that."

"Yes, you do. Every girl does."

"I don't. Really I don't. Thanks just the same."

He arranged for a hansom cab to pick them up at theater or restaurant and drive them slowly along quiet streets on a roundabout way home. He said little on these midnight rides, and she sat in a kind of dream, listening to the clop-clop of the horses' feet, half remembering the sound of Grampa's Old Bell and Tim's Mavourneen treading sand, ledge, and gravel, feeling the jolt of the cobblestones, and staring at the gaslights in Louisburg Square, only faintly disturbed when his arm lay across her shoulders or his hand sought hers.

He was again taking her out every week. Their dates had always been on Saturday nights because she had no classes on weekends and was off duty Saturday afternoons and Sundays. He was now trying to persuade her at least to come for a walk with him on midweek evenings, though she never did. In the short time she could stay awake after work she could walk by herself or with other girls.

One night in the clop-clopping cab he drew her against him and tried to kiss her.

She drew away and said sharply, "Don't do that."

"And why not?"

"It doesn't mean anything."

"What makes you so sure? I incline to think it does. Who knows why, but I may be falling in love with you."

"That's absurd."

"If that's what you think, I hope it isn't true."

He withdrew to his own corner, and did not move or speak when the cabbie stopped before the nurses' home, but let her get out and hurry alone up the brick walk. She was sure then they would never go out together again, and she could hear Granny assuring her that it was better, much better so. But he had already told her he had tickets for a concert for the next Saturday night. When the time came, he rang her bell and she went with him, avoiding his somber eyes, and chattering nervously, still determined to miss nothing of the city that he would show her and that she almost certainly would never see or hear unless with him.

The concert on the Common ended early and he did not have a hansom waiting or whistle for a taxi, but took her elbow and steered her quickly down a narrow street.

"Where are we going?"

"To get something to eat. Aren't you hungry?"

"No."

"Neither am I. But I need a drink."

He had never said before that he needed a drink.

They went down an alley and through a door into a small, dim, smoky room crowded by a bar running the length of one side and tables for two placed so close together that it was not easy to draw out a chair without entangling it in the one behind.

He seated her, helped her out of her coat, spread it across the chair back, touched her shoulders lightly, sat down across from her, sighed as if in vast relief, and smiled at her.

"This is good. I don't mind telling you I've had a rough week."

"Have you? Why?"

"I was afraid you wouldn't come."

"I told you I would."

"But that was before I . . . I thought afterward I might have frightened you. I see now that was ridiculous. You are a very self-confident young woman . . . Mm-m-m, I'm comfortable for the first time in days."

Alice was not comfortable. She set herself to listen to the popping of corks, the ring of glasses, the gurgle of liquid at the bar behind her while he spoke to the waiter using names she had never heard.

When the order came, it was two tall drinks and a divided metal tray with popcorn in one end and potato chips in the other.

Alice looked at her glass and asked, "What's this?"

He lit a cigarette and smiled at her.

"A highball, darling. Your very first."

"Pietro, you must know I wouldn't—"

He leaned toward her across the small table, his long, narrow face lighting up in that dim room, coming to life as she had never seen him do before except when he talked of other girls he knew, and bringing that life so close to hers now that it was impossible to overlook, to ignore.

"Of course I know it, Alice. Yours is only ginger ale on ice with a slice of lemon."

"You didn't order ginger ale."

"Oh, yes, I did. By a name that *means* that, but *sounds* like a real drink. It's for people who don't drink but don't want to be conspicuous where others are having highballs."

Alice would once have said, "Not for people like me. That's silly." But it was too late for that, too late to tell Pietro that anything he did was silly. Probably it had always been too late. She sipped her drink in silence. It was ginger ale.

"Alice, let me tell you what I want to do."

"What?"

"I want to take you to New York."

New York!

"You think Boston is exciting. Boston is just a bigger country town. New York is a city. Oh, it's not Paris or Florence or Vienna or even London. I'll take you to them later. But you're ready for New York now. We've *done* Boston. Darling, we could begin in New York this very next weekend. Shall we?"

"Next *weekend!* You know I have only Saturday noon to Sunday night!"

He laughed, not gruffly as usual, but with music in it, and his eyes shone.

"Oh, I know very well what a stickler you are for duty, my dear. You probably haven't missed a class or a shift yet, not even an hour of them."

"No. I haven't."

"Well, well, a day and a half will do for the first time. We could catch the one o'clock train, be there in time for a quick dinner before going on to see Carmen in O'Neill's *Anna Christie,* and have supper afterward, maybe with her if she isn't tied up. Then we'd have all Sunday to tour the city and take an evening train back. You'd get only a glimpse, but it will be all you need to want to go again and again. I *know,* darling. I've watched you in Boston. If Boston excites you—"

See Carmen Ferrari in an O'Neill play . . . any O'Neill play . . .

"Would we stay with her?"

"Who?"

"Your sister."

"If she has enough room. I don't know what kind of digs she has. She hasn't phoned since she got into New York. This is a play she did in Chicago last winter and it's being tried out for two weeks in Yonkers preparatory to opening on Broadway this fall. If you say you'll come, I'll find out where she is. I can call her agent. I can't *tell* you what a marvelous experience it would be for you. I simply don't have any words. You've never given me any words for the way you feel about what you see. It's all in your face and I understand the language but can't speak it . . . Will you come, darling?"

There was much in his face now, too, but she did not understand the language and could not read it.

"I'll have to think about it, Pietro. You know I have to think about things."

Was she really intending to think about it? She did not know. All these years later, Alice still does not know.

"Yes. Well, all right. You think about it. Think about Boston and try to imagine it multiplied a hundred times and more . . . You'll even love the trip. Have you ever ridden through Rhode Island and Connecticut? We'll be in a parlor car with deep chairs that turn in any direction you want them to, and a porter to bring us whatever we want. And when we get there, the first place you will see is Grand Central Station —a far cry, I can tell you, from Boston's North Station where you came in from Maine. Maybe we'll have dinner in Grand Central. One of the Alice Foote MacDougall's restaurants is there—like a courtyard in some old Spanish town. I think you would like that place. I know you would . . . But one thing, darling, you must let me get you some clothes. Now, stop! Don't say no again! You know how long I've wanted to, and this is the time. I know just what I want you to have. I've seen them on Newbury Street, and I'll order them sent out tomorrow, in time for you to get small alterations made if you want to. I'm sure I know your size, so they won't need much. They won't be anything you might think extreme or call gaudy. Boston doesn't have that sort, and if it did I wouldn't choose them for you. Just an ensemble for traveling—a blue and white print dress with a cashmere coat in blue lined with the same print as the dress, a white straw cloche and bag to match, and another dress—pink lace, I think, with a brief white silky piqué cape, and a little white evening bag for the theater. Maybe a few pairs of white gloves and some silk stockings . . . Do you have white pumps, darling?"

"I have my graduation slippers."

But she said this only because it was too late to say, "Don't be silly." If she had ever thought she might consider seriously going to New York with Pietro Amalfi, she knew now she never would.

"Fine. They'll probably do. I hope so, because I couldn't safely choose shoes for you, and I know you'll think you're too busy to do it . . . Darling, I believe you're coming . . . I'm all but sure you're coming!"

He sounded triumphant. His eyes glowed. His tall glass was nearly empty. She had scarcely touched hers.

"Give me one of those, Mac," he said to a waiter passing with a tray.

"These are ordered, sir. I'll bring you one at once, sir."

"Don't make it too light."

"No, sir."

Alice said, "Pietro, we should go. You know I have to be in by twelve."

"Trust me, little law-abiding Alice. I'll see you make it. We'll take a taxi this time." He spread his hands, leaning so far across the small table he could have touched her. His white teeth flashed. "But next Saturday night you'll have no deadline to meet, darling. You *must* see how crowded Times Square is at two to three o'clock in the morning. It's the brightest, liveliest hour of the twenty-four there."

"If I didn't get in until three or four o'clock, I'd be dead on my feet next day. Remember I have classes all Saturday mornings. And this Monday I start my first assignment in the operating room."

"On weekends, my dear, you should forget the hospital. Totally. As if you had never been inside it. I do."

A freshly filled tall glass was deposited before him, frosty and dripping, staining the small paper napkin with the scalloped edge. He lifted the glass without looking at it and drank several swallows in rapid succession, his glowing eyes on hers across its rim.

"Do you really?" asked Alice.

"Do I what?"

"Forget the hospital when you aren't there."

"It's the only way, darling. Otherwise the carbolic smell that maddened Carmen would seep into our very souls. We can't let that happen. We have to live our own lives, separate from all that. Our own lives are all we've got, and time rushes on . . . You know how to do it. You certainly aren't thinking of the hospital when an orchestra is tuning up or a stage curtain lifting."

"No. I can forget it for a few hours. But not for a whole weekend . . . I think the hospital and what goes on in it *is* part of my own life, not separate . . . I think even in the few hours I'm forgetting it I'm unconsciously storing up feelings inside myself to take back to it. Feelings I hope make me a better nurse . . . Pietro, I'm just realizing this is the first time we've ever spoken to each other of the hospital where we both work. Or even of our professions. Ever. In all these months."

He seemed to be listening to her, still smiling, his eyes fixed on hers, but she was not sure he heard until he shook his head and said:

"Oh, Alice, what a strange girl you are! At first you seemed to me so typical, so transparent I'd never have asked you out if Carmen hadn't brought you up so often I began to think she had seen something in you I hadn't. I've always been attracted only to girls I couldn't fathom. The fun was in unraveling whatever mystery was there. I figured that in two dates at most I'd have you unraveled. But you—you're unravelable! Every time I think I may be getting close to the real secret of you, I come up against the ivied wall of a new secret. You're transparent, yes, but only as far as that stupid ivy. When you talk, I don't know what you mean, whether you really mean what you are saying. When you're silent, I never know what you are thinking. Now, all of a sudden, you're acting like a dedicated nurse. I don't recognize this Alice. You are mystery upon mystery."

Too late to say, "That's silly."

She said, "Only to you, because of the difference in our backgrounds. I *am* dedicated to nursing, was before I came into the hospital, and get more so all the time. You've been taking me a little way into your world, and I've enjoyed it and been busy absorbing what I could of it. But it's not my world."

She thought, "And I've never tried taking you into my world. I couldn't have even if I had wanted to. You would never have come, even as far as I've gone into yours."

"But it's going to be, darling," he exclaimed exultantly. "You've just finished an elementary course. Next weekend you'll advance, and we'll go on from there. And someday soon I'll uncover one of your secrets and understand that much of what makes you tick. But I'm convinced now you'll always have more in reserve. Always, as long as I know you. Lord, I do love you."

"Pietro, I have to get back."

"I know. I know."

He drained his glass, threw down some money, helped her into her coat, and with a hand on her shoulder guided her quickly to the street. A line of taxis were drawn up before the

theater across the way. He sang out her address to the driver
of the first one in the line, they were inside, the engine roared
—and Pietro Amalfi had Alice in his arms, immobilized, forced
her head back with the drive of his mouth on hers, pushed her
against the seat, and was kissing her in ways she had never
known kissing was done.

She clenched her teeth and waited. It seemed a long time.
She wondered if it would ever end.

When it did, he moved away from her, and they rode in
silence until he growled, "It's no use, is it?"

"No," Alice said miserably.

She had nothing with which to compare what had just
happened except Tim Corcoran's kiss. And there was no comparison. Her mouth tasted of whiskey and tobacco. She felt
unclean, degraded. For the second time in her life, and for a
diametrically different reason, she wanted to die.

She turned her face away and looked out the window, saw
the city lights, and hated them. She wanted to be out of
Boston. She wanted to go home.

Then she saw a street sign which told her they were near
the hospital, and was startled by her response; an almost dizzy-
ing lift of her spirits and the accompanying revelation—faintly
curious to remember years later, but nevertheless an accurate
prophecy—"As soon as I brush my teeth, I'll be all right."

Now for the first time she could have a thought for Pietro,
humped up over there and staring straight ahead, all his tri-
umph died aborning, all his exultation, all his glow gone; as
miserable as she if not more so. Poor Pietro!

She could even bring herself to put a hand lightly on his
arm and speak to him gently.

"Don't feel bad. I do understand. You thought you loved
me so you thought you could make me love you. You were
mistaken, that's all. *I* think you were mistaken on both counts.
I don't believe you really love me. I don't see how you could,

I'm so different from you. That's why you call me strange . . . Maybe what you did would do what you wanted it to to some girls, but I'm not one of them. If I could ever have loved you, I should have loved you long ago. You've been very good to me, and good for me, in many ways, and I'll always be grateful. But the fact is we don't know each other and never will. I really don't keep secrets, and maybe you don't, but you are as much a mystery to me as I am to you. One difference between us is that you like to ferret out secrets and I'm content to let them lie until they reveal themselves . . . Pietro, I think maybe you're just lonely. You're not at home in Boston. Shouldn't you think about trying for an internship in New York, if that's possible? I don't know about such things, but you must . . . Anyway, we won't go out together again. For both our sakes . . . "

The taxi stopped before the nurses' home. He walked with her silently across the uneven brick.

"Goodbye—Dr. Amalfi. Pretty soon you'll laugh about this. If you ever think of me, it will be of that strange probationer from Down East who lived for the day she would get a white cap."

At the door he took her hand and kissed it.

Too late to say, "That's silly."

When he straightened, he was smiling the wry smile which had been the first she saw on his face.

"I hope so," he said. "Goodbye, Alice McIntire."

13

This is the day Melissa's family is coming to the island to take her home, and it will be the occasion of a great and rare happening. All of Alice's descendants and in-laws will be here together. There are more of them than there have been the few times they have assembled before—once for the first Christmas after Phil and Delores were married, once for Emily's wedding (Delores and the boys did not come with Phil), and the last time for Harley's memorial service, when Weston and Gary remained in California with their mother and Rhonda came with Phil but Sue, Desirée, and Margery were not yet born.

Now Phil is on vacation, and his sons, back from Canada, have been for two days on the island, helping him pack the camper in which the family will cross on the boat tonight. Pictures the boys took on their trip have persuaded Phil and Rhonda they must see more of Canada than they have, and so must their daughters. Phil and his family are leaving the island to return to Oak Park by way of Quebec, the St. Lawrence, Montreal, and Ottawa.

"We might have stayed another few days," Phil said to Alice yesterday, "but we don't want to feel hurried along the way. Besides, if we cross to the mainland with Emily's family we'll see that much more of them."

"That will be nice," Alice answered. "You have so little chance to be together."

Phil, his five children, and Melissa were building a beach oven yesterday in front of Alice's cottage for today's clambake. Melissa calls it a clambake, but here the clams are quahaugs.

"Shouldn't you pick up and go home, too, Mother? Even if you have the cottage rented for another week? I don't like to leave you out here alone."

Alice smiled and shook her head.

"I know you thought we'd be here longer. We did, too."

"It's all right, Phil. I could never feel alone on the island. No knowing when I'll be back again."

Alice is up before the sun. She stands for a minute looking down at Melissa. How deeply children sleep even at the dawn-

ing of a day they know will be eventful and which will bring
many changes! She gathers up clothing laid out last night and
tiptoes as quietly as she can down the creaky stairs to shower
and dress. She measures out coffee and connects the cord to
the outlet.

Now she can stay inside no longer. There is still no sound
from Melissa. She goes to the door. The pale morning sunshine
is bathing the world. There is no movement anywhere except
that of the surf, which is never still, and of the birds. Season
after season, generation after generation, age after age, the
waves come rolling one after another against these ledges,
running up this hard-packed sand, bringing nourishment to
small shelled creatures beneath it, to tiny winged creatures who
race silently across it on feet made almost invisible by their
speed, and to the great white gulls dipping and soaring above
it. Only the gulls are talking, and no one has ever translated
what they say, season after season, generation after generation,
age after age. . . . The creatures do not know who is bringing
their food. The waves do not know they bring it. Each is doing
only what it is its own nature to do, for its own joy.

Alice walks up and down in front of her cottage, close to
the water, and Harley is with her. He is always with her unless
she is with someone he does not know and with whom he has
no connection, or is in a place where he has never been. Not
the memory of Harley, only now and then a reliving of one of
the countless experiences they have shared in the past, but
Harley himself, the man whose life has been more and more
steadily interwoven with hers for half a century. She does not
often speak to him or he to her. From the first they have not
had much need of words. Harley is a quiet man, and Alice has
always been happy to be quiet with him.

But now she says softly, "To think they'll all be together
on the island today! Philip and Rhonda; Emily and Jim; Gary

and Weston; Vicki, Chris, Melissa, and Doan; Sue, Desirée, and Margery. Isn't it lovely to look forward to?"

He answers, "Yes. Only it will have its surprises. Don't let anything that happens today worry you. Remember they're all under great pressure at their ages. More than we were, even."

"You think that, too?"

"No question about it. This is the era of uncertainty. They have to try to avoid the same abysses we did, but fear quite as much as the abyss the possibility, even the probability, that as they move on they may be going nowhere. Doubt is in the air they breathe."

"Even on the island?"

"They haven't met here yet. We have to wait and see. It wasn't here for us, was it?"

"No. This was one place where no worry intruded. You're right. We must try to keep it that way. At least for us."

"Because they must move on and we know they are going somewhere. The periods of youth and middle age are so demanding it often seems the stress will continue until it crushes us. But the truth is it lasts only a minute against the backdrop of eternity, and the time comes when we know that beyond all question. The struggles of mortals are as soon over, in God's sight, as the sting from an inoculation for a baby, or the pain of a bruised knee for a little boy. We are all here for a purpose, and that purpose is achieved by every one of us, even if we never have an inkling of what it is."

"I know . . . But I might forget sometimes if you didn't remind me . . . "

"Garmie!"

"Yes! . . . Yes, Melissa?"

Melissa's tousled head and bare shoulders have appeared at the bedroom window.

"I'm getting dressed! You should have waked me! It's past

seven o'clock and the boat gets in at ten-thirty. We have to hurry!"

"Not really. Everything is just about ready. Put the bed to air before you come downstairs. I'll be right in and start breakfast."

Salad makings are in the refrigerator, next to stacks of ears of island corn. Yesterday's rolls from the Island Food Shop fill the breadbox. And late last night Alice took from her oven three big pies made of island blackberries, needing now only a froth of meringue to be crisped and gilded by the broiler.

By eight o'clock Phil has been over to build the fire which will heat the stones of the beach oven, reporting that his boys are digging quahaugs and he will pick up lobsters on his next trip.

At ten o'clock he is back in the rented dune buggy and deposits baskets of clams in the cool shade beneath the back porch, tosses lobsters into old black tubs filled with salt water, and piles more wood on the fire. Rhonda on the front seat takes Margery on her lap and puts Desirée between her parents, leaving room for Alice and Melissa in back with Sue. Sue says, "Get in the middle, Garmie." She does, and they are off.

"Go as fast as you can, Uncle Phil!" shrieks Melissa.

Alice is pleased.

She thinks, "The child hasn't seen her own family for a month, and now she can't wait to. That's the way it should be. She has had her visit out, as Granny used to say."

"We'll be in plenty of time!" Phil shouts back. "Anyway, Gare and Wes will be on hand to meet them. They left when we did, headed for the dock on their bikes."

"But I want to see the boat come in!"

"You will."

They do. After a few minutes when the adults sit on

weathered benches at dockside in blinding sunlight, keeping a half-shut eye on small ones drawn as if by magnets to small strangers and to leashed dogs little and big, Rhonda says: "Here it comes!"

They all rise at the signal. In two long strides Phil singles out and picks up Margery, sets her on his shoulder.

"See the boat, honey? Aunt Em is on that boat. It looks small, but you watch it. It looks small now but you watch. It will grow."

"Where's Desirée?" asks Rhonda. "Sue, find Desirée! Quick!"

"I've got her," says Melissa, hurrying up, panting, pulling an unwilling Desirée behind her. "Here she is."

"I was playing with the doggie," Desirée whimpers.

"Sh-h-h. The boat is coming in," Rhonda tells her, reaching for her hand.

"I can't *see* it! Daddy, take me up on your other shoulder!"

"I know I've got two shoulders," Phil says. "But only two hands, and Margie wiggles like a tadpole."

Weston drops off the fence along the edge of the dock, where he has been lounging beside Gary, says, "Come on, mite," and tosses Desirée to a seat even higher than Margery's. Squealing, she grasps a handful of his hair, and he says, laughing, "Ouch! Take it easy, mite."

Gary stays where he is, rocking slowly back and forth as if about either to plunge face down onto the scarred planks of the dock or to go over backward into the harbor. A glance at him, so precariously balanced, is enough for Alice. He must know what he is doing. He is twenty-five years old. She turns her gaze toward the open ocean, shading her eyes with her hand.

The *Islander* is growing, as Philip promised, smoke spurting out as its whistle blows, its outline and proportions recognizable, the design of its flag clear against the bright blue sky. It is like an old friend to Alice, who has come in and gone out on it so many times, so many other times stood here as now trying to catch sight of loved ones on the upper deck.

Now she can see a crowd of faces. Tiny faces. Tiny arms waving. Everyone on the dock waves back, except those waiting to board and drivers of trucks sent to pick up mail and merchandise.

"That's Em!" shouts Philip, suddenly. He thrusts Margery into Rhonda's arms, leaps like a boy onto a bench, and swings both arms high above his head.

Alice, trying in vain to separate her daughter's face from all the others, thinks contentedly, "All these years living such different lives so far apart with people neither of them knew when they were growing up together can't have destroyed the bond that used to be between them. Emily is still the only sister Philip will ever have, and he her only brother."

She remembers when Philip came home on college vacations, while Emily was still in high school, and she and Harley took them to spend evenings with his relatives. Emily would have chattered on endlessly about Phil's grades, the fraternity he had been asked to join, the essay his economics professor had entered in national competition, if shy Philip—perhaps out of embarrassment—had not interrupted to say Emily was doing all right, too, and he supposed they knew she had been elected president of her class but maybe they hadn't heard she had just been given the leading role in the senior class play, though she was only a junior.

She remembers Harley's father looking around at Harley and remarking indulgently, "Your children sound like publicity agents for each other"; and Emily—whom nothing could embarrass—rubbing her chin against Philip's coat sleeve and saying pertly, "Why not? We're a Mutual Admiration Society."

"I see her now, Phil!" cries Alice, snatching off her kerchief to wave. "Hi, Emilee-ee-ee!"

It is Chris who hears or sees her. He turns to tell his mother, pointing at Alice, picks up Doan and puts her on his head, and Doan and all the Eustaces are waving now to Alice and Melissa and Phil and his family. Crew members in white caps with visors are running along the edge of the deck. One stands with a coil of rope around his arm, ready to hurl it down for the tying up. The gangplank waits to be pushed out for the foot passengers to pass over. And the Eustaces suddenly disappear. . . . When the big doors open in the hold, Jim's van is the first to come through, and the Gilmans and Melissa trail it until he can find a parking place. Before he comes to a full stop, Eustaces are spilling out, everybody exclaiming in only half familiar voices, men shaking hands, slapping backs, women and older girls hugging one another. Sue, Desirée, and Margery stare curiously, and Doan hugs Chris's leg, hiding behind it all but one eye, one fat, pink cheek, and one corner of her dazzling, delighted, and delighting smile.

"I here, Gamie," trills Doan. "Chrissy bring me on boat. Big boat."

"Yes, Doan, yes!" cries Alice. "You all came. We're all together on the island."

And there is someone else. Emily is introducing him. A tall, lean black boy in desert boots, faded Levi's, and a shirt which looks as if it had been dipped into a Hawaiian sunset.

"This is Greg—Mom, Rhonda, Phil," Emily is saying eagerly. "Greg Saunders. Vicki's friend. Ours too since he began coming over. He and Vicki have been working together all summer. He's never been offshore before, and he simply has to begin to know the island. I've told him we used to be here all summer long when we were kids; weren't we, Mom? *You* remember, Phil! Oh, it's lovely. Don't you love it, Melissa? The air smells exactly as it always did on this old dock. I'd know where I was if I'd just waked out of a sound sleep—"

Everybody shakes hands with Greg, who nods and says nothing, is unsmiling. Vicki is talking eagerly to Weston. Gary has come off the fence, landed on his feet, and stands on the fringe of this family reunion, watching it idly, listening as if faintly amused by it, but not yet seriously considering paying the small admission charge to go inside the tent.

"Well, we'd better be getting along to the beach," says Philip. "Get the bake started, and then some of you will want to go for a swim—"

"Yes, let's go," Emily responds. "Oh, Vicki, Greg, you two think you know what swimming is, but wait till you get into this island surf. There's nothing like it, is there, Phil? Even the deep pools after the tide goes out—remember you taught me to swim in them? Jim, while the other kids battle the waves, let's find one of those pools for Doan."

"Chrissy," says Doan. "Chrissy—swim me."

"You little nut," says Chris fondly. "If you think I'm going to flub around in a pool today!"

"Chrissy swim me," Doan states confidently.

They are all climbing back into the van and the dune buggy. Gary and Weston roll their bikes into line, and rev them up.

"We'll give them an escort, Gare!" shouts Weston. "Just like royalty. I'll go up front and clear the way. You bring up the rear." He shoots ahead.

Greg speaks for the first time. His voice is deep and musical. "Come over on this bird, did you?" he asks Gary.

"Never travel any other way on land if I can help it. Just got back from Canada on it. Came through from the West Coast before that . . . Care to hop on and bounce back to the beach with me?"

"Yeah."

From a corner of the back seat of the dune buggy Alice turns to watch these two who are the final entry in today's Gilman parade across the island. Almost equally dark-skinned—Gary has his mother's complexion and is deeply tanned—they are of much the same build and they lean with the same ease and grace as they round a curve. Gary's long locks fly out like a pennant, while not a hair of Greg's head is disturbed. Neither wears either helmet or goggles, and Alice fervently hopes there is no island law on these matters. Their eyes are like dark slits against the wind made by their own movement, and their lips are parted, showing their white teeth in what may be grins of enjoyment or grimaces of annoyance that they cannot go faster while staying in line.

Vicki, who is beside Alice, does not look back. She pushes her spun-gold hair away from her face, which is too thin—Alice sees hollows in her cheeks—and tosses it up from her hot neck, gives a long sigh which sounds like one of relief, ducks her head to nuzzle Alice's shoulder, and murmurs, "Oh, Garmie, it's so good to see you again."

"I was afraid maybe you couldn't get away to come. Your mother wasn't sure."

"I finished yesterday. I really need two weeks to get ready for school."

"Of course you do."

"Weston's a nice kid, isn't he?"

"I thought you and he were hitting it off."

"Did I ever see him before?"

"If so, it was when you were too young to remember it now."

"I wonder if we'll get a chance today to really talk . . . Funny. I feel as if there is a lot I'd really like to talk over with him."

Alice once wrote, "I'd love a chance to talk all by ourselves . . ."

"Maybe you can."

"Funny," Vicki says again. "He seems like a guy who can put handles on things. So they won't keep slipping away . . ."

She slides far down in the dune-buggy seat, knees hunched to her chin, rests her head on the back, and closes her eyes.

"The child is tired out," thinks Alice.

Beyond Vicki, perched on Chris's knees, Doan squeals, "Wawa! Chrissy see more wawa! Vicki, wake up! WAKE UP! More wawa!"

Jim's van has turned into the back yard of Alice's cottage. Weston's bike has stopped against the underpinning of the porch. The dune buggy trails the van and Philip turns off the engine. Gary and Greg leap off, and suddenly Gilmans are shooting out and buzzing off in all directions like so many bees.

Alice climbs the steps, crosses the back porch, and pauses in the middle of the cool, sparsely furnished cottage living room to watch them through the picture window, all framed in strips of roughly finished pine turned brown by time.

They come into the picture from both sides, squeezing through openings in the wild-rose hedge, wading through the tall sea grass, clambering over the rocks. Gary and Greg reach the beach first, from one side, then Vicki and Weston from the other. There they stop, a little apart, gaze out to sea, and turn, a bit uncertainly, to watch the others coming toward them. Chris, though carrying Doan, is next, closely followed by Sue. Now here comes Emily, with Philip carrying Margery, Jim leading Desirée; and they gather at once around the bake oven. The children are set down and instantly scamper toward the waterline, like the sandpipers; but only Alice's eyes follow them until they stand still and then kneel on the wet sand, holding out their hands to the birds. Emily is chattering away, probably explaining to Jim how the dinner will be prepared, and Philip keeps nodding and putting in a word or two when he can. The boys and Vicki and Sue draw nearer to listen. Vicki asks a question and Philip, turning quietly approving eyes on her, answers it. Rhonda and Melissa are the last to appear, coming slowly. They not only squeeze through the hedge, but see and smell the roses; not only wade through the grass, but sense its dryness, sharpness, pale gray-green color; cross over not only rocks but forms, textures, relationships; and when they reach the sand pause with bent heads, as if studying it, as if planting themselves, like trees, to draw nourishment from it.

Light heads, dark heads, ruddy heads, all bare. Long thin legs, short fat legs, all bare and brown. Broad shoulders, narrow shoulders, sloping shoulders. Big square hands, smaller tapering hands, children's hands, baby hands.

Where have all these people come from . . .? And why are they there, together, all caught in the frame of one window?

Because of Alice and Harley. Harley Gilman and Alice McIntire.

Even Doan. Even Greg.

The love which sweeps through Alice is like a wave too strong to stand against. She puts a hand on the frame to steady herself.

She is honest. She does not love them all equally. The only two people she has ever known between whom she had no preference, could under no conditions make a choice, are her own children. She always knew she loved Grampa more than Granny, though at the time she felt this was unfair and wrong, and had pangs of guilt about it. She has never felt the slightest guilt that she loves her children more than those they married, or that Melissa is her favorite grandchild. She could, if she would, list her grandchildren in close order of her preference for them; and she readily admits to herself that she can never love Doan as much as the others, not because she is Vietnamese but simply because she is not Alice's own, and she can never love Greg, however long and well she knows him, even as much as she loves Doan, because she never saw him until he was grown. To Alice, this is natural and reasonable. It is Emily whose maternal feeling has no limits; not Alice . . . Yet the sum, the total of what she feels for those in her picture is almost overwhelming. She must master it before she can join them. If she were to go out there with this "all hanging out," as Vicki would say, some of them would notice it—most likely Melissa—and it could not be explained to them.

She sits down for a minute, facing the window, and calls up thoughts to blur her feeling and so ease its poignancy.

How did it happen that it was Jim, not Rhonda, who led Desirée across the sea grass and the stones? That it is Rhonda, not Emily, to whom Melissa is staying close? That Vicki seems to have established some sort of instant bond with her Uncle Philip as with his younger son? That Doan chooses to cling like a little leech to Chris, though surrounded by people who love her? That Sue, too, trails Chris? That Gary and Greg are drawn to each other?

She thinks she knows the answers. If they are wrong, no one will know, for no one knows the questions have been asked.

Jim is nothing if not kind, and he relates to other men. If Philip carried Margery and Desirée was there, not quite so small but still small, Jim would take her hand as a matter of course. Dear Jim! . . . Melissa was born to give, and in giving receives. Emily wants nothing Melissa can consciously give; Emily seems to Melissa fulfilled, complete; Emily gives without needing to receive. Philip is happy to be with his sister again. Rhonda needs Melissa; without Melissa Rhonda would be alone . . . Vicki is under stress. She wants above all things to be just like her mother, but she is not her mother. She wants what her mother has, but cannot have it. She sees the spontaneous affection between Emily and Philip. She cannot have that. She has no older brother. But Philip is her uncle, his son who is so like him is her cousin and older than she. She has a right to her own uncle and her own cousin, hasn't she? . . . Maybe Doan left big brothers behind in Vietnam, and Chris feels to her as they felt to her . . . And Sue. Sue has had scant cuddling. She trails Chris and Doan at a little distance, imagining that she is Doan being carried and tossed, Doan screaming with laughter, Doan trusting and confident, sure she is safe and loved . . . As for Gary and Greg, they feel apart from the others —a separation of their own choosing—and this has brought them together . . .

"Garm! You in there? Unhook the screen!"

"Coming," says Alice.

It is Vicki and Weston.

"The men have got the fire raked out," says Vicki. "Kids are pulling in the seaweed. We've come for the clams."

"AND the lobsters and corn," adds Weston, peering at Alice through the comparative dusk of the cottage. "What are you still inside for, Garm? Don't you like us?"

"I like you all right," says Alice steadily. "I'm here for the same reason you can hardly see. Had as much sun as I wanted for a little while. I'll be on the beach long enough soon enough. Corn in the refrigerator. Lobsters and clams in baskets under the back porch. Full rations for a small army. I estimate delivery to headquarters will require several trips."

Weston and Vicki run through carrying armfuls of unhusked corn as if it were stovewood, or run past the end windows with a basket of clams between them, and finally ask for buckets with which to transfer the lobsters from the tub. Alice goes to point out the buckets, carrying Doan, whom Chris has deposited unceremoniously on her lap in order to follow Gary and Greg into the basement, where all three are kicking off boots and disreputable tennis shoes, tossing shirts and pants into a heap on the old stepladder. Alice knows what they are doing because Doan, with her fifth wild scream of protest, escaped from her adopted grandmother's gentle grasp and was halfway down the basement stairs before she could be recovered.

Now Doan's tear-stained face breaks into smiles and she shouts, pointing where Alice is pointing, "Pail for Doan! Pail for ME, TOO!"

"Of course there's a pail for Doan," says Melissa. "A little pail for Doan, because Doan is a little girl. A red pail. A red, red pail just for Doan."

Melissa has come in with Rhonda and Sue, who are changing Desirée and Margery into romper swimsuits. Melissa takes Doan from Alice.

"We'll take off Doan's dress," she says, "so it won't get wet while she plays in the pool with her red, red pail."

"It's *my* red pail!" shrieks Margery in sudden, uncharacteristic fury.

"No, it's not, either," says Sue. "It's Desirée's. Yours is blue. And even if it were yours, you could share, couldn't you, for goodness sake?"

"*I* can," says Desirée with angelic, almost cloying sweetness. "Doan can use *my* pail if she wants to."

"Mine," says Doan happily to Melissa. "Red. Red, red pail."

They go off, linked together in a Gilman chain, to the pool Emily has found for them, tested with a hand, with both feet, gloated over for a minute, and then returned, carrying her shoes, to Jim and Philip by the bake oven.

The boys, having galloped across the beach like three great spiders, are shooting through the waves like so many playful seals.

Briefly, Alice is again alone.

Consciousness of being alone is always an emotional experience, but what a range of emotions it can produce! All depends not only on the situation but on the personality of the one alone and on his current mood. To the recently widowed the realization of being alone is a deep, fresh wound one is convinced will never heal; surely the flow of blood from it will never be staunched. To the parent looking into a beloved child's bedroom on the evening of that grown child's wedding day it is a yawning void he cannot believe will ever again be filled. To the person of any age who lives only in and for contact with other human beings, who has no inner resources he can or dares to draw on, it is the threat of imminent death. To the old and ill and weak, who feel totally forgotten by all who remain of those they once thought loved them, who lie like driftwood on a deserted winter beach, it is heavy, dull, constant heartbreak in a tight enclosure from which there is only one open gate, and every night they pray to be led through it before another dawn.

But for those to whom, after a time, association with others becomes overstimulating and exhausting, to be alone is a blessed relief; and for those who have much to do, much to think about, much to observe and appreciate which can only be done, thought, observed, and appreciated when one is not preoccupied with responding to others, periods of being alone are vital. Solitude is essential nourishment, a longed-for opportunity for self-fulfillment, a time for gathering in and storing up what tastes sweet now but will have a far better flavor and far greater usefulness later on.

Alice thinks, "It came to me a little while ago that Melissa stays close to Rhonda because otherwise Rhonda would be alone today. I'm sure that's true. Melissa thinks that Rhonda alone is sad. But is she? Rhonda relates with difficulty to people, but so naturally, easily, creatively to landscapes. Is she least alone when no one comes between her and trees clinging to the crevices of a barren ledge, between her and the waves ceaselessly rolling in, between her and patches of sunlight and shadow, between her and the wild-rose hedge, wind-whipped laundry on a line, the half-open door of a long deserted house? Do all of us, with the best of intentions—even her own husband and children—intrude so much on Rhonda and her world in which there are no people that we imprison her, cut her off, make her an exile, fill her with terror that if she can ever get home again she will have forgotten the language, will have become blind, will not be accepted, will be turned away? . . ."

"Mom, what *are* you doing?"

It is Emily running in on bare, brown feet, with soot-blackened hands and wrists and a smudge on her forehead where she has pushed back her hair.

"It's almost time to open the oven," says Emily. "I came in to wash, but what good it will do I'm sure I don't know. The kids keep asking why you haven't come out."

"I stopped to think," says Alice. She was not obliged to say anything. Emily does not require or wait for answers. If Alice had said nothing, in an instant Emily's lilting voice would have begun again, gurgling over the yellow pebbles of whatever came into her mind. But Alice likes to answer Emily. Her daughter is the only person she knows to whom she can say whatever occurs to her, provided only that it is brief, and who is never surprised by it, whatever it may be. "Don't you ever stop to think?"

"Me? No," says Emily, laughing, from the kitchen, where

she has turned on a faucet and is splashing at the sink. "Any thinking I do is done on the run . . . Phil looks more like Dad all the time, doesn't he? It's uncanny."

"Especially when he smiles," says Alice, "and he's all smiles today, he's so glad to see you. He's attracted to Vicki too, probably partly because he associates her with you when you were her age."

But Harley grew in confidence every year he lived, while Philip, always shy and somewhat introverted as a boy, has in maturity grown a little and then slipped back, by turns, so that each time his mother anticipates seeing him she finds herself wondering where she will find him now.

"She isn't a bit like me," says Emily. "Vicki's a funny girl. For instance, I haven't the slightest idea how much she likes Greg. I think he's fascinating. I hope you get home before he goes back to school. I want you to hear him sing. His voice is fantastic. We've asked his family over for dinner Wednesday night. There's just his parents and a sister about Melissa's age. I want Melissa to know Felicity. Felicity is a dancer. She's already a member of a Boston ballet troupe—"

"He obviously likes Jim, too," says Alice.

"Greg?"

"Philip."

Emily comes in from the kitchen, shining clean, and stands over Alice, her hands on her hips, looking down with an expression of faint accusation in her smile and of frank curiosity in her eyes.

"Everybody likes *Jim* . . . Mom, you haven't been listening to a word I said!"

"Oh, yes, I was. I heard them all. But I hadn't finished thinking about Philip. Where does Greg go to school?"

"The University of Chicago. But hold it, Mom! Would you want to swear you don't harbor a bit—not even a smidgeon

—of prejudice against Greg because he's black?"

"No," says Alice. "I'm not that thoroughly acquainted with myself. But I'm not aware of any. As far as I know, he is just another boy whose name I was told when he came off the boat and who rode over here with Gary."

"Why did you ask where he goes to school? Come on; weren't you hoping it isn't where Vicki is going?"

"I wasn't thinking of Vicki at all. I was trying to show the interest in Greg you apparently wanted me to."

"So you don't feel any spontaneous interest?"

"Not just because he is black, Emily," says Alice quietly. "Any more than I would in some other boy just because he was white. And what else do I know about him except that he worked with Vicki this summer, and you like him, and he goes to the University of Chicago? He does have a beautiful speaking voice, and I should like to hear him sing."

"I get it, Mom," Emily says with a good-natured shrug. "You're telling me again I'm too impulsive, too headlong, rush in where angels fear to tread, and all that. Well, I admit I'm not much for all this waiting and seeing you always advocate. Life's too short. I've never waited and I've seen a lot."

"We see, whether we wait or not," says Alice, rising. "We all see a lot in a lifetime. Now my thinking's done, let's go to the beach before they decide you're lost trying to find me, and send out a search party."

Emily laughs and, as they go down the cottage steps, tucks a hand companionably under Alice's elbow.

"Rhonda seems awfully quiet and sort of withdrawn. Is it your impression she and Phil are getting along all right?"

"Rhonda is always like that. I think the summer here has been good for both of them. Melissa has been a tremendous help, too."

"Melissa?"

"She admires Rhonda very much."

"I thought it looked that way."

"Rhonda is doing a great deal of painting, and Melissa has fallen in love with her pictures. She has drawn Philip's attention to them."

"How could she do that? If Rhonda couldn't?"

"By being Melissa. Melissa has her own special gift. What she sees and feels is contagious."

Emily calls joyously, "Phil? You think everything's done? It must be, it smells so marvelous. Exactly as it always used to, doesn't it? I'd almost forgotten—"

She releases Alice's arm and runs ahead, leaving the imprint of her strong, narrow feet in the sand, to hug Philip and then reach for Jim's hand, standing between them with the sun on her bright face and the wind off the water rumpling her hair.

"She is still so young," thinks Alice. "Younger even than Vicki or Melissa or Sue. Perhaps she is the youngest of us all, younger even than Doan, because she has been surrounded by love all her life, always knew it, never questioned it, took it for granted. Perhaps, being Emily, she will never quite grow up."

As if at a signal, the boys are racing each other out of the surf. Rhonda and the five younger girls come down the beach from the pool. All approach the bake oven dripping. Vicki's blond head and thin, tanned face appear over a ledge, and she moves slowly nearer across the uneven rocks, swinging her hands until they meet in front and then in back; forward and back, forward and back. Weston sees Vicki, waves to her, lopes off to meet her. Greg and Gary stoop to pick up seaweed left by the tide, and come draped in cool, wet, slippery garlands to partake of the Gilman feast.

"Chrissy! Chrissy!" squeals Doan, pattering toward him on sandpiper feet, climbing him as if she were a chipmunk.

"Time to break out the salad, kids," calls Emily.

"Where's the stuff? We'll get it," offers Weston.

"In the fridge," Emily answers. "I peeked and saw it. Three big bowls.

"Bring the breadbox, too," says Alice. "It's full of rolls. And there's a package of butter, Vicki, beside the top bowl."

Vicki springs off toward the cottage, Weston close behind her.

"What's to drink, Garm?" asks Gary. "Plenty of beer?"

"I have no liquor license," Alice tells him. "There are thermos jugs of lemonade in the basement, and boxes of paper cups."

"Beer's not liquor, you know, Garm," Gary tells her indulgently.

"I think I heard that somewhere, but I didn't pay much attention. It's intoxicating and that's all I need to know. Neither your grandfather nor I ever offered anybody an intoxicating drink, and I'm certainly not beginning now. You'll find my lemonade very good."

"Garmie makes the best lemonade I ever tasted," says Melissa, dropping down on a rock beside Alice. "She makes it the way *her* grandmother made it. All fresh lemons, and lemon pieces all through. You'll like it, Gary. Really you will."

"Well, we'll see about that," says Gary, ostentatiously reserving judgment. "Anything wet and cold will be better than nothing. Come on, guys, we're the lemonade brigade!"

He looks around for Greg, but Greg doesn't hear, being on the other side of the bake oven, watching Philip and Jim beginning to rake away the steaming seaweed from the big iron pans . . . Gary looks around for Chris, but Doan has dragged him off to "swim me" in the pool.

"A brigade of one, it seems," says Gary with a shrug. "Well, so be it." From a step or two away he turns and asks,

"What do you think we drink when we're where people do have liquor licenses, Garm?"

"I take it for granted you all behave yourselves as well when you're out of my sight as when you're in it," says Alice. "Get along with you, Gary Gilman. You aren't the only one who's thirsty."

Suddenly Philip's shadow looms before her, and he stretches himself on the hot sand at her feet, his hands under his head, a satisfied expression on his face.

"I think we're coming out just about right," he says. "It's one-thirty and I've put the coffee on. Rhonda'll want her coffee. Maybe some of the rest will too. Remember Dad always wanted coffee at a clambake, no matter how hot the day was?"

"And cream in it. I didn't think of planning for coffee today. You must have brought it."

"I knew Rhonda would want it."

But he turns his head toward Alice, and she knows he has not come to talk about coffee, or even to rest. There is something else he wants to say and he doesn't know how to begin. It has always been difficult for Philip to begin saying what he most wants to say. His mother waits as she always has.

"Don't let Gary's talk worry you, Mother."

He has heard what Gary has said to her. Perhaps not her reply.

She says quickly, "Oh, I don't, Philip. I think he has some drive to try to shock his grandmother a little. If he were really what he half pretends he is, he'd have brought his own drinks or go to get them."

Philip's eyes search her face, she has convinced him, and he rolls to his back again with a sigh of contentment, closing his eyes against the sun.

He says, "I've got pretty well acquainted with my boys the last few days. More, I guess, than I expected to be again. And they're good boys. I don't know how it happened, but there's a lot of good in both of them."

"Had to be," says Alice loyally. "I don't know why you're surprised. I'm not. They're your sons and your father's grandsons."

Weston and Vicki, passing with arms full of salad bowls, spray sand on him, and Weston says, "Sorry, Dad." Philip grins and makes a motion with his hand which means, "No matter." Running back for the third salad bowl and the breadbox, they shower him again, and Weston says, "Give up, Dad. Many feet sure kick up a lot of sand. You might as well get going and rake out the clams."

Philip sits up, watching them go, watching Gary coming toward him with a thermos jug under each arm and a package of paper cups in each hand.

"Their life has been nothing like mine was, or Dad's either. I don't know how they've got hold of anything to help them make sense of things. But they have."

"Weston has," thinks Alice. "I don't know about Gary. If I were to worry, it wouldn't be about what he *says*—"

"What's born in a person is more important than what he rubs up against," she tells Philip.

Gary is near enough to hear her.

He says, "There are two schools of thought on that, Garm. One is for heredity and environment. One is for environment. Nobody is all for heredity."

"I am," says Alice, calmly. "I say anybody with a father and grandfather like yours is bound to—"

"Like your lemonade?"

"That, among other things."

"As I suspected, you two were talking about the Gilman black sheep. GREG! I've earned my clams. You earn yours, will you? Bring down two more jugs like this from the basement?"

"Where in the basement?" asks Greg, approaching.

"I know," says Melissa. "I'll show you. I don't think they've got the plates yet, Garmie. I'll bring them."

The two go toward the cottage together.

Gary crouches beside Philip, setting one jug on the sand beside him, the other between his knees, and tears open a box of paper cups.

"So let us continue my analysis by testing my reaction to the contents of this object, shall we?"

He fills up a cup, takes a mouthful from it skeptically, then drains it, pours another, and raises it toward Philip and Alice.

"I yield," he announces, "to forces I am powerless against. I am obviously how-do-you-say son of my father and grandson of my grandfather. Your lemonade, Madame, is superb. Want a cupful, Dad, for the road?"

"Drink yours while it's cold," says Philip. "Then I'll have one."

"Garm?"

"Not yet," says Alice. "Later."

He drinks his second more slowly, stopping once between swallows to stare into the cup and shake his head in amazement.

"Wouldn't have believed it," he murmurs. "No way . . . You sure it isn't intoxicating, Garm?"

"Positive. Now give your father his before his throat parches."

Greg and Melissa come back, and Greg drops two more thermos jugs beside Gary.

"Fine," says Gary dreamily. "Keep 'em coming, Mac."

But Greg, and Melissa, who is carrying stacks of paper plates, go on to where Rhonda is sitting by herself. Melissa speaks eagerly to Rhonda, and then comes back to the bake oven with the plates, leaving Greg alone with Rhonda. Standing a little uncertainly, he seems to ask Rhonda a question. She studies him silently for a minute, and begins to talk slowly with long, thoughtful pauses. Greg is listening closely, watching her face. His own is brightening. Suddenly he drops on one knee beside her, letting handful after handful of sand slide between his fingers without looking at it, still watching her; and when she is no longer speaking asks another question, or perhaps makes an observation, at which her eyes widen and she laughs.

Philip and Gary are standing now, holding empty cups, grinning at each other.

"Come back here, Phil!" yells Emily. "Your coffee's leaping right out of the spout, and Jim's itching to pull out the lobsters but I won't let him until you've checked."

"You gotta go, Mr. Indispensable," says Gary.

They go together, the same height, the same strolling gait, each carrying two thermos jugs.

Melissa runs up to Alice.

"Do you see?" she whispers conspiratorially. "See Greg talking with Aunt Rhonda?"

Alice nods.

"I asked him if he knew Aunt Rhonda is an artist. He didn't. He was surprised. He said he thought we were all business people. I told him no, just Uncle Phil. He didn't even know Daddy is a lawyer. Isn't that funny? But he said he couldn't think of any more to say to lawyers than to business people. He just likes music and dramatics and sports—and art. He says his father is a designer. He designs fabrics, Greg says; you know, to be made up into draperies and coverlets and clothes, things like that. Greg says he's painted some pictures himself, but he doesn't like them and never has shown them to anybody. I told him Aunt Rhonda is going to have a show of her paintings in Chicago this fall. Did you know that's all settled, Garmie? It is! Uncle Phil has engaged a gallery for the first week in November. She just told me today. Remember you promised we'd go out? Remember?"

"I remember," Alice says, smiling at her.

"Oh-h-h," breathes Melissa. "I'm so excited! I'm so happy, Garmie. I *like* our family when it's all together. It's got so many different kinds in it. I didn't think Greg liked us very well. He only liked Gary at first, but now I think he's liking Aunt Rhonda because she's an artist. Isn't that lucky? And he acted as if he kind of liked me after we talked. I don't see why Vicki doesn't talk to him more, do you? If he's her boy friend?"

"Maybe he isn't."

"Maybe Mommy just thinks he is. Mommy's always—always—"

"Jumping to conclusions?"

"Yes."

"I know. She jumps to a good many right ones, but I suppose she may jump to some wrong ones, too. It's not easy to be sure how two people feel about each other, unless you're one of them; and often even then you aren't really sure, at least until you've known each other quite a while."

"Did it take you a long time to find out Grandfather was your boy friend?"

"Longer than Greg and Vicki have known each other."

"Did you know sooner than that that you wanted him to be?"

"Yes. The very first time I saw him."

"Then was it awful—waiting to find out?"

"No. No, I was happy just knowing he was in the same world with me."

Dear Harley . . .

"Like I feel, knowing you're in mine? Even when you're not where I am?"

Alice is halted on the road she was traveling and slowly

turns back, hardly believing she has heard these words from Melissa, almost on the point of asking, "What did you say?" But she looks down into Melissa's eyes and does not need to ask, for the words are still written there. She remembers for the first time in many years that the feeling she had as a child about her grandfather was in that way a beginning of, a preparation for, what she felt the first time she saw Harley.

Melissa's hand is on Alice's knee. Alice strokes it with one finger, smiling at Melissa.

"A little like, maybe," she says. "I suppose we all feel some of it about people we love. Only when you feel it about a boy you want to have as your best friend all your life, it is multiplied more times than you can count. So big, so strong there's no way to describe it; but when it happens, there's no mistaking it. Just before it happened to me I had reached the place where I felt no lack of anything I couldn't get for myself. I thought that anything I would ever want I could learn or earn or somehow achieve alone. But the minute I saw him, all that changed, and I knew that whatever it was I wanted most could come only as a gift from him. It doesn't always happen as quickly as it did to me. It didn't to him. But it happened to him gradually. And all that time he was giving me his first gift just by being there . . ." Alice laughs softly. "I could hardly get to sleep at night for knowing I would surely see him again the next day . . ."

"Mom! Melissa!" calls Emily. "Didn't you *hear* me yell 'Come and get it'?"

"Oh, my goodness, Melissa," says Alice. "We have to run or it'll all be eaten up before we get some. Give me a hand. I think I'm grown to this rock."

They work their way into the tight Gilman circle around the bake oven. Hands extend paper plates, and Phil and Jim heap them with lobsters, clams, and ears of corn; Emily spills butter over them; Vicki and Weston pile salad on other plates;

Sue adds rolls; Gary is still standing guard over the thermos jugs and Greg and Rhonda have joined him, holding trays of cups for him to fill; Chris is settling Doan in the middle of a beach towel with her roll, salad, ear of corn, and cup of lemonade. Melissa and Alice give the same attention to Desirée and Margery, though each of them has demanded one clam and one lobster claw for her plate and now looks at them askance. Margery says, "You don't *eat* them, Des. They're *hard!*" Desirée tells her, doubtfully, "Garmie's taking the hard off my clam. It looks like a big, bare bug." Alice pops the clam into her own mouth. It is luscious. Desirée wails loudly, "Garmie ate my clam!" Margery says hastily, "You can have mine. Garmie'd take the hard off again." Desirée: "Don't want it. Big, bare bug." Margery, pleading: "You eat mine, Garmie?" Alice says, "Happy to oblige," and does so.

Now everyone is moving away from the oven, finding ledges on which to put heaped plates and brimming cups, the older ones sitting down there, the younger ones walking about or standing with plate or cup in hand by turns. They eat with the hunger of fishermen in from a long day at sea, saying little until that hunger begins to be satisfied, but surrounded by the water, the sand, the island fields which have produced the food, browning in the sun and wind, the long, bare legs of the young glistening with salt.

"Just see them, Harley," says Alice silently. "So many of us! And, as Melissa said, so many different kinds of us! Tell God how much we love them all. Ask Him to keep close to them—take care of them—"

Emily and Jim are sitting cross-legged on the sand near Doan on her towel. Emily passes Chris her empty plate; he stuffs his mouth and goes chewing to refill it for her. Emily drops her head on Jim's shoulder. Jim goes on eating. Doan topples over fast asleep. Emily laughs. "Look at the baby, Jim."

Jim glances at the small body suddenly stilled, nods and grins.

Philip is sprawled beside Rhonda, leaning on his left elbow, plying a plastic fork with his right hand. They are a little apart from the others. Anyone with Rhonda is always a little apart. Not far enough from Alice but that she hears Philip say, "You drinking lemonade? I thought you'd want coffee. I made some for you," and Rhonda answers, "For me? . . . Oh, Phil, I do want some." He looks pleased, puts down his fork, and starts to get up. She puts her hand on his shoulder. "No. Greg will bring it to me. Really, he'd like to, Phil. We've got to be friends. He told me he didn't want to come today, but he let Emily persuade him; now he's glad he did. Greg! Would you bring me a cup of coffee, please?"

He turns from where he is standing with Gary and Vicki and Wes, his eyes light up, his teeth flash in a quick smile, and he puts down his plate.

"Sure thing, Mrs. Gilman. What do you want in it?"

"Nothing. Bring it just as it comes from the pot."

Greg hurries down to the bake oven, stands alone beside it, pouring Rhonda's coffee, the sky and water brilliant blue behind him, and hurries back.

She takes the cup, nods her thanks, and smiles at him.

"Want anything else?"

"No, thanks. This is just what I want."

"Sing out if you want more."

"I will."

He moves back toward the group and on the way throws out his arms as if joyously taking in the whole island, lets them fall as if dropping the shell of a clam consumed. The three to whom he returns are talking animatedly. He picks up his plate and eats, listening closely, critically, to what is being said, and watching intently the faces of the speakers.

"They don't know it," thinks Alice, "but they are being judged. I suppose we all are. Maybe Vicki knows it and that's why she—but she looks so much more rested than when she came off the boat. Today is good for her. Good for us all. I hoped it would be. I thought it would be."

Rhonda says, "This is marvelous coffee, Phil. You always make good coffee, but this is really—nectar. I'm so glad you thought of it."

"It's this air," says Philip.

"The air is delicious. But so is your coffee."

A smile touches his lips as he tilts his head to look up at her, squinting in the sun.

"I wonder you've never painted a cup of coffee."

"I wish I knew how to paint this flavor."

"You'll figure it out someday . . . I'm going for more food. Want any?"

"No. Just—"

"Just what?"

She looks full at him. Rhonda rarely looks full at anyone. Alice has never before thought her beautiful.

"Just—come back."

Standing, he stoops suddenly and kisses her forehead.

"I'll be back," he says low, but Alice hears him and the tremor in his voice, "before you know I've gone."

Melissa is still with Desirée and Margery. All three seem to have had enough to eat and drink. She is between the little girls with an arm around each and apparently is telling them a story.

Sue comes out of nowhere and flops on her back along Alice's rock, her head in Alice's lap.

"Oh, Garmie, I wish you were going to Canada with us."

"I'd love to, but then you're going on to Chicago. How would I get home?"

"You could come home with us. You could come and live with us."

"Oh, but I couldn't. Not now."

"Why not?"

"I have my own home. And my work. This is my vacation. When I leave the island my vacation will be over, and there are old ladies who need me to take care of them."

"How old are those old ladies?"

"In their eighties. Some of them."

"How old are you?"

"Seventy-one."

"When you're in your eighties, will you come and live with me and let me take care of you?"

"Maybe. That would be nice, wouldn't it?"

"Yes. How many years will that be?"

"Ten. Or so."

Sue is adding.

She says, "I'll be nineteen then. How old is Vicki?"

"Seventeen."

"I'll be older than Vicki. I'll be all grown up. So I'll know just how to take care of you."

"Of course you will."

Sue sighs rapturously and closes her eyes. Alice plays with her hair.

"Oh, Garmie, I love this island."

"We all do, Susie. It's part of us."

"You're going to be here after we go, aren't you?"

"Yes. For another week."

"I think I'd like being here all by myself."

"Maybe someday you will be. When you're old enough."

"When I'm taking care of you, we'll come here every summer and stay a long, long time."

"That won't be quite all by yourself."

"No, but almost. I'd walk a lot on the beach and stop on the rocks and think. The way you do . . . If you can't walk very well, we'll have a nice comfortable chair on the porch and you can sit there and think . . . Then I'll come back and sit on the steps or lie in the hammock and we'll tell each other what we've been thinking."

"That will be fun, won't it? We'll probably surprise each other, we'll have been having such different thoughts with only a strip of beach between us . . ."

Emily and Jim are standing now, looking down at the sleeping Doan. Jim bends to gather up the corners of the beach towel and picks her up as if in a cocoon. Swinging her gently, with Emily holding his other hand, he goes toward the cottage.

"Put her upstairs on my bed if you want to," calls Alice.

"Better to make a pile of rugs and put her on it just as she is," Emily calls back. "Then she won't have far to roll off. Nothing but a fall will wake her for a couple of hours. She's out like a piece of driftwood."

Alice feels a quiver inside at the simile. Does Doan ever *feel* like a piece of driftwood? Will she, as she grows older? Did Greg, riding with Eustaces to Falmouth and coming over on the boat?

Melissa calls, "Can Margie and Desirée use our bed, Garmie? Margie's having a hard time keeping her eyes open."

"Yes, of course," Alice answers.

Rhonda looks over at the three and says to Philip, "Let's go tuck them in."

He nods, and they go together to the three, stand for a minute talking to Melissa; then Philip picks up Margery, Rhonda takes Desirée's hand, and they stroll up toward the cottage.

Now only Alice and the young people are left on this stretch of beach.

Melissa sits alone for a minute gazing at Greg, Gary, Chris, Vicki, and Wes, springs up, and runs down to join them where they lie in a rough circle on the sand.

Her passing rouses Sue, who stares after her, shading her drowsy eyes.

"I wonder what they're talking so much about."

"You want to go down and find out? . . . Maybe you'd better. You don't want to fall asleep."

"I don't want to leave you."

"Nonsense. Run along and let me think."

But when Sue reaches the circle, Vicki, turning to look at her, and at Melissa, begins to get up, as if their being there released her. Now she walks slowly back to the bake oven, gazes at the coals, drops her plate on them, and comes to Alice with her cup in her hand.

"I've had a better time than I expected to today, Garmie."

"I thought you looked more rested."

"I really like Wes. We had a good talk. He says if I send him my address after I get to school, he'll write to me . . . I told him about the mix-up Mom's got me into."

"What mix-up?"

"Oh, you know. With Greg. Him, too. I mean, he's in the same mix-up, poor kid. Just because he asked me to go in to the concert in the park with him one night. I don't know why he asked me. He doesn't know why he asked me. I guess because he wanted to go and didn't want to go alone. I don't really understand that because he's naturally a loner. At least, as far as girls are concerned. Anyway, he asked me and I went because I didn't have anything else to do. Anyway, you know Mom. She *took* to him, and she's kept him on the hook ever since. He doesn't really like us, but she won't let him stay away from us. She simply *dragged* him over here. Now she's asked him and his whole family to dinner next week. They don't want to come, he says. Why should they? His father's best time to work at the studio is from late afternoon to midnight, when nobody else is there, and his mother'll miss her choir rehearsal. It's going to upset their whole schedule, and bore us all to death, just because Mom's set on it."

"Why do you suppose she is set on it?"

"*You* tell *me!* . . . All I can figure is that she thinks it's a Big Thing, Greg's being black. Or else she's trying to prove it isn't a Big Thing. Anyway, he hates it, and so do I. It's nothing to do with us, and here we are all mixed up in it."

Alice is puzzled.

"What I don't quite see, if it has nothing to do with either of you, is why you should both be mixed up in it. If Greg didn't want to come to your house the first time your mother asked him, why didn't he just thank her and say he already had plans for that evening? Or day, whatever it was."

"Well . . . probably he wasn't sure then he wouldn't like it."

"But as soon as he found out, why didn't he make an excuse the next time she asked him?"

"Oh, I don't suppose he *did* have any plans. He's really at loose ends now he's off the beach, until he goes back to school. And Greg wouldn't say he had plans if he didn't. At least, Greg's honest."

"I'd think he could have made some plans. Fast . . . Or you. If you don't particularly enjoy each other, and he told you he didn't want to come there—or here—why didn't *you* tell your mother? I'm sure she wouldn't have gone this far if she had realized—"

Vicki shakes herself in a spasm of irritation.

"Oh, Mom's so hard to convince. She thinks we're all so great she takes it for granted everybody else—Besides, Greg bugs me."

"How do you mean?"

Another spasmodic shake.

"At first I was going to try to get him out of it. But he kept on talking and said too much and I got mad. Since then I've hardly spoken to him. You'd think Mom would notice that, wouldn't you? Last night he rang me up and talked on and on about how he didn't want to come to the island and his folks didn't want to come to dinner, until I hung up on him. I was so furious I hardly slept all night . . . Partly because when I came out of your part where I'd gone to answer the phone because Chris was fooling with the baby and she was squealing —I never for a minute thought it would be Greg, *hoped* it was somebody else—Mom looked like the cat that ate the canary and said, 'That must have been Greg. You talked a long time, didn't you?' And I'd hardly said one word!"

"Under the circumstances, I can see why your mother annoyed you. But why were you furious with Greg? He was only saying what he'd said to you before, wasn't he? Being honest, which you admire."

"Yes, but he'd already said too much about it. That made *three times* he'd said it. Once was enough. I was getting mad before he finished the *first* time."

"Why, Vicki? Try to explain to me why."

"Because—because there's not that much wrong with my family! Mom goes overboard, kills everybody with kindness, and *he* may not like it, but it's not the worst fault in the world. And what's the matter with Dad's being a lawyer? Be a funny world if every man in it was either a designer or a musician. They've both tried to be friends with Greg but he won't let them. And Chris is really a neat guy. He'd like to talk sports, but Greg doesn't pay any attention to him at all, says he's just a kid. Now, if Mom wants to lay to and put on a big feed for his family, why can't they take a night off and come and eat like the Merrifields from across the street do when she takes it into her head to ask them? And not make such a fuss!"

Alice smiles, sighs, and shakes her head gently.

"Oh, Vicki, Vicki . . . No doubt they could. No doubt they will. You don't *know* that they've made any objection at all. Maybe Greg just thinks they don't want to come because he doesn't want to and doesn't want them to. If they're coming and have said in the privacy of their own home that they'd rather do something else, it's none of your business and it would be better if you didn't know it. I expect your mother and father and Greg's father and mother can take care of themselves, and it will turn out to be a pleasant evening. *If* you and Greg don't spoil it . . . Now, think. Greg isn't your boy friend. You aren't his girl friend. You are just two young people who worked together this summer and are about to go your separate ways to school. Neither of you is threatened. What other people may think doesn't matter. What you both know is what matters."

"But now Mom's got us all mixed up!"

"Wait . . . You're getting old enough to keep your affairs in order even if your mother, with the best of intentions, or anyone else, moves in to change a course you don't want changed. That's going to keep on happening the rest of your life because we live surrounded by other people all the time. You have to steer your own ship, not blaming everybody who gets in the way, but trying to understand what their needs are, and still holding to your own channel. I don't think you should be angry with Greg. What he did was a call for help. Maybe you hadn't given him reason to suspect how much loyalty you feel toward your family, and he has no idea yet what made you mad. It seems to me you should be able to get everything unmixed very easily."

"How?"

"Talk with Greg. Honestly. The first chance you get. Tell him why you've been mad. Tell him if he and his family really don't want to come to dinner, you will get them out of it. If he says again they don't, tell him to tell them they are under no obligation to come, and then tell your mother the exact truth about the whole situation. If he says, well, maybe they do want to, then tell him it's up to you and him to make the evening a success, the Eustaces entertaining the Saunders family, and the Saunders family being entertained by the Eustaces. Only before the dinner you should tell your mother Greg doesn't wish to be invited again; then you and he need never see each other afterward unless you want to. And when you're both off to school, the Saunderses and the Eustaces can develop a friendship or not as they choose."

Wes calls across the sand, "Race you to the point, Vicki!"

Vicki starts, blinks, and begins scrambling to her feet.

"Thanks, Garmie. I'll think about it," and she darts off to take Wes's hand and run with him toward the water.

The four parents are coming back from the cottage. Alice rises a bit stiffly and meets them on the way.

"Nobody needs to listen for the children, Mom," says Emily. "If that's what's on your mind." It is. "They're all three out like lights, and now it's our turn to get into that water and cool off before we pack up."

"I should think so," says Alice. "I'll just sit on the porch and watch you. I've had my fill of sun for today."

"Only don't you dare try to wave us in if you think we're too far out," says Emily. "Remember how she used to, Phil?"

He nods at Emily, with an affectionate glance at Alice, and says, "I understand that better now than I did then."

"At last!" says Alice in mock relief, and goes on contentedly toward the haven of the shady porch and the cretonne-covered cushions of its chairs.

When, comfortably seated, she looks seaward again, she sees Emily and Jim diving in and out of waves with clasped hands. Chris and Sue are walking in shallow water, heads low, spying out crabs or shells. Vicki and Wes swim toward the sand, stand up where the water is no more than knee-deep, and wade slowly toward the ledge, talking as they go. Alice hopes Vicki is telling or will tell Wes what Alice has told her, and he will agree this is what Vicki should do; but perhaps Vicki needs to talk with Wes about something else altogether. At seventeen there are so *many* uncertainties . . . The three heads halfway to the lighthouse are Philip's, Gary's, and Greg's . . . But Rhonda hasn't gone into the water. She is moving about quietly, painstakingly gathering up plates and cups and piling them on the fire, or on the spot where the fire was. Melissa is staying with her, picks up the rake, and pulls seaweed over the litter. Alice hears their voices but not their words . . . Her eyes seek the bobbing heads. Now she can count only two. Has one of the boys outdistanced the others and reached the lighthouse already? She can see no movement among the rocks out there, and the buildings and rock-edged lawn of the island on which they are isolated at high tide are completely still, as if deserted. She counts the heads again. Two. *Which two?*

Then suddenly, with a soft, indrawn breath, she sees Greg striding out of the water onto the beach. His eyes are on Rhonda and Melissa. Melissa said, a little while ago, "I didn't think Greg liked us very well. He only liked Gary at first, but now I think he's liking Aunt Rhonda . . . And he acted as if he kind of liked me after we talked . . ."

But Vicki has seen him. Perhaps she and Weston have watched him swimming in.

Vicki calls, "Hey, Greg! Come on over!"

Poor Greg! But he hesitates only an instant. He goes.

Vicki tries to encourage him, from a distance.

"Had enough of the water? I have. But Wes hasn't."

"No way," says Weston, leaping off the ledge. "If you aren't going to stay out there and show up those two guys, Greg, I am."

He runs along the beach until he meets Greg, puts a hand on Greg's shoulder and says something to him, grinning, and plunges into the surf. Alice watches him. He is a strong, fast swimmer, and scrambles up the lighthouse rocks before Philip and Gary reach the grass on which all three throw themselves at full length.

Alice is sorry for Rhonda and Melissa not to hear whatever Greg may have come back to say to them. She is sorry for Greg not to have the chance to say it. She is sorry for Vicki to be going through the process of untangling her mix-up. But she is glad for Philip and his boys to have this little while entirely by themselves where no one else dares or cares to go; glad they have one another, that Emily and Jim, and Rhonda and Melissa—even Chris and Sue—have each other, and that the three little girls are sleeping so soundly in the midst of a family reunion of which at least the older two may have some faint, sweet memories many years from now. Only Vicki and Greg are troubled, and perhaps even their trouble is already fading as it should, for it is only an incident along the road of growing up.

This is the hour of peace. Such peace as comes rarely where so many of such a range in age have been brought together.

"It would be, if anywhere, on the island," thinks Alice . . . *Harley's island* . . .

She slides a bit lower in her chair, rests her head on its back, and closes her eyes . . .

She does not think she slept, but Jim and Emily have come out of the water, chasing each other like teen-agers, shaking the wet out of their hair.

"My goodness, aren't they wonderful?" cries Emily.

"They've got everything cleaned up! Rhonda, Melissa—you're angels!"

"We even took the pans and thermos jugs and salad bowls and everything back to the cottage," says Melissa. "We went in the back way and left them in the basement, they're so sooty and sandy; but we went right by the porch four times and Garmie never heard us. She was asleep."

"Good thing if she got herself a little shut-eye," says Emily. "Well! Time to get going. The four of us better clean up and dress. Then I'll yell for the others, and the boys can use the basement and the girls the downstairs while we get the babies ready for a boat ride."

As they troop past her, Alice says, "Don't think I haven't heard every word you've said. I'm NOT asleep."

"You were when we took the stuff in," says Melissa. "Wasn't she, Aunt Rhonda?"

"I hope so," says Rhonda. "She's been doing so much for us all this summer she's certainly earned a little rest."

"Why, Rhonda!" Alice says, surprised and touched. "I haven't done anything *but* rest. It's been a lovely summer."

"Yes," Rhonda says softly. She looks out to sea and then back at Alice with a slow smile climbing toward her eyes. "It has been, hasn't it?"

She follows the others into the cottage. Splashing has already begun at the sink, and the shower is running in the basement.

"We tried to get Mom to come home with us today and save her all the bother of closing up the cottage alone, and taking the bus out of Falmouth," shouts Emily above the noise. "But she says she'll go back the way she came down."

"We tried to get her to ride with us through Canada and fly back," says Rhonda, "but she doesn't seem to think she can take the time."

"Oh, another week is the most she'll allow herself," says

Emily, laughing. "She knows there are sick people waiting for her. She doesn't know who they are yet, but she knows they're there . . . Anyway, as long as she doesn't want to come with us, we'll have her rooms to spread out in tonight. I'm so glad you're all going to stay over with us, but I promise we'll let you get on the road early. It's just so nice we can stretch out this visit a little. It's such fun being together. I'd almost forgotten. We should do it oftener. Lucky Gary and Weston have their sleeping bags. I've figured up, and we'll have just beds enough for the rest. Okay, now I'll call in Phil and the kids."

Emily appears in the doorway, brushing her hair.

"Vicki! Vick-ki! CHRI-IS! *Sue!* . . . Oh, Phil and the boys are almost to shore, Mom. I know you're glad of that . . . EVERYBODY IN! HURRY UP NOW! DON'T WANT TO MI-ISS THE BO-OAT! . . . Vicki heard me. She and Greg are getting up. They'll round up the others."

She disappears.

Melissa is saying, "All of us that go out to Aunt Rhonda's show will be together again in November. If you and Daddy come with Garmie and me—"

"Oh, I wish we could, Rhonda," says Emily, "but honestly I don't see how we could *all*—of course, Vicki'll be in college, and even if we took Doan with us—and she *would* be a bother—that would leave Chris alone in the house—because he'll be all tied up in basketball by then—and I know he's old enough, but we never have—"

"We'll see Greg at the show," says Melissa. "He told Aunt Rhonda he'll be there as soon as the gallery doors open."

"Greg?" Emily repeats.

"Of course he'll be nearby, at the university," says Rhonda deprecatingly.

"Why, yes, of course," says Emily. "Why didn't I think of that before? Vicki may want to come, if she can get away.

In that case we should be able to work it out about Chris. We have to begin *some*time."

Alice smiles to herself, watching Vicki and Greg joining Philip and the boys, Vicki tucking a hand in her Uncle Phil's arm and laughing up at him, Greg falling in beside Gary, Weston dropping back to walk with Chris and Sue, and all moving toward the cottage. When they reach it, Philip and the boys follow the path to the basement. Vicki and Sue come up the steps.

"Hi, Garmie," says Vicki cheerily, rushing past. "What time is it? Mom! What time is it?"

"Hi, Garmie," says Sue, pausing for an instant beside Alice and looking at her as if she might be an illusion. "We found a whole boxful of nice shells. I gave them to Chris because I don't have room to take home any more . . . Aunt Emily! Aunt Emily, I gave Chris all the shells we found!"

"I'm so lucky," thinks Alice. "I'm probably the luckiest woman in the world. They all came. Every single one of them. We've had a lovely day. And now they're getting ready to go home."

The children's high-pitched voices are mingling with Melissa's and Rhonda's overhead. Emily goes running up the stairs. It is Vicki and Sue who are splashing at the sink, and Philip, Weston, Gary, Greg, and Chris keeping the shower running. Alice hears Jim opening the back of the van behind the cottage and beginning to load up. Philip joins Jim.

He says, "I don't know how we stow it all away and still have places for everybody to sit, do you?"

"It's always nip and tuck," Jim answers. "But so far—"

"Can't you get the sand pails inside the spare?" Philip asks. "Oh, there you are, Wes. Wes is driving me to pick up the camper. Then he'll return the dune buggy. I've just been renting it. Next summer I may get one of my own. We're thinking about buying the house we've been staying in. Rhonda likes it, and there's no place like this island for me in the summertime."

"That's good news," says Jim. "Did you tell Emily?"

"No. Somehow didn't get a chance."

"She'll be pleased. She's been talking to me today about our renting a cottage here next summer."

"Say, wouldn't that be great?" exclaims Philip. "Get our kids all together to grow up the same way she and I did! ... Okay, then. I'll be back in a few minutes. Coming, Wes!"

Next summer ... Next year ... The island. Harley's island ... Next year ... Next summer ...

Van and camper follow two motorcycles, Greg riding behind Gary, Vicki behind Weston. Everyone rides wherever he could get in. Alice finds herself between Melissa and Sue.

Sue says anxiously, "How will you get back to the cottage, Garmie? Both the cars are going on the boat."

"There are always taxis at the dock," Alice answers her.

"I hate to leave you, Garmie," says Melissa.

"Hoh," scoffs Alice. "Just for a week? In another week I'll be right back under the same roof with you."

"I won't," says Sue. "I won't be with you again for a long time."

"Remember she'll be at your house in November," says Melissa. "We both will."

"Will you come Christmas, too?" asks Sue. "Garmie, will you come Christmas, too?"

"I *wish* she'd stay home *one* Christmas," says Melissa.

"Christmas is too far away to plan," says Alice. "I can't think past November."

"You have her all the rest of the time," grumbles Sue. "We want her every Christmas."

"You've been here with her all summer. I was here only a few weeks."

"Well, you stayed right in the same cottage with her. Ours was way up the beach."

"Look! Look!" cries Alice. "The boat is in! We're not a minute too soon!"

Gary, Greg, and Weston are already aboard. Philip and Jim drive on without stopping, to be sure of their space. Everyone scrambles out. Alice is caught in a tangle of hugging and kissing.

"There," she says breathlessly. "I must run or I'll be carried off, and all my doors and windows left open. So glad you all came. Greg? Greg, I'm glad you came."

"So am I," says Greg, with flashing smile. "I had a real great time. See you at the Rhonda Gilman show in Chicago in November."

"I'll go back to the dock with you, Mom," says Philip.

"No, no, no. You might get left behind. I'll be there in a trice. The whistle's blowing! All ashore that's going ashore—and I am! See you in November, Philip. Next week, Emily—"

She stands on the dock, where she has stood so many times waiting for those she loved to come in, watching those she loved go out . . .

"Goodbye! Take care of yourselves!" . . . "Bye! Don't swim too far out, Mom!" . . . "Bye, Garm!" . . . "Bye, Garmie!" "Bye! Bye, honey!" "November" . . . "Next week" . . . "Bye, Mom!" . . . "Bye—"

She can still see their faces; Philip, Jim, and Chris holding the little girls high; Sue and Melissa leaning over the railing of the top deck, blowing kisses; Vicki and Weston standing tall, waving, waving . . . They blur into the crowd around them . . . The boat is gaining speed, growing smaller . . . smaller . . .

"Never watch anybody out of sight," Granny used to say ominously. "Not if you ever want to see them again."

Alice obediently, resolutely, turns her back on the tiny boat riding the great blue expanse of sea and walks slowly, in a state of suspension, through the green curtains of the island world. She has said she would ride, but she will not ride. She will walk, making her way one step at a time into a land of solitude.

14

Right foot, left foot, right foot, left . . .

There is the island post office, but she has no mail to send, and is expecting none. She has been inside once, early in the summer, but the people there were all strangers. She asked that day for Mr. Westmoreland, who used to be the postmaster— how Harley enjoyed Mo Westmoreland and his talk of going, as a boy, on his father's boat, fishing off the Grand Banks— but they said he had retired a dozen years ago and had died since. She has no reason now to stop at the post office.

She passes the Island Food Shop. She might go in, but she is not hungry, needs no food. Once she would have gone in anyway, just to say hello to Dottie, watch her swiftly counting out hot molasses doughnuts, boxing jelly rolls, tying up jars of beach-plum jelly she and Guy made last fall after the season, and catching glimpses of Guy in white ducks, white shirt, and tall white chef's cap, turning out a dozen blueberry pies at once from the kitchen ovens. But Dottie and Guy don't come over to the Food Shop any more. Their daughter Rose and her husband have taken over the business, and all the famous Food Shop recipes.

Rose was—is—the same age as Emily. They used to be in the same class at Sunday school, summers. Emily envied Rose not having to leave the island at summer's end.

"Maybe Rose would like to," Harley said once. "Maybe she thinks it would be fun to spend part of the year off-island."

"No, she doesn't," Emily answered quickly. "When I tell her how lucky she is, she says, 'I know it.' I'd know it, too. I'd never leave this island if I didn't have to."

But she had to, and did. When she was in college, she never wanted to leave college. That is Emily's way. She has always seemed happy in her father's house. Wherever she is she seems to belong. Now wherever Jim is, Emily is at home. All she really needs is Jim. But she has so much else, takes on so much else, risks so much else. . . . There's Vicki, who gets mixed up and is leaving home and family in a fortnight to go to college. College life is not what it was when Emily lived on a campus. Vicki will have little or no protection from herself or others, little or no guidance, whether or not she wants it. Will Vicki ever do what she will later sadly rue? . . . There's Chris. He seems so like Jim, but *is* he like Jim? And what would even a Jim do, becoming eighteen, twenty, twenty-two now, toward the end of the twentieth century? Will Chris be another Gary, forever searching, never finding, always half hoping to come upon something perfect, all ready-made, never stopping long enough anywhere to *make* something, *build* something . . . And precious Melissa. What will these times do, what will life do to wide-open, throbbing, volatile Melissa? . . . Does Emily worry about her children? If she does, Jim calms her fears . . . And now there is Doan, only two years old. Will Emily be able to meet all Doan's extraordinary needs? Emily will try staunchly, as she tries to meet every need she sees or thinks she sees . . . Emily will be all right, as long as she has Jim. But if she suddenly didn't have Jim? Or if she were gradually losing Jim? . . .

"You go on," Alice tells herself. "Whatever happens, you go on. Emily would go on."

There is an antique shop. A little Victorian cottage

painted the color of spruce gum, with gingerbread trim and porches around three sides. The porches almost touch the sidewalk. Alice pauses in the shade of an ancient maple tree to look at the pinkish clapboards and sharply pitched roof against the island green. Inside the small-paned windows there are bits of colored glass. On the porches there are crockery jugs and jars, a shoemaker's bench, a big spongeware cider pitcher, a barrel churn, and a rackful of butter molds.

Alice likes the cider pitcher. Granny had one like that. She wonders if Philip remembers it. Perhaps he would like to have this one for Christmas. But she doesn't know whether Rhonda would find a place for it in Oak Park. As far as she knows, Rhonda has nothing in her house that is old. Alice really knows almost nothing about Rhonda except that she married Philip and is a painter. She wishes Rhonda were not so detached—even from her own children, even from Philip. But perhaps a painter has to be detached from everyone, everything except what she is painting or thinking of painting. If she loves Philip enough, if Philip loves her enough, surely they can discover together the combination by which to open the safe at will . . . If not, Rhonda will drift away, perhaps as if in a dory without oars, perhaps to disappear into some anonymous art colony to live and work beside but not with others as detached as herself. It is too easy to think of Rhonda going somewhere —anywhere—and never coming back. Perhaps she would return to Nebraska, where Philip found her after he escaped from California when everything there had become intolerable to him and he was trying to lose himself in a part of the country where neither he nor Delores had ever been. Perhaps Rhonda still has family there, though Alice has never heard so. They have never mentioned visiting in Nebraska, or having visitors from Nebraska, to Alice . . . May Rhonda have known a grandmother? Might a Nebraska grandmother have had a big spongeware pitcher? . . . Philip would still have the children. If Rhonda ever goes away to stay, it will not occur to her to take the children. Sue, Desirée, Margery—how could Philip care for them? It was surprising that he married a second time. He will never marry again.

"He could bring them to us," thinks Alice. "I might be able to fill in for Sue. Jim and Emily wouldn't hesitate a minute to take two more little ones to grow up with Doan. But we'd never fully understand them, not even as much as we do Melissa. Those three are unique children. They're Rhonda's children . . . And what would become of Philip? Nobody ever needed his own family more than Philip. He needs the kind of family Jim has. But he doesn't have it. Because he isn't Jim . . ."

How do people bear tragedy, or what seems to them to be tragedy?

. . . Granny had a barrel churn, too. And butter molds. Alice sees no beauty in them, but there is beauty and a sudden surge of serenity, of peace, in the memory of Granny on churning day, seated in the ladder-back, basket-bottomed chair on which Grampa had shortened the legs so that when tiny Granny sat in it she could plant her short, square feet firmly on the wide pine boards of the kitchen floor. Granny with one veined, bony hand clutching one knee, the other hand pushing the handle of her barrel churn over and pulling it back; her mouth determinedly set, her eyes fixed on what no one else could see; her small body, obscured from neck to wrist to ankle by a dark calico wrapper and darker calico bibbed apron, swaying rhythmically, as if she rocked a baby in a cradle, when what she rocked was cream gathering slowly into butter . . . Granny at last standing on tiptoe to snap up the heavy metal clamps which released the cover of the barrel, peering inside through steel-rimmed glasses snatched from her apron pocket; nodding, satisfied. "Butter's come." Granny setting a shiny tin pail under the bottom of the still barrel and pulling out the bung to let buttermilk, thick, faintly yellow, pour out. "Take this pailful down to the dairy, Alice. You may want a cup of it with some gingerbread when it's cold. Better when it's cold . . ." Now only butter is left in the barrel. Granny lifts it out into a big wooden bowl. It must be heavy. She sets the bowl on the kitchen table, rolls back her sleeves—the skin on her forearms is soft, loose, puckery—and begins to work the butter, squeezing, kneading it until the last drops of whey have been forced out, adding salt. Now she takes the molds from the cupboard, the round mold with the picture of a cow on it, and the boxlike mold with the initial "P." Each mold will take, she says, exactly a pound of butter. She briskly packs it in with a wooden spatula, smooths it off, and pushes it out onto a pan covered with a white tea cloth. When the pan is filled, she covers it with another tea cloth and tells Alice to take it to the dairy. "Mind your step now, on the stairs. Better keep an elbow on the railing. Be an awful thing if you was to tip all this over onto the cellar floor . . ." Tomorrow morning Granny will be up early before Alice is awake, filling the round painted boxes with covers which Grampa will put in the shade of his wagon seat and take to customers. There are a good many in the village, she says, who won't touch any butter but hers . . .

As if she rocked a baby in a cradle, when what she rocked was cream—

Alice never knew, until she was near despair because, after Philip, it began to seem that she could not bring another pregnancy to full term, that Granny and Grampa had been married fifteen years before her mother was born.

It was spring of Philip's first year in school, and he and Alice had come to spend his Easter vacation week with Granny and Grampa. He loved to be with Grampa. It seemed to him completely natural that while he climbed a pile of boards sawed out of pasture pines last fall, and jumped off, and climbed it again, and jumped off, Grampa leaned gratefully against another board pile in the thin spring sunshine, leaned back to the board pile and forward with both hands on a cane gnarled as they, his eyes twinkling at Philip, his lips smiling at Philip around the stem of the pipe he never smoked in the house, knowing how Granny would sniff her disapproval. They would both smell of pine pitch when they came in, and probably have some on the seats of their pants.

"I'm hoping again, Granny," said Alice, almost apologetic yet longing to tell someone and unable to bring herself to tell Harley, again. "But not very much."

"That so? How many now, since Philip?"

"Three."

"How long'd you carry the other two?"

"Not long. Three months the first time. Two the second."

"How long now, with this one?"

"Oh—almost no time. I've known only a couple of weeks."

"Well, try not to think about it, long as you can. Put it right out of your mind. Don't expect anything, can't be disappointed. That's what I done. Best I could."

"You?"

"Lord, yes. First fourteen years I was married I had nine misses and stillborns."

Nine . . .

"Oh, Granny! You never told me . . ."

"Never said anything to anybody. More'n I could help. What can't be cured must be endured."

"Didn't you and Grampa talk about it?"

"No. What was the use to carry on and worry him? I'd go along and get sick and get better and go along again. 'Course

for the stillborns he had to get Aunt Sarah Hendrick over—
everybody had Aunt Sarah for birthing here in them days; she
was an awful good hand at it—and he had to bury 'em. But
we never talked about it . . . It was all made up for when we
got Emma, ten solid pounds of her. I guess your grandfather
couldn't believe his ears when she let out her first yell, Aunt
Sarah holding her up by her heels like a little pink pig. I mind
he'd gone to bed upstairs, and the minute he heard that his feet
hit the floor overhead, and down he come. He was still pulling
on his galluses and looked as if he'd just heard Gabriel's trumpet. I couldn't help laughing at him. He stood there in the
doorway, staring at me, and says, 'Lissy! Have we got a young
one?' I said, 'Yes, praise the Lord. See for yourself!' By then
Aunt Sarah had a blanket round her . . . There never was any
more. But neither Molly nor Em ever had any. So we was all
thankful for the one we got. As you ought to be for Philip. You
got him right off and you're sure of him. If you never get
another one, well, that's the Lord's will and His will be done.
So you put it right out of your mind. Much as you can."

They had Emma. They were three, like Alice, Harley, and
Philip. But Emma grew up, fell in love at seventeen with a
chopper down from Canada to work at Hendricks' sawmill, ran
off and married him, and went to live with him in his tar-paper
shanty. She was expecting to go to live with him in Canada
when his chopping was done, but one day a tree fell on him
and killed him. The funeral was to be in Granny's parlor, but
that night Alice was born and Emma died. Then Grampa
thought best to send Jack McIntire's body home to his folks.
They had not known Jack McIntire very well. Emma was
buried beside her grandparents within the fence of the Plaisted
cemetery on the pasture hill. Granny and Grampa now lie on
Emma's other side.

Small wonder they did not want Alice to fall in love with
Tim at seventeen.

But it was Harley Alice fell in love with at twenty-one, and married two years later; and her fourth pregnancy brought Emily, almost certainly because Alice told Harley the whole story of her and Granny as soon as she reached home, and Harley did not put it out of his mind but had her begin at once a series of shots to prevent miscarriage. When Alice took the children home, put Emily in Granny's lap, and told her about the shots, Granny said triumphantly, "Well, wonders will never cease! Now that comes of being married to a doctor! Only, like I told you, 'twouldn't have happened if 'twa'n't the Lord's will!"

And Emily—her coming, her being here—has always seemed a kind of miracle to Alice, to Harley, who knew well the limitations of preventive treatment, and even to Philip . . .

Alice smiles, remembering those months when she could first speak to Harley, to others, of "the children." She has not, she thinks now, ever ceased to feel a deep inner tremor at the wonder of it. Not "our child," or "our little boy," or "our son," each time, but "the children" to be called to supper, to take their baths, to be sent to bed, to get off to school, to teach, to watch and listen to and try in vain to foresee the future for . . . And now there are twelve of them . . . Twelve . . . A minute ago they were all here. Now they have all gone, riding bravely into the unforeseeable future . . .

Here, where Alice is, there is only now.

She has reached the end of the sidewalk. The black hard-top road goes straight on toward a rambling old frame hotel at the eastern point, the very tip of the island. But Alice is not going to the hotel. Nor is anyone else. If hotel guests came off the boat, they have already driven past. The road is empty, deserted, still. But Alice leaves it for a white sand path, a shortcut across the interior of the island where sheep used to graze and which has turned into miles of rolling dunes. Pink-blooming heather has overrun them, completely obscuring the sand except in the winding, narrow path underfoot. Mo Westmoreland, descended from the first settlers, called this rosy cloud which extends in all directions as far as she can see "huther." He said some of the old ones brought it with them and planted it here, to ease their homesickness for Scottish moors, and it flourished and spread. He said he heard this was the only place outside of Scotland where it did that. Mo didn't tell Alice. He told Harley. Harley told Alice. . . . She bends and breaks off a branch. It grows scarcely knee-high. The island does not miss the one branch. It is crisp, dried in the sun, its fragrance very faint, like nothing else but "huther." Mo's huther. And Harley's. And Alice's.

She has come through the green of the island, through the low-lying, rose-colored cloud, and reached the firm white road of the beach beside the turquoise blue at the edge of the world, at the end of time, beside the boundary between the familiar here and the totally unknown there. She has gone far enough, as far as she has any right or reason to go, as far as she can, as far as she wants to today. Here she takes up her station, seated on a friendly boulder with a spray of pink "huther" lying across her lap.

She does not feel alone. She never feels alone. But now, as for some years past, she is farthest from being alone when there is no one with her whom anyone else could see, if anyone were watching . . .

A conversation is going on, though there is no sound but that of the waves rolling in from the horizon.

"Some experts are saying another ice age is starting down from the north and may cover half or more of all the land area of the earth."

"Your experts have little knowledge, and can use only what they have."

"If it does come, will all the people know it? Will they see it coming, closer and closer? Like a flood? Will the air grow colder every day? As if the fires of the sun were dying?"

"If it comes, they will know it is coming. But not when it will recede. Nor what treasure it may leave behind when it goes."

"Others tell us it is a great drought which is coming. Forty years of drought, bringing famine to half the world or more. The suffering, they say, will be beyond our imagining, and the effects on human relationships unfathomable."

"Much is unfathomable to the human mind. Its wrestling with what it does not in the least understand is what causes man's worst suffering. The fortunate man is he who concentrates on doing each day whatever he can do best, content to leave to others what they can do better than he, and the rest to God."

"What can mankind do about an ice age? Or a forty-year drought?"

"Nothing. Such things are part of the rest. Neither ice nor drought nor floods nor war nor pestilence has yet destroyed the human race. Which is not to say they never will. Neither an individual nor a race is to know the manner of the inevitable end. Man is not on earth to study on what he cannot know, but to love and bring forth his seed in its season and help his neighbor and make what provision can be made by men against present and closely approaching hardship. If it is growing cold, he must seek ways to provide heat. If reservoirs are drying up, he must find new sources of water. But above all he must love, for without love his light will surely be extinguished."

"What is love?"

"Caring. Sharing. Trusting. And something beyond all that which you have no words for. You could say it is the divine spark in the human heart and mind which man cannot put out but which he douses to his eternal peril, or tends steadfastly to his true enlightenment and everlasting joy. But that is only skirting the fringe of what it is, because even such a spark is too hot for man to bring forth and hold in his hand, too bright for his eyes to look upon. It is concealed for your own good from your view and your touch and your attempts at analysis. But you know it is in you or you are no longer human. And you see its glow in every man you meet, sometimes as faint as the fragrance of heather, sometimes in a golden fountain of which he is the center, shooting golden streams skyward, scattering golden drops far and wide, lighting up distant pools which until then were dark and still . . . Most often the intensity of the light is somewhere between these two extremes. But there is some of it in everyone. *Every man, woman, and child . . .*"

Alice does not know whether she is talking with Harley or with God. It no longer matters.

She says, "Granny used to sing sometimes around the house. She had kind of a cracked little voice, and didn't sing very often. She stopped if she thought anyone was listening. But I liked to hear her. The song she sang most was about love."

Alice sings Granny's song softly at the edge of the world, at the end of time, beside the boundary between Here and There.

> "Once in the dear dead days beyond recall
> When on the world the mists began to fall,
> Out of the dreams that rose in happy throng
> Low to our hearts love sang an old sweet song—"

"That's what you mean, isn't it?" asks Alice.

"That's a way of describing the advent of the divine spark on earth, in living matter."

"Then it was here before Jesus came."

"Of course it was." Suddenly Alice remembers Kablu, the boy who came down to the plains of the Indus, who had been taught to worship the sun-god, to whom a flame was his church, his Sunday, his everyday, his prayer, his Bible, his minister; for he had no other. "It has been in all human life from the beginning. It is what makes you human. But at times it dims. Jesus came to renew it."

"Is it dimming now?"

"It has never been kept bright enough, steadily enough, to make earthly life what it might be. It often needs renewing. But man can always renew it if he will. Jesus showed the way."

". . . The people are confused. From experience with cruelty, coldness, selfishness in others many reject it violently, and often along with it all forms of discipline, seeing discipline as unwarranted, insupportable suppression of the self. In some the violent rejection leads straightway to violent rebellion against all authority, all established standards, all sense of respect for whatever has long endured; to a blind, raging drive to tear down anything not brand-new. And that is nearly everything, because when so much time and effort are being devoted to destruction, little is being built . . . Some, out of the same past experience, turn instead to total tolerance, to passivity, permissiveness, noninterference. They make no requirements, give no guidance—doubtful if they have any right, or if they would do more good than harm by speaking—and try to expect nothing of anyone lest they expect too much. These sooner or later find themselves, and perhaps their children reared in this philosophy, overpowered by the rebels, the marauders, with nowhere to turn for protection; their own children may have joined the guerrillas, if only to satisfy their own longing to be shown what to rebel against, what opposition feels like. . . . But you know all this."

"I know all this. And you are not speaking now of love but of power and how it is used. You did use the word 'overpowered,' you know. So far mankind has tended to associate power with evil; and not without reason on the basis of the human experience. The power of evil is great, can make tyrants of the strong, and transform the weak into monsters. But let the day come when the power of good is released and spreads until it shines into the darkest places, and yours will truly be a new world. Only that will renew it permanently. Good will destroy nothing. Gradually evil will destroy itself, defeated by lack of supporters, dwindled away from neglect. Good will have its own discipline. Good discipline must be imposed from without unless and until it is imposed from within. It is neither kind nor unkind; only wise, and essential. Good will expect much and have its expectations joyfully met. Love is the basis. Not passivity, permissiveness, noninterference, but a love both strong and tender as that of a good man for his chosen woman taking hold of the world and turning its face to the light. . . . Gradually, remember. It will not come overnight, but slowly. And don't wait for it. Work for it. If enough of you work hard enough for it, believe hard enough in it, you can achieve it *before* ever the ice comes down from the north, *before* ever the reservoirs dry up . . ."

Granny is singing again.

"Even today we hear love's song of yore,
Deep in our hearts it dwells forevermore,
Footsteps may falter, weary grow the way,
Still we can hear it at the close of day,
So till the end, when life's dim shadows fall,
Love will be found the sweetest song of all.
Just a song at twilight,
When the lights are low,

And the flick'ring shadows
Softly come and go—"

"Granny—why did you stop singing?"

"What? Oh, my Lord, just come to, what I was doing. I can't sing. Never could."

"I think you can. I like to hear you."

"Mercy sakes alive, pity if you're that hard up for something to listen to. Better put a record on the graphophone. Your grandfather likes to hear it a-going when he comes in from the milking."

Alice opens a canvas trunk with leather straps and buckles, takes out a brown cylinder on two fingers thrust inside and holds it close to the lamp to read the printing on the edge. "Under the Double Eagle March"; Edison Record; the Columbia Military Band. Grampa doesn't especially like band records. He likes fiddling better. She puts back the brown record and takes out a black one . . . "The Preacher and the Bear."

"Hurry up," says Granny urgently. "He's coming through the shed now."

"The Preacher and the Bear" will do while Alice looks again for fiddling for Grampa.

"The preacher went a-hunting upon a Sunday morn,
Of course 'twas against his religion but he took his gun along.
He got himself some very fine quail and a fat and juicy hare,
But then—"

"Oh, THEN," roars Grampa, "he met a GREAT BIG GRIZZLY BEAR!"

"Hush up, Joel," exclaims Granny from the dark end of the stove. "Let the feller on the record do the singing. You can't carry a tune any more'n I can, and you know it."

But Alice can hear something like a happy little giggle in her voice; and so can Grampa. He sets the milk pails in the sink, raises his bushy eyebrows, and rolls his eyes extravagantly first at Granny, then at Alice, then at Granny again.

"Don't you get your dander up, woman. Never mind my singing," he says. "What have we got for supper, besides this apple pie I see a-setting here?"

"Some salt fish and potato chopped up together," says Granny smartly, "and browned in a mite of pork gravy left over from noontime."

She stands turning it over in the spider, making sure the flavor will be all through it and no crumb burnt on. Grampa comes up beside her.

"What's in your little kittle there?"

"Beets. And 'most the last of 'em, too."

"Anything in the oven?"

"Why don't you look and see?"

"It might fall. Maybe you put a dozen eggs in it."

Granny makes a derisive sound. "A dozen eggs! Pretty likely!"

He opens the oven door a crack, and the fragrance of corn meal comes stealing out.

"Johnnycake!" says Grampa, purring like a big cat. "To tell the truth, I was afeard to look. It could have been biscuits again."

"What's the matter with my biscuits, I want to know?"

"Just one thing. Just one thing's the matter with your biscuits. They ain't johnnycake."

"Oh, go along with you and fill up the woodbox."

"I will fill up your woodbox, Lissy," he says solemnly. He goes as far as the pantry door and turns there, almost touching the casing all around, and regards both Granny and Alice solemnly, though still speaking to Granny. "I will eat your fish hash and your buttered beets and your johnnycake and—is your mustard pickle all used up?"

"I just brought up a jar from the cellar. It's on the table."

"—and your mustard pickle and your apple pie and Formosa Oolong tea. And then—THEN—"

"I s'pose you'll meet a great big grizzly bear," says Granny.

"I won't care if I do. But what I was going to say is—then I'm a-going to sing like no man ever sung before. Better than that En—Enrico Caruso. Better even than Harry Lauder. Wait and see if I don't."

The door closes behind him on his way to the shed.

Alice realizes with a start that the record is still running. The preacher is just finishing his fervent prayer in the top of a very tall tree.

"Oh, Lord, if you can't help *me*, for goodness' sake don't you help that bear!"

She hastily lifts the needle, pushes the lever to stop the cylinder, takes off the black record, puts on a brown record—she has found the right one now—winds up the machine, pushes the lever, sets the needle; and when Grampa comes back through the pantry, a fiddler is playing jigs and reels.

"Now, that's the ticket!" he says. He stops in the middle of the kitchen floor, his arms full of all the wood they can carry, a pile which rises to his stubbly chin, beams around, and begins to dance a quickstep.

"Now," sighs Granny in pretended despair, "I s'pose he thinks it's Fourth of July and he's at a picnic on the mountain, wearing out the soles of his boots on the Flat Rocks."

"That's right where I met my girl," Grampa, feet flying, tells Alice. "I looked around and see her a-setting there in a green sunbonnet, and that minute I lost all track of the fiddling and been dancing to her tune ever since."

"So dance right over to the woodbox and get rid of that wood," says Granny. "Then wash your hands and eat your supper. It's ready."

Grampa drops the wood into the big pine box—CRASH. He dips water from the pail by the sink from which Granny has just snatched out the milk pails and pours it into the washbasin—SPLASH. Alice watches him blot face and hands on the roller towel hanging on the cupboard door, take a comb from the comb case and make familiar movements before the tiny looking glass to cover his bald spot.

"Hurry up," says Granny. "It's all getting cold."

"You ever noticed," Grampa asks Alice, "how, soon as it wouldn't blister the roof of your mouth, she says it's getting cold?"

Alice is turning off the graphophone. They are all in their places at the table. The lamp chimney shines because Granny washed and polished it this morning. It lets light spill over the crisp brown hash in the thick yellow bowl, the squares of ruddy-brown johnnycake, the circle of Granny's butter with a cow on top, the scarlet beets, the mustard-colored pickles; to the red checks of the tablecloth, the heaped plates, the tumblers filled with water from the well, the bone-handled knives and forks and thin coin-silver spoons . . . over the moving hands . . . the comforting, comfortable faces.

So Alice learned early what love is. Not passivity, permissiveness, noninterference, but love strong and tender . . . wise and merry . . . always there . . . *Footsteps may falter, weary grow the way, Still we can hear it at the close of day* . . . expressed differently by different people and at different times . . . but constant, come what might . . . expecting much and having its expectations joyfully met . . . And always there . . .

That was good at work. Perhaps it was not perfection, but

Alice at five, at eight, at ten, saw no flaw in it when the wood
fire in the kitchen stove crackled, the lamp was lit, Granny
sang, Grampa danced, and they had fish hash, johnnycake, and
apple pie for supper.

If only everybody—

But *gradually, remember.*

Alice, for one, has already seen what love can do, and not
only in Granny's kitchen.

15

The days and nights drift by, and she hardly knows when or
where she sleeps. As often as not she is far from the island on
which she chose to spend this precious week, caught and lingering in other places, other parts of her life, as in a silken web.

Walking by the sea, watching the waves, listening to their
thunder, drawing in deep breaths of the salt air, she thinks:

"How we take our senses for granted! How inexcusably
ungrateful of us! What is more miraculous than that I can see
this tumbling water, reflecting the color of the sky, the ledges
it rushes forever upon, breaking into white froth, and the sun
strewing it with diamonds . . . the fine white sand . . . the
roofline of the cottage, and the steps running up to the door."

But how many other things she has seen. So many every
day she has lived. For so many days . . . They come swarming
now, one after another in rapid succession, filling her mind's
viewfinder for an instant and then yielding to another.

The crab-apple tree in full flower outside their bedroom
window the first time she and Harley came to the farm after
they were married. The magnolias in the walled-in garden they
looked down upon from their third-floor, walk-up apartment on

Marlborough Street. The white enamel sink in that apartment, with brown stains on it which she finally gave up trying to get off. Harley in his "whites" bending over her in the delivery room as Philip is being born; she can see only his eyes, how they shine; and he says quickly, "It's a boy, Alice! A fine boy! . . ."

More and more what flashes before her is unidentifiable with anything she specifically recalls, yet she instantly recognizes each one as seen somewhere before.

The apron of shade flung on a field by a tree reaching exuberantly toward the sun. A carpeted stairway with black walnut newel post and banister. *When lilacs last in the door-yard bloomed . . .* only old dooryard lilacs never die but, if left untouched, continue to spread and bloom for every Memorial Day, generation after generation. A sunset reflected on a weathered Christian door. The profile of a girl in white looking up at her new husband, and his as he looks down at her. That of a mother bending over her sleeping child, and of the father standing at her shoulder, holding a light. The dazzling green of May after the rain, fogs, and mist of April. The long, thin, quiet fingers of a woman asleep at last on a hospital bed after hours of pain and fear. A heavy rain dimpling the gray water of a lake. Waxy pond lilies floating. A conductor running crabwise along the side of an open trolley, swinging by one hand as he makes change with the other from a holder attached to his belt. The catcher in a Little League game putting on his mask. A letter found in the mailbox, addressed in a familiar hand, with a familiar return address, and a familiar postmark. A country auctioneer standing on a library table in a farmyard, holding up a Lowestoft helmet pitcher without a handle. ("What am I bid for this old pitcher? I know it's minus a handle, but you can put a handle on or leave it without a handle. Two dollars I'm bid. Who'll make it three? I've got

three. Who'll say four?") A soft-colored Oriental rug with worn
spots here and there. A man and woman waving from the
platform of the last car of the train. Little girls in alternating
pastel colors dancing around a maypole. A Christmas-tree ornament shaped like a trumpet . . .

Her inner eyes grow tired. She closes them with an act of
will, as one leaves a museum when the warning bell rings, or
as one puts aside an absorbing book when the print begins to
blur and turns out the light. But the museum will reopen, the
book will be on the bedside stand tomorrow night when the
next day's work has been done. Will Alice ever see again the
same pictures she saw tonight, and those she might have seen?
Oh, surely, surely—

In the darkness, to comfort herself, she thinks of sound.
. . . If she cannot see, she can hear . . . The voice of the owner
of a little corner candy store trying to explain to a grimy
five-year-old why there is no change coming back from the
nickel he gave her for the ten-cent cone she has just handed
him: "What you had was just right, Butchie," she lies, then
looks up at the next customer in line and says, "God love him."
A whippoorwill singing in the dark of night. The rush of an
incoming subway train. The ring of the telephone, the turning
into the driveway of a car for which you have been eagerly
waiting. The Fifth Symphony. The incredible range of Galli-
Curci, rising, rising, and still rising. Rain pelting against a
window, bouncing off a shingled roof, sluicing down a metal
gutter pipe. A camp bugle blowing Taps. The placid, sleepy
lowing of young stock spending the summer in the hills. A dog
suddenly barking, then telling himself in muffled, exasperated
tones that he has wasted his breath again, barking at nothing.
"Well, 's time you're back! Where you been so long?"?"; it's
Granny. "What s'pose I found coming out of the woods after
we fit fire last night? This little baby rabbit. Look!"; it's

Grampa. The birdlike sounds of the newborn being wheeled along a hospital corridor for delivery to their mothers at daybreak. College boys singing on the roof of a fraternity house. The passing of a mounted policeman. Big Ben in the Sunday silence of London. A querulous old voice complaining that there is no milk on the tray for her tea. A breathless child's voice in the doggerel to which she times the swinging of her skip rope . . .

Taste . . . If one can neither see nor hear, perhaps he can still taste . . . Warm gingerbread and a glass of cold buttermilk. A red radish pulled, brushed off on a sleeve, and chewed with nine-year-old teeth in the late afternoon; it had a name: *"French breakfast."* Checkerberries found in the moss under the pasture fence, all to be gathered for Granny save these last five. Wild strawberries to fill a saucer for Grampa, and after the saucer is heaped . . . The first bite of turkey at Thanksgiving, of goose or roast pork or beef at Christmas, of salmon and new peas on the Fourth of July. Curried shrimp on rice with a sharp green salad. A paper cup of sweet cider just pressed out at the mill. A spicy pizza. Tacos. Tea and scones in England. A dish of oatmeal on a chill fall morning in the Lake Country of Scotland. An omelet in France. Black-cherry preserve in Switzerland. Chicory-flavored coffee in the Farmers' Market in New Orleans at midnight, and a plate of Creole gumbo soup for lunch next day in the courtyard of a house with lacy iron railings on its balconies. Gooseberry pie in East St. Louis. Grits and black-eyed peas in Sebring, Florida. Chilled melon on a hot evening in a little restaurant looking out on the Golden Gate Bridge. An apple from a bin at a roadside stand when you have driven a long way and still have far to go. A slice of sprouted wheat bread toasted, with a skim of guava jelly, at bedtime. A seedless white grape, or a blue Concord grape. The meat of a hickory nut you have broken open with a hammer and picked out with a darning needle. The filling for a pumpkin pie, drunk from a cup . . .

Or touch . . . Rain on the face, as warm as tears; or snow in icy pellets stinging already half-frozen cheeks. The body held suspended, swinging slowly in a hammock. The prick of a thorn. The head of the newborn pressed to the breast or cupped in the hand. The satin of the bark of the birch tree, the rough strength of the hickory, the stickiness of the pine. The yarn looped around your fingers as you knit mittens in a Norwegian design. Paddle pulling to shoot the canoe ahead, pushing to slow it down and turn it in toward shore. A ball. A box. A pencil. A broom. A chopping knife. A paring knife. A mixing spoon. A swab. A bandage. A hypodermic needle. The only half-conscious drawing up of a wool blanket on a cold night and moving toward the warmth of him who lies beside you and who may rouse a little and take you in his arms. The trusting child's hand in yours as you cross a busy street. A steering wheel. A velvet ribbon. A cow's sleek neck. A horse's firm rump. A cocker's curly ears. A cat's long tail. A baby chick's downy feathers. The exciting shock of the day's first plunge into Atlantic waters. The shoulders and shoulder blades of the bed patient getting a back rub, narrowing to the waist, broadening and softening to the hips. Putting on clothes; taking them off. Bare feet on carpet, linoleum, boardwalk, macadam, stones, sand, lawn grass, field stubble, wherever there is no sign up, "NO BARE FEET." The handclasp or quick hug of a welcoming friend. Opening a door with knob or latch. Trembling poplar leaves you push through to stay on an overgrown old path. Scottish tweed. Irish linen. Lace. Digging with your hands into the good earth. A cold drink in a hot, parched mouth; a hot one when you shiver . . .

Or smell . . . Spreading a thin glaze of maple icing over a devil's food cake. Bread just out of the oven. Mayflowers no one can see. Scent of watermelon in the air where juicy green lawn grass has just been cut. Brooks flowing through deep woods with ferns clustered along their banks. Hot-sun-on-berry smells. Rich, dark swamp smells. Seaweed and clam shells. Old-fashioned roses—cinnamon, Hundredleaf, Seven Sister, and tiny, white Scotch roses. Long-stemmed carnations from a florist's box. The "Y" swimming pool. The subway station, telling you why in other countries this is called the Underground. The cabbage patch after the first hard frost. Haymows before grass was baled when dry. Hamburgers cooking on an outdoor grill. Trout browning in a guide's frying pan on the shore of a wilderness lake. High mountain air so pure, so crystal clean your unaccustomed lungs ache from its entry. Sweet fern. Bluegrass at mowing time. And perhaps most precious of all, the unique, individual aroma of each of those you have loved most who could not or did not conceal or eradicate it with deodorants and artificial perfumes. In groups, these combine to blend neighbors with one another and make them all one with the place where they are. To Christmas concerts in a one-room district school, men came in boots they had worn for the milking, women had dressed just before cooking a hurried but hearty supper, best coats and shawls were lately out of mothballs, pine knots were burning in the stove, the Christmas tree was only twenty-four hours from the forest, and all doors and windows had been tight closed since midafternoon . . .

"All this I have had I shall always have," thinks Alice, "as long as I still think and feel . . . And I cannot conceive of a heaven where there is not play of thought and feeling."

What wealth to have been granted, to have been allowed to store up!

But where is it all stored? What gave it such color, flavor, meaning? And what is the magic preservative which has kept and is keeping it untouched by time, as fresh and crisp as home-grown lettuce and tomatoes just picked in the cool of the early morning?

Sandpipers skitter along the beach, at the edge of the water. But if they don't know where they run, where they are running to, what they are running for, and do the same tomorrow, not even remembering they did it yesterday, then they gather no wealth to store, have no receptacle in which to store it, live only in and for the present moment.

In Grampa's pasture the partridges must have heard approaching footsteps, because a whole family of them would suddenly rise up out of underbrush in which they had been completely hidden and rush away from danger with a frantic flutter of wings. And the rabbits must have heard the child Alice, too. If they were near their holes, they vanished into the earth; if one of them was too far from home, he became instantly immobilized, as in a trance, eyes glassy with the effort to appear not to be there at all. Years came and went and no partridge or rabbit ever learned that Alice was only looking for mayflowers or berries or pussy willows, so they never taught their young that Alice was no threat, and all kept on being afraid of her. Did they hear sounds which did not frighten them—the wind in the pines, the gurgle of the brook, the feeding of the cows in the open places where the sun shone and grass grew? If so, did they know they did? Or were they aware only of the sound of danger?

Even the cat. She lies on the kitchen rug, curled into a beautiful furry ball, and sleeps awhile, then slowly rises, stretches luxuriously, may wander over to rub against a chair leg, an ankle, is stroked along her back, gets scratched behind her ears, and returns to the rug, lies on her stomach with feet tucked under or on her side, in complete abandon, with all four legs thrust out, tail spreading like a plume, and goes back to sleep. Does she know she is with people who love her, will keep her warm and feed her? Or only that she is not hungry and is not cold? If tomorrow she were to find herself a hundred miles away, what would she remember except the way back to where she was not hungry and was not wet or cold?

Or the dog. He follows at his master's heels, sits by his mistress's chair and puts his chin on her knee, stays by the grave of the one who dies, may even die himself as if of grief. But is he loving? Or yearning for no man knows what? He is called man's best friend. But is he? Does he want to be? Is man the only substitute he has for whatever it is that he really wants? Mankind typically has a strong attachment to animals, both wild and domesticated, but have they any real attachment to him? Is it possible to form attachments if you cannot think, are keenly aware only of physical discomfort or threat of danger, do not remember, having no storage space or anything to store? Perhaps there is much more or less unconscious pity in the feeling we have for our non-human brothers. We tell ourselves they suffer less for not knowing, not trying to know, not peering into the future, not suspecting there is a future. Oh, but there is, for most of us, more than enough joy to make up for any suffering which comes with knowing, feeling, and learning from what we know and feel.

She remembers vaguely a poem read years ago. Not the words of it. Not even a complete line or the title of it, nor the name of the poet; but the point it was making: that one in despair has no patience to listen to or read what is intended to give him hope, because for one in despair no hope exists. Hope to him is a cruel illusion or a stupid hoax. What he needs, the poet says, what he craves is proof that others are as bewildered, hurt, angry, lost, hopeless as he; that it is absurd to struggle for answers, for there are no answers; that this is a not uncommon dilemma and thus he is not alone.

She remembers thinking as she read the poem as she thinks now:

"I am sure there are people who do need that, whose only possible reassurance it is. But there are a great many more fortunate whose struggles do produce answers, who in times of trial feel their hope flagging and are frightened, needing above all to have it reinforced because they have never been without it, do not see how they could live without it or why they would want to. Hope is as natural to most of us as breathing, though it is constantly under attack, and in these times the attacks seem to be growing in intensity. There was another poet, an earlier poet, who said, 'Hope springs eternal in the human breast'?"

She thinks now, "If that is true, as I am sure it is, the divine spark must contain the elements of hope as well as of love. Or is each a part of the other, inseparable from the other? Without love we could not hope. Without hope how could we love? Is there any difference between hope and faith? Or between love and faith? If we want one name for the divine spark, shouldn't it be faith? . . . But *He* called it love, I think. Perhaps because the ability to love is the prime essential, basic to the others. A baby loves and knows that he loves long before he knows what hope or faith is . . ."

But more is a unique part of being human. A baby does not love until he knows what he feels, or possess hope or faith until he consciously feels and recognizes them. Until he feels with more than his body, as long as the only sensations he is aware of are discomfort and spontaneous, nameless fear, he is not yet differentiated from the pasture rabbits and the partridges.

Kablu's father told him a very important truth when he said, "Man is he who thinks." But man would not be man if, equipped with his magic senses, he could do no more than think, could feel only with his sense of touch. What would be the thoughts of such a creature with no sources of emotion? Where is this source? For that matter, where is the source of thought? In all the centuries of study and experimentation, neither has been found, though there has never been any doubt of their existence. Then are they, too, in the divine spark? If so, why do they ever make mistakes? Well, our hopes are not always borne out, nor is human love without flaw. Because, of course, even with our divine spark, we are human . . .

Where, though, does hate come from? Such reactions as despair could, surely must, come from the fading, the almost dying of that vital spark. But hate, even if restricted to just one person, one landscape, one situation, even if only temporary, is active, aggressive, burning hot, as alive as a tooth in which the bared nerve is jumping. If it spreads and deepens, and becomes constant, it is an inferno, consuming whatever it can reach . . . Someone has said that hate is akin to love. Alice thinks so. Closer than that, she thinks. What can hate be but love itself—love trapped, love blocked, love furiously forcing its way through channels never meant for it, becoming diseased, and reaching the surface, if at all, with an entirely different consistency, an altogether different color from that pure transparent liquid gold it was in the beginning?

No, no, hate is not a sin, though sinning along the way adds to it. Hate is the dread sickness, the one which makes all other ills flesh is heir to seem minor; tuberculosis, malignancy, leprosy, heart disease, muscular dystrophy, all health by comparison with hating. Where it is not cured, others cannot help fearing the victim, for he is dangerous. All possible precautions must be taken to prevent an epidemic, for hate is contagious. But sympathy for those so ill can never be wanting, or the knowledge that there, but for the grace of God—

"Oh, it is good," thinks Alice. "Good to have, at last, time and quiet in which to sort out a tangle of long accumulating half thoughts, tie them together, and wind the strand into a ball you may have use for later. As on a winter night Granny used to wind the lengths, short and longer, of string she had saved from store-bought parcels and packages sent by mail-order companies."

What was in Granny's mind then as she sat silently tying and winding her twine, while Grampa read his paper, Alice studied her spelling, the kitchen clock ticked, the wind hurled the snow against the dark windowpanes? Nobody ever knew. And no more does anyone know what Alice is thinking now, as she sits beside waves rolling in upon the island and rolling out again, over and over, along the boundary between Here and There.

Once she becomes vaguely aware that a figure moving on the beach is growing larger. When it is large enough to have a shape, a sharp silhouette against the white sand and the blue sky, she thinks perhaps she has seen it before, possibly more than once. But she does not recall when, whether yesterday or a week ago or early in the summer; or even where, except that surely she would not recognize it as it is now after seeing it on a city street or getting off a bus or going down the stairway of a subway station. It is of no importance. It is no one she knows.

Her gaze returns to the surf, and she sees Philip, a tall, thin, grave little boy in rolled-up dungarees, filling a pail and carrying it as fast as he can, as carefully as he can, to the sand's edge where Emily, a short, chunky, merry little girl, is on her knees beside a hole she has dug, peering into it and squealing, "Get nuvva vung, Philly! Nuvva vung, quick! It's almost gone out! Quick!"

Alice says to Harley beside her, "Poor Philip! She wants another one before he can bring this one to her!"

"If your train of thought should be interrupted, do you think you could get it back on the track?"

Alice turns, startled. This is the voice of a stranger. She has not heard a strange voice in a long time. The figure has approached to within perhaps six feet of the jutting ledge on which she sits, and paused. It is a man in swimming trunks. A rather big man, very brown all over, with a crest of crisp white hair.

She stares at him, disbelieving.

He smiles a little and says, "Forgive me if I—"

She is annoyed with herself. Is this what time and quiet have done? Has she forgotten how to walk in any place where she has not walked before? Forgotten how to respond to an unexpected question? Is she disoriented? Is she—old?

She says to herself, "Come *out* of it, Alice! For goodness sake—"

She says to him, honestly, "If I was *that* lost in thought, it's time I was roused. Nothing to forgive. Accept my gratitude. How is the water?"

The silliest of all questions, asked over and over every day on every beach of anyone who is wet. That question alone is proof enough that she has not fully recovered herself.

But he says, "Fine. It's always fine. I swim twice every day here. Before breakfast and before dinner."

"My husband and I used to. Now I usually get in only once, around noon."

"I've seen you then. I walk the length of the beach every day before lunch."

"You sound like a person—with a firm program."

"I hadn't thought of it that way. I swim and walk because I'm restless."

"Restless? On the island? I didn't know that was possible . . . Have you spent the summer here?"

"Oh, no. Just this week. Visiting my daughter and her family. They've been here all summer. They bought Sunny Villa two years ago. That's the cottage on the other side of the next point . . . Have you been here all summer?"

"Yes. We built Sunny Villa. After we sold a farm in

Maine that—was left to me. Later we sold Sunny Villa to buy a house in Brookline. By then the children were growing up. The island is ideal for children. As for anyone, of course, who likes it. This summer my son and his family rented Whiteoaks. That's a mile up the beach. Toward Weyanoke Point. They're thinking of buying it. Now my daughter is beginning to talk of renting a cottage for her family next summer. They've all been here, but went home a week ago. I stayed on for a few quiet days. I'm going tomorrow."

Until she has said this, she has not known that it is tomorrow she goes back to Brookline.

Her easy flow of words has encouraged him. He crosses the space between them and stands leaning against the ledge beside her.

"You like quiet days, don't you?"

"Oh, very much . . . You don't?"

"I used to . . . Frankly, it was my growing impression that you did which eventually led me to venture to speak to you. You seem extraordinary—to me. I've seen you several times every day since I came here. You are always alone, walking or sitting or swimming, always quietly. Several times others have been quite near you. A few times I have been. But you seemed not to be aware of any of us. Completely absorbed in your thoughts—but not unhappy. Alone—but somehow not alone . . . You have thoroughly baffled me."

Alice laughs, and with the sound her mind is cleared of every lingering wisp of reverie. It is his turn to look startled.

"Why do you laugh?"

"I'm not sure. Maybe because a woman enjoys being baffling, and at my age it is a rare experience indeed to be told you are. You don't expect anyone will notice what you are doing as long as it doesn't bother them, no matter how peculiar it is, how apparently antisocial—"

"But it does bother me. Because I don't see how anyone

can be—as you seem to be. I don't understand it."

"And you *want* to understand it?"

"Of course I do."

She laughs again.

"You mean, as some of my grandchildren would say, it bugs you?"

"Is this what they mean by that?"

"Sometimes. It often seems to me young people nowadays have very limited vocabularies. One word or phrase that they can manage to bring out comes out over and over again, meaning at least a dozen different things. Very confusing to those of us to whom each word has its own single meaning. Well, never mind them now. You really want to know what I've been doing this week? *Just* this week? For if you had been here all summer, with your two swims a day and your noon walks, you would have noticed—if you noticed at all—a Grandmother Alice, a Mother Alice. They're different. This week I've been mostly—just Alice."

"Just Alice. Just this week," he says, sitting down. "What have you been doing, walking so quietly, sitting so quietly, swimming so quietly, alone?"

"Well, I'll tell you. I've been thinking, which is one of my greatest joys. And remembering, which is my greatest relaxation. I always manage to do a great deal of both, if only in bits and pieces. But this week, free to concentrate, I have been, you might say, organizing my thoughts and memories. Like clearing out and tidying a cluttered desk . . . And I have not been alone. I am never alone. My husband is always with me."

He turns his face toward her, silently inquiring.

"Yes," she says. "He died ten years ago. But I have been married to him for nearly fifty years. We are inseparable."

He stares at her for a minute, then turns away, staring at the sea.

"Do you suppose that happens to many couples?" he asks. There is strain in his voice.

"I don't know. I should think it would, when people have been part of each other that long."

"You—has it been like that the whole ten years? Since—the very beginning?"

"You mean since the minute Harley died? No. I think my first reaction was black shock. I had known he was going, but was not prepared in the least for how I would feel when he went. I doubt if anyone ever is. For a while I thought I was alone. But increasingly I realized I had been mistaken. He was still with me."

"How could you think that? . . . When you couldn't see him . . . you couldn't speak to him or—touch him—or do any of all—"

Alice thinks about this, tries to recall some details of that time before Harley came back. So long ago now . . .

She says slowly, "Perhaps at first by choice, though this was entirely unconscious, for I had no idea I had a choice. I know I longed for him, day and night, for weeks; and it seems now that suddenly he was there. But probably it wasn't sudden. Probably, being me, I was doing a good deal of thinking about what I was longing for, a good deal of remembering what I had had that I was so lost without. This longing, thinking, and remembering must have generated at least a mustard seed of faith that such a bond as we had forged could not be broken. Either that, or a special miracle was wrought, and I'm not much of a believer in on-the-spot, out-of-the-blue special miracles. Anyway, one night Harley was with me again, and it didn't feel like a miracle. It just felt natural. And right. It felt like—like a broken bone mending; like a high fever dropping; as if from a dream of struggling through dark woods, trying hopelessly to find my way out, I had come upon a road, and it was a familiar road with my own house just ahead, all its windows lighted, and Harley standing in the doorway, looking out into the dusk and wondering what had made me so late getting home."

He is still staring at the sea. She doubts whether he has listened to what she was saying until he says hoarsely: "Oh, God! . . . I wish to *God* it was like that for Janice and me!"

"Is that a prayer?" Alice wonders. "If so, maybe that is how he is to begin."

There is silence again for a while. The waves rush in, crash, and recede . . .

Then, "When did Janice go?" she asks.

"Two years ago." As if not sure he has spoken aloud or expressed himself precisely, he clears his throat, turns toward her, and says quite loudly, "Janice died two years ago. Suddenly. With no warning at all."

Alice nods, almost matter-of-factly.

"How long had you been together?"

"Seventeen years. Not quite seventeen years . . . Wonderful years. Perfect years. I wouldn't have had a minute of it different in any way from what it was."

He turns back to the sea; really looking at it now, she thinks.

"In that you are fortunate, aren't you?" she says softly. "Too many live with vain regrets. Usually silly ones. There was something I might have given him, or her, and didn't; things I should have said, or done, but failed to. Probably we all dwell on that at first. But when they get through to us they tell us, 'Nonsense. I may have thought I wanted it then, but only for an instant. Or my wanting it may have been all your own idea. Anyway, I understand completely now why you didn't give it, or say it, or do it. It no longer matters to me, to anyone except you. I have with me only warm and lovely memories . . .' "

"But I do have regrets," he says savagely. "Not for anything I didn't do for her while I had her. I honestly don't remember ever having failed her when I had her. She certainly never failed me. My regret is that I had her only not quite seventeen years, and that is nobody's fault but mine."

"Your fault?"

After a minute he lowers his gaze to the sand at his feet and speaks rapidly:

"Janice and I were classmates in college. We went together all our senior year. I loved her and she loved me. But when I asked her to marry me, she said she couldn't, because she was Catholic and I wasn't. She said it wasn't so much her own feeling but her family's, and she couldn't disappoint her family that way."

Tim . . .

"I should never have accepted it. But I did."

"What else could you have done?"

"I could have persisted! If that didn't work, I could have converted!"

"Why do you think you didn't?"

He sets his jaw, castigating himself.

"Oh, I was arrogant. I didn't think it should matter that much to her, *either* her religion or her family. I thought if she loved me she would marry me anyway; or if she did love me and preferred to be a martyr, let her be a martyr . . . There was more to it than that, but I know now that was a good part of it, though in later years I worked hard at convincing myself I let her walk away from me our Commencement night so she wouldn't have to keep on struggling against me, so she could be carefree and happy again the way she had been when I first knew her, not suffering as she was, more and more, the last few months. I thought I was convinced of what I wanted to think, but it wasn't true—at least, only partly true. I know now how it *was* . . . and it tears me apart . . . All those years lost! . . . I went to New York, got on a paper, took courses at Columbia—and one night read in an alumni magazine of her marriage to a Ronald Toussaint, another classmate of ours. He was Catholic, I knew, for he'd been president of the Newman Club on campus. Within a week I'd thrown up everything and booked passage on a tramp steamer out of San Francisco. For months I wandered, hardly knowing where I was. Then I met Brooke, who was studying art in Paris. Brooke was a great girl, stunning; I don't know what she ever saw in me, but she helped me pull myself together. When I left to come home, she said she would be back in the States in a couple of months, and gave me a number to call, after that, if I felt like it. I called her, we were married the next spring, and she died a year afterward, when Margo was born. Brooke was one of the finest people I ever met. I respected her tremendously, was deeply grateful to her, relied on her—too much. But I never loved her as I loved Janice. I've never felt responsible for—anything that happened to her."

"Both my parents died the day I was born," says Alice. "My mother's parents brought me up."

"Brooke's parents brought up Margo. Oh, I went to their place weekends. When she was old enough, had her at my apartment for weekends. Turned up at her school for parents' nights when I could, and all that. But her grandparents were more her parents than I was, and brought her up very much as they had brought up Brooke. Margo is almost Brooke over again . . . Most of the time she was growing up I was buried in the paper, fighting to forget that I was alone. Without Janice, that is . . . And by then I was beginning to see that my condition—and whatever hers might be—was caused by my own arrogance."

"Most young men are arrogant. Especially in love."

"Not many, I hope, pay the price I did."

"What price?"

He looks at her quickly, with something like sharp irritation if not anger.

"I thought I had told you. When we were graduated, I was twenty-two and Janice twenty-one. At the time we were married, I was fifty-six and she fifty-five. That's *thirty-four years lost*. And then we had not quite seventeen years together."

"But you had almost seventeen. Wonderful years, you say. Perfect years. If I dared, I'd ask how many men you suppose begin, at the age of fifty-six, almost seventeen perfect years. If I dared, I'd say it sounds to me a little like calling a cup partly empty when it is almost full . . . How did you find Janice again?"

"The '22 class letter (which I always read, as I did the alumni news notes in the magazine, for news of her which never came) reported Ronald's death. It said he was survived by his widow, Janice Cawley, '22. I wrote to her. It took me ten days to do it, but I tried to make it appear spontaneous, while working in, to sound like evidence of my understanding of bereavement, that my wife had died in 1925. After a while she replied, thanking me for my sympathy, and asking if I had children, saying she did not. Then we corresponded, not often at first. Eventually I asked if I might come to see her when I would be in Minneapolis for a speaking engagement a few weeks later. She was then living in St. Paul. She said she hoped I would."

"What a joy that must have been for you both! What an opening up!"

"But it was another year and a half before we were married. Of course, then a whole new life began. But it didn't last quite seventeen years . . ."

"A year can be as a day. Or a day can be as a year. It is

as we—or events—make it. Or as we see it."

With a jerky motion he bends forward and turns to look up into Alice's face. His own is contorted with pain.

He says, "I *want* to see my marriage as you see yours. That's what I *want.* But I don't know how. Tell me how."

"I doubt if anyone can tell another person that. The circumstances are always different. More important, the people involved are individuals, and this makes every relationship and shared experience unique."

"Try. Please."

"I think I've already told you as much as I can of what might interest you in how I see my marriage. I couldn't judge how you should see yours . . . No, the best I could possibly do would be to say how it looks to me on the basis of what you have told me. And that might do more harm than good. Should we risk it?"

"Believe me, it does good just knowing you are going to try . . . Go on . . . How does it look to you?"

"You will hear it simply as one outsider's view?"

"From a new angle. Yes, yes. Tell me."

Alice laughs a bit nervously.

"You make me feel like a soothsayer . . . Well, I see your marriage as all you have said it was, and so as the finest, most rewarding, most lasting achievement any man and woman can have in a lifetime. Such a marriage cannot end. As soon as it has begun, it begins to change and change steadily, as it should and must to meet changing needs; but it never ends. Harley and I know it doesn't. Janice knows it doesn't. Only you, of the four of us, have the slightest doubt. By trying to think what we think, you might come to believing what we believe and thereby learn what we know . . . The reason you haven't yet, I would guess, is at least partly that, during those thirty-four years, your thinking and feeling that you were alone because

Janice was not within your reach made a rut; and even after seventeen wonderful years with her the old rut was still waiting, though so long unused, for your thinking and feeling to slip back into. That rut has to be filled in, made smooth, grassed over, and forgotten . . . Another thing. Have you ever thought that it was not *intended* you and Janice should marry before you did?"

He frowns. "Intended?"

"Yes. It happens that I believe whatever works out well for us, on the whole, was planned for us and we, however unconsciously, followed the plan . . . If at twenty-two you had not been too arrogant, as you call it, to persist, and Janice had been unable to keep up the struggle against you, and so had married you against her parents' wishes, against the teachings of her Church, is it likely it would have been the marriage it was when she did come to you, when presumably there were no barriers to it? . . . You may wish you and she could have had children—"

"I've never thought about that. With Janice, I felt no lack. All I wanted—all I want now—is Janice."

"You *have* Janice. And Janice has you; she also has the knowledge that she never knowingly hurt or worried her family; and she has her God. She is completely fulfilled. And so should you be. For your 'arrogance,' coupled with the love proven by your constancy, helped her to earn it all . . . Didn't this occur to you during those seventeen years when she must have revealed what her faith meant to her? Didn't you realize then that for Janice, aged twenty-one in 1922, to marry you would have been as hazardous, even perhaps as wrong, as she sensed it would be?"

"I told you," he says stubbornly. "I could have converted. And I would have. To please her. To ease her mind."

"Did you? Before or during your marriage to Janice?"

"No. The possibility was never mentioned. There simply was no problem. We *had* no problems. Our wedding was very quiet, attended only by her brother and his wife and Margo and John, and conducted by her priest, who knew I had been brought up in the Episcopal Church, in which my father was a bishop for twenty years, and that I had been increasingly active for some time in our church in White Plains, where I lived. Janice had told him, and I had told him. He gave us his blessing without reservations. After our marriage I went to early mass with Janice every Sunday morning. Nothing else would ever have occurred to either of us. She loved early mass and so did I. Then at ten-thirty she went just as naturally to the Episcopal church with me, and helped as readily and capably with all its undertakings as any Episcopalian. We traveled a great deal— Janice had a lively interest in seeing the world, and I became a columnist to give me the freedom to take her wherever she wanted to go—but nowhere that on Sunday mornings we could not go to early mass and later to another church service, though we couldn't always find an Episcopal church . . . As I say, we had no problem."

Alice nods.

"Janice would not have been made happy by your going through the motion of changing your faith to please her, to ease her mind. If you had done it for that reason, it would not have eased her mind. She knew that fifty-five years ago . . . Oh, the more I hear about Janice the more I admire her! . . . And now I believe I must go in, for the sun is setting and I have things to do—things like packing, cleaning the refrigerator, calling Cora Watkins to find out whether she wants me to lock the cottage and take the keys to her or leave it open, keys on the kitchen table—"

"Cora Watkins?"

"Cora owns the cottage I've been renting."

They have both risen. She moves slowly toward the cottage steps. He walks beside her.

He says, "Believe it or not, I am basically not a gloomy person."

"Oh, I agree with you. I can see that. You have worked at it, and I don't know why you did. It seems perverse to me. Where there is so much to be enjoyed—"

"I should have been telling you how much fun Janice was."

"Then she is. Whatever she was she still is. Only more so. Try to believe that."

They have reached the steps. Alice stops.

She says gently, "Sorry I can't ask you in. Simply too much to do. Besides, you have to get back to Margo's or you'll be holding up her dinner."

"You—couldn't take time to come over to the hotel for dinner with me?"

"Goodness, no. The hotel? I've nothing here I could wear into the hotel."

"Then for some lobster rolls we could take out to eat on the rocks? I'd come by for you whenever you say. We needn't be gone an hour."

Alice laughs.

"We would be, though. You know you have no end more to tell me about Janice, and I haven't told you anything yet, really, about Harley . . . No, I do have to get at my packing, and eat up what is in the refrigerator, and you have to be a good guest. You're here for only a week with your daughter, you said. Make it count."

"Will you—be back next summer?"

"I hope so. Somewhere on the island. Meantime, have a good year."

She runs up the steps, turns on the porch to smile and wave, and disappears into the dusk of the cottage.

16

A few minutes later, lights on, she is at the telephone.

"Cora? This is Alice Gilman. Thought I should remind you I'm leaving on the morning boat tomorrow. Should I lock up and bring you the keys?"

"Oh, no, no. Don't lock up. Just leave the keys on the kitchen table. Some of us'll be over before noontime to do whatever's needed there. A family's coming in day after tomorrow to stay through Labor Day. Been a good season. Haven't had a vacancy all summer. Hate to have you go, Alice, even though I haven't had a chance to see much of anything of you, I been so busy. You coming again next summer?"

"Oh, I expect to. Philip is buying Whiteoaks."

"He is? I knew Roger was thinking of selling it, but I didn't know as he had made up his mind. Well, we all like to have Gilmans on the island."

"I think Emily may bring her family over, too. But they'll rent. At first anyway."

"Good, good. Tell her to let me know if she decides to come. I might have something she'd like. But she ought not to put it off too long. A lot of people reserve a year ahead, and I try to hold one cottage for ones who can get out only for a week or two. They ought to have some chance, I always say."

"I'll tell her . . . Now, there was something else I wanted to ask you, Cora. What was it? . . . Oh, could I buy a book I found on the shelf by the fireplace?"

"Buy a book! What book?"

"The title of it is *Ten Boys Who Lived on the Road from Long Ago to Now.*"

"*Ten Boys*—never noticed it. Take it, for pity's sake, if you want it. People are always leaving something when they go, and if they don't write and ask us to send it, I figure they don't want it."

"This one has probably been here a long time. It was published in 1885, so it is quite old. And it's small, which would account for your not noticing it. But I have no idea of the value of it. I just like it because it reminds me of books my grandmother had when I was a child. If you'll price it, I'll leave the money with the keys—"

"Put it this way. If you ever sell it, you can send me half of what you get for it. *If* it's worth putting a stamp on, which I misdoubt. If it's small, you can just drop it in your handbag and have something to read on— Or is Emily or some of her folks meeting you in Falmouth?"

"No. I told them not to. I'll take the bus into Boston. I like the bus—"

"Then, as I was going to say, just pop your ten boys into your handbag and let them out along the way if you get lonesome for some company. Won't that bus driver be some surprised?" Cora laughs heartily. "Okay, so tomorrow noontime while I'm poking around to find a roll of dust under your bed, knowing well as I want to there's none there to find, I'll think of you jouncing along up the road to Boston. As I say, hate to have you leave, but every good thing comes to an end, I guess. Take care of yourself this winter, and now you've found the way out here again, don't be such a stranger. If any of you want a rental for next summer, or any part of it, let me know as soon as you can."

"We will, Cora. And as soon as the season is over you get a good rest."

"Rest! After October we have five solid months here when there's nothing to do *but* rest. Even if we want to. And I can tell you that after two or three of 'em, we want to!"

Those who have lived all their lives on the island are always "we"; off-islanders are "you" or "they" regardless of how long they stay or how much they are liked by the natives.

This, Alice thinks, is logical and right.

Later, with everything done which can be done that night, she goes out and walks for a while on the beach, sits for a while on her favorite ledge, gropes her way up the dark steps for the last time, and sits for a while on the porch. The moon is almost full and makes a silvery-gold path across the shallow hills and valleys of a quiet sea. The sea is the mother, the ledges the cradle, the white beaches the homespun blanket covering the island child. Alice and Harley have loved this child. It has been a great joy to her to come back to it this summer, to embrace it, and find it in many ways the same beloved child; but it is not their child. They are attached to it, not it to them. It belongs only to itself and the sea. In no other way could it preserve itself, maintain its special character, be what it is, all that endears it to those who respond to it and its Davy Jones' locker filled to the brim with ageless wisdom.

She will miss it, but it will not miss her, has no need of her and never will. Whatever need it has, its own will meet. So she can leave it in the morning in pursuit of those who do or may need what she has to give, without concern for its safety, without anxiety about its welfare. It has, she feels, its own program for the cold months. "They" may think it sleeps all winter, like a bear, and "we" are careful to say nothing that indicates otherwise; but Alice, not really one of "them" and certainly not one of "us" with knowledge of what the island chooses to keep secret, is convinced that when the last of the summer visitors have vanished over the horizon, all the bells ring out a great festival. Perhaps the mother sea snatches her child from the cradle and spins it in a mad dance of joy until they both collapse, panting and laughing, on the white blanket. Then maybe they run away together to some other place, some place no one but them has ever seen, and have their own season —such a season as no one but islanders have ever known or can imagine . . .

The morning is bright and warm, as if summer must be yearlong.

The linens which Cora supplies are in the hamper, the blankets neatly folded on the foot of the bed, all the windows wide open to the salt air and the sun. The refrigerator is empty and scrubbed, the iron sink lubricated with oil, all the stove switches turned off, toaster disconnected, coffeepot polished. The suitcase is packed and snapped shut, handbag and coat piled on top of it. It is always cold at some point of the crossing, if not all the way.

Alice, in a dark blue skirt, dark blue sneakers, and white, sleeveless crewneck cotton jersey tucked inside her belt, with a blue and white kerchief covering her hair—the crossing is always windy—is waiting for the taxi when the telephone rings. She stares at the telephone. It rings again. Before she can cross the room it rings a third time.

"Hello?"

"Oh, good! You haven't gone, Alice—"

"No, Cora. I'm expecting the taxi any minute—"

"Yes, well, this will only take a minute. I've got kind of a funny thing to ask you. Do you know a Mr. Floyd?"

"Mr. who?"

"Mr. Floyd."

"No. I don't think so. Isn't that a first name?"

"I thought so, but I guess it's his last one. Anyway, he just called me up, and that's who he said he was. I wrote it down, in case I didn't catch you before you left and had to write to you. He spelled it out for me. F-l-o-y-d—"

"Cora, the taxi's here!"

"Yes, well, it sounds funny, but he says he's visiting his daughter at Sunny Villa and there's something he wants to write to you about, but he doesn't know either your name or your address. I told him I had it all here in my files, and if he'd wait a minute I'd read it off to him. But he said no right off, real sharp. Said he didn't think I should be giving out your address without your saying it was all right for me to. Said he'd called me because he'd heard you were a tenant of mine. As I say, don't make any sense to me, but I told him to hang up, and I'd find out if you were still at the Blue Heron. If he knew where you were, I don't see for the life of me—"

"All right, Cora. Hermie's blowing his horn, and time *is* short. Of course I don't know what this is about, either. But tell Mr. Floyd I said he may have my address. And thanks for all your trouble—"

"No trouble, long's I caught you. Take care now—"

"I will. You, too. Hermie's just come in and grabbed my suitcase. Here I go-o-o!"

"I sounded," thinks Alice, "like the Wicked Witch in *The Wizard of Oz* when she was melting away."

But Alice is not melting away. She is bouncing away in Hermie's taxi, briskly walking across the old dock, boarding the *Islander,* standing on the deck, hearing the blast of the farewell whistle, watching the water widen between the boat and the shore, seeing the island recede until it becomes only a white fleck on the ocean and disappears.

She has spent a long summer moving easily back and forth between Then and Now, a week on the border between There and Here, and she has ended her journey. Today is Now, today is Here; and she is part of it, belongs to it.

She stands by the rail, at the side of the deck, looking neither forward nor back, but at the clean white froth thrown up out of the blue sea by her passing, and at the endless, cloudless blue sky above water, boat, and passengers.

The wind pulls at her kerchief and, smiling at the sensation, she tightens it firmly. The wind grows chill, and she puts on her coat, which is warm from the sun and warms her bare arms, her back, her neck.

"I'm alive," thinks Alice. "So alive. So glad to be alive . . ."